JIGSAW

M. LEE PRESCOTT

Published by Quicksand Chronicles
Copyright 2014, Quicksand Chronicles
Cover design by Lees River Studios
ISBN: 978-09855614-5-1

This book is a work of fiction. Names, characters, places, and events are products of the author's imagination or are used fictitiously. Any resemblance to actual people (alive or deceased), locales, or events is entirely coincidental.

For my family, always

PROLOGUE

The gloves snapped as he slipped them off, disposing of them as he always did after an outing. A deeply satisfying sound, the snapping of latex, powdery dust feathering up into the air. Brother loved it. Just as he had loved Rosie in those final moments as she begged for her life. "Oh sweet Rosie," he crooned lying back on the musty cot in the darkened room, his lair. "You made me soooo happy."

Already the euphoria was ebbing away, sucked into the insatiable maw of time, eroding his pleasure, washing away his joy. Try as he might, Brother was powerless to stem the flow, the precarious happiness seeping away only hours after the outing until all that remained were powdery smudges dotting his furrowed brow.

CHAPTER 1

July 27, Thursday

"Alright ladies, take the field!"

Bobby Gagnon, coach of the Flint Flames of the greater Fall River Women's Softball League, frowned watching 'his girls' take their positions. In his forties, a twice-divorced, recovering alcoholic Gagnon still looked like the triple A ballplayer he had once been. While his hair was thinning on top, his wiry, muscular frame looked much as it had in his twenties thanks to years as a brick layer.

"Jesus Christ Peters! Put something into your throw—anything! I haven't seen a rag like that since—

"Souza! The catcher, Souza, the catcher, for Christ's sake! Her mitt's where it always is, at the end of her goddamn arm!

"That's the way Gladys—stretch for the throw.

"Wilson! Center field's that way! Atta girl!"

As Gagnon continued yelling, coaxing and browbeating, the occasional compliment thrown in, his eyes scanned the street. Finally, the person he'd been waiting for hopped out of a dark green pick-up, J & T Limited lettered in black and gold on the cab's door. The pick-up took off and Bobby turned back to the field, feigning indifference as the latecomer jogged onto the field.

The explosion came as she reached the bench, stooping to tie the laces of her cleats. "Whitman, it's about goddamn time you showed up! I wanna talk to you!"

"Hi Bobby, nice to see you too." Julia "Juls" Whitman smiled, straightening to her full height, gray-blue eyes regarding him without a hint of consternation. She stood at least six inches taller.

"Where the hell's Mikawski?" Bobby resisted the urge to hop up on the bench to continue his harangue. He didn't much care for women looking down at him.

"Isn't she here?"

"No, and if she doesn't show in five minutes, you're pitching."

'But I—"

"Put a sock in it and start throwin'. I gotta date tonight and we're starting on time for a change. Belles have been warming up for forty-five goddamn minutes."

"Rosie'll be here. She'd never miss a game," Juls called over her shoulder trotting out to the mound.

Fifteen minutes later the game was underway with Juls pitching—still no sign of Rosie Mikawski.

By the third inning, Juls, agitated and distracted, allowed three runs to score, two of them on errors.

Gagnon blew up. "What the hell are you doin' out there, Whitman? Jesus Christ!"

"Watch your language Bob, there are kids watching," called Dan Powers, husband of Ruby, the Flames second baseman.

Powers' words had little effect. After the next pitch yielded a triple, Bobby charged out to the mound, arms flailing, eyes bulging, curses punctuating the night air.

Juls endured his screaming for several minutes before exploding herself.

"Stop it Bobby! I didn't want to pitch and you knew it! How do you expect me to concentrate when I'm worried about Rosie? This isn't like her, I talked to her this morning and she was psyched for this game. Something's wrong."

"You got that right, and you're it!" Gagnon snarled, worried himself, but unwilling to show it.

"Look, you've had it," he continued, turning towards the outfield. "Mendoza, get your fanny in here, now! And you, get out there where you belong."

"Fine," she mumbled, turning towards left field.

"Juls," he called after her, his voice softer. "She's fine. Forget about it and play ball. We'll go over to her place right after the game, okay?"

He watched Juls' retreat, her long straight back knit with tension. Even in league issue orlon, she was just short of gorgeous with those long, thin legs and slender hips. Juls Whitman had commanded his secret admiration since the day he'd volunteered to coach the Flames. Her hair had been long then, tied back in an unruly braid that reached her waist. Shoulder length now, the auburn hair was tied back in a ponytail that stuck out above the strap adjuster on her cap. A smile to die for and lips that begged to be kissed, the woman had no idea of her effect on men, least of all, middle-aged Bobby Gagnon.

Tuck Potter, Juls' partner in a suburban caretaking business was a boyhood friend of Bobby's younger brothers. Tuck had coached the Flames for five years, but the business had grown to the point where it was impossible for both partners to be unavailable three or four nights a week during the summer. Tuck had described the team as a "great bunch of ladies" and he had been right. Coaching the Flames had been Bobby's salvation.

Years earlier, the J and T partners had had a brief affair, but nowadays, Tuck described Juls as "one of the guys." It was bullshit, of course, since Bobby knew damn well that Tuck still harbored more than friendly feelings for his partner. Juls had prevailed, and she now kept Tuck, and most men for that matter, at arm's length.

Gagnon hadn't failed to notice the tears rimming his pitcher's eyes and she was right, it wasn't like Mikawski. The Bedford Belles were their biggest rivals and Rosie would never have missed this particular game voluntarily. All the punch knocked out of him, Bobby withdrew to the bench, glumly taking his place alongside his players.

The game dragged on, Juls' dread mounting with each inning. The Belles finally put them out of their misery, burying the Flames under a merciless barrage of hitting. The ump called the game in the seventh, Belles-12, Flames-1 as darkness descended over the Globe Corners field, the headlights of passing cars a distraction the Flames would no longer have to endure.

Juls gathered her things scanning the crowd. "Where's Tuck?" she asked to no one in particular. "He was supposed to pick me up! He should have been here hours ago. The one night I really need him!" She waved at her teammates who were heading for a beer at Archie's across the street.

"Go in and call Mikawski," Gagnon yelled, tossing the equipment bag into his trunk. "If there's no answer and Tucker isn't here by the time you're back, I'll run you over."

"You sure?" Juls asked, dropping her bag at his feet. "What about your date?"

"Screw that, now get goin'. Give her hell so we can go in and get a goddamn beer to drown our sorrows after this fuckin' game from hell."

"Thanks Bobby, watch my stuff okay? Be right back."

Gagnon threw her bag into the car, starting the engine and pulling the Impala up in front of Archie's. Knowing Rosie Mikawski as well as he did, there was no way he'd be havin' a beer in the foreseeable future.

Two minutes later Juls appeared, "No answer," she said, hopping in. "Let's go."

"You know she's probably all fucked up, three sheets to the wind at the Bluebird right now doncha?"

"No way."

Gagnon didn't believe it anymore than she did. Softball and her teammates were Rosie's whole life.

Bobby had spent many evenings with Juls, Tuck and Rosie drinking, playing cards, enjoying cookouts on the beach, going to concerts, out to dinner. Just last weekend they had all sailed to Nantucket on a friend's boat, camping on the beach, all the men in one tent and Rosie, Juls and two other women in a tent up the beach, giggling all night long.

Mutt and Jeff he called them. When the two friends walked into a room, one was first struck by the contrasts—Juls' tall, slender beauty, alongside the handsome, but shorter, stockier Rosie. The latter's coal black curls wild and unkempt, her dark eyes dancing with light mirrored her personality. Rosie was gregarious, loud and physical in her affections, whereas Juls, although friendly, was quieter, more reserved. Beneath the facades, however, dwelt two kindred spirits and together, they created a whole, distinct from their individual selves, a palpable warmth radiating from the pair that enveloped all around them in its warm, comforting embrace.

Their easy camaraderie was nearly impossible to resist and people were drawn into their circle of friendship. For Bobby Gagnon—to whom women had always been strange, elusive creatures—the friendship with Juls and Rosie had been a revelation.

The "girls" as Tuck called them, had known each other since grade school, remaining close friends through high school and college despite long periods of separation. Bobby never tired of listening to the stories of their growing up years. The Whitmans had never approved of Rosie Mikawski from the Flint, but that hadn't mattered a wit to their daughter. During her high school years, Juls was sent away to a boarding school in the Berkshires, while Rosie stayed at home, but the friends wrote, sometimes five or six letters a week, calling as often as they could. Weekends, if Rosie could get away, she'd coerce a friend into driving her up to visit Juls, sneaking her out of the dorm.

As he started down Willett, Bobby began praying. "God make everything be okay," he thought, as he pulled the Impala up to park across the street from Rosie's building.

"What?" Juls asked, looking over at him.

Not realizing he'd spoken aloud, he mumbled, "Nothing," adding hoarsely, "Come on let's go give her hell."

CHAPTER 2

Dan "Tuck" Potter walked into Archie's Tavern not three minutes after Bobby's Impala rounded the Globe Corner rotary, disappearing from sight.   Spying the Flames clustered at their usual tables by the jukebox, he waved, grabbing a beer on his way to join them.

"How'd ya do?"

"We stunk up the field," Karen Ramos replied, her leg slowly extending, pushing an empty chair towards him. A come hither move if he'd ever seen one and he'd seen most of 'em.

"No?"

"Yup. Lost twelve to one," Ann Greeley said, rising to fetch another round. "It's okay. We have two more shots at 'em. Besides, we were missing players. We'll get 'em next time, you wait."

"Gagnon must be a happy camper. Where is the lad anyhow and for that matter, where's my partner?"

"They've gone to Rosie's. She didn't show for the game, Bobby's pissed and Juls is a basket case."

As Ann prattled on, Karen leaned back in her chair eyeing Potter, her eyes leaving little doubt as to her intentions. The team uniform—baggy on most of the women—fit Karen like a second skin. The top was stretched tight across her ample bosom, nipples clearly visible under the thin, white orlon. Reddish blonde curls—frisky even after three hours shoved under a baseball cap—ringed her heart-shaped face and her dark eyes danced with mischief. Karen was pretty and she knew it.

She had always had the hots for Tuck, but her interest had never been returned. He barely knew she was alive except when he needed to locate one of his buddies, Juls, Rosie or Bobby. Fuck him, she thought, not my type anyway, too preppy with all that tousled, sandy hair and sea blue eyes. His tan canvas slacks were worn and ripped, but she had to admit, they looked gorgeous on his trim athletic body. A faded blue work shirt fell loosely over the broad shoulders and although Karen had never seen what lay beneath the shirt, she could imagine.

"Well, ladies, gotta go. See you at the next game."

He had barely sat down and now he was rushing off, as usual, trailing after Juls. It was always Juls, more like a marriage than a partnership, Karen mused, grabbing his untouched Pabst, calling "thanks" as she turned back to her teammates.

"Phew," Tuck mused as he headed towards the North end, driving at least twenty miles over the speed limit. "Cat's on the prowl tonight," he said aloud, thinking that Karen Ramos was trouble with a capital T. He'd just broken up with one bitch and he sure as hell didn't need another.

After Gracie had packed up and left a year and a half ago, Tuck's lady luck had taken a decidedly sour turn until Marcia came into his life. In the beginning, their relationship had been sweet indeed. A friend of a friend, they'd hit it off from day one and Marcia had fit right into the gang. Then, she moved into the beach house he shared with J and T's office and things had gone downhill fast. Juls didn't like Marcia, but hell, Juls hadn't liked any of his girlfriends except for crazy Annie from Boston. Juls claimed he only dated bitches, but she and Annie had hit it off from the start until Annie had fallen in love with big Jim and run off to Colorado to run a saloon. They still sent Christmas cards.

He had to admit, Juls was right, he did attract bitches, no doubt about it. As soon as Marcia moved in she started screaming, a continual screech that never let up except when Juls was in the office, which wasn't often. During Marcia's residence, Juls had avoided the office as much as possible. Too much of an effort to be pleasant.

When the whole gang got together, it was easier for his partner to keep her distance, but in the office it was impossible. From day one, Marcia insinuated herself into every facet of the business and once she grabbed hold of a project, there was no wresting it away from her. Tuck had initially encouraged his live-in's involvement, but things had quickly gotten out of hand. He smiled, remembering Juls' long overdue explosion after a particularly trying day with Marcia.

"That's it Tuck! Either she goes or I do! No... that's not right. I'm not going, Marcia is and you're telling her as soon as she gets back!"

"Telling me what?" Marcia purred, voice smooth as silk as she sauntered in from the kitchen.

Taking in the saucy stroll, the self-satisfied grin—Marcia had a wicked smile—and the haughty flip of her silky blond hair, Juls took a deep breath and let her have it.

"Marcia, I started this business with Tuck almost twelve years ago. It's a good business, we make a decent living, we get along and our customers are happy."

"So what'dya want, a medal?"

Tuck cringed, fearing he was about to witness a murder.

Juls ignored the sarcasm, "Then you come along and suddenly Mr. Longfield's calling saying you've insulted his wife. We've got dirty units that you were supposed to have had cleaned and we've got a phone bill that's three times what it usually is. Then there's the—"

"Can I get a word in?" Marcia interrupted, her voice squeakier than usual.

"I'm not finished."

"You're just jealous, that's it isn't it? You can't stand it that Tuck and I are partners now and doing a great job without you!"

Tuck intervened at this juncture. "That's enough Marcia. Juls is right, it's our business, hers and mine and you've been screwing up. It's my fault, I take the blame for encouraging you to become involved in the first place. Stupid move on my part. Sorry hon, you're gonna hafta bow out. It's not working and if Juls hadn't spoken up, I would have. The Longfields are two of our oldest customers; they've been with us since the beginning. There was no reason for you to treat Janet like that, calling her dog..."

"A fucking guinea pig! I can't believe what I'm hearing! The little rodent bit me, for crying out loud, and all you care about is the old bat and that decrepit husband of hers! What's the matter with you people?"

"What's the matter with us is that J and T is built on good will and friendly service neither of which you seem able to deliver," Juls replied. Her voice had lost its fire, but her cheeks were flushed and blotchy, betraying the anger still smoldering beneath the surface. "And we don't have the money for all these hour long phone calls to California, New York and wherever else you're always calling."

Jaw set, her face flushed and angry, Marcia glared at the partners standing side by side behind the desk. "Fine, I'm outta here. Screw the both of you and your cozy little partnership. No one could step between you two and live to tell about it anyway! I've been offered a job in New York starting next week so good riddance!"

"What the—?" Tuck stared at her.

"That's right. I'm leaving Sunday so you can go back to your pathetically chummy existence."

So, Marcia had departed and Tuck had heard nothing from her and didn't expect to. Something told him that Karen Ramos would make Marcia look like Pollyanna. Best keep his distance from that one. Besides, it wasn't as if he needed lady friends. A coed working for J and T this summer had already caught his eye and if he and Kerry hit it off, the last thing he needed was Karen breathing down his neck.

Marcia had been right about one thing, he and Juls did lead a chummy existence. However, he doubted that Juls had ever been jealous of Marcia or any of his girlfriends, she just didn't have it in her. He had known his partner for nearly fourteen years. She was warm, funny, stubborn, practical in business matters, athletic, compassionate, opinionated, a fiercely loyal friend, a forgiving opponent, a hard worker, a loving daughter and sister, but jealous? Not Juls.

They'd met in Laguna Beach, California where they were both attending an advanced workshop on the craft of leaded glass construction. Amazed to find fellow Fall Riverites so far from home, they had sought each other out during the workshop, spending their free time together during the six week course. At the workshop's conclusion, they extended their stay for four weeks, traveling up the coast to Northern California, Washington and Oregon. A brief romantic fling during that trip had ended the day they stepped off the plane in Providence.

While a fierce attraction lingered, by the time they arrived at home, they had decided to go into business together and Juls had insisted romance give way to friendship if they were to work together. By his own admission, Tuck had already dated and discarded more women than he could remember and she wasn't about to start a business only to have it fall prey to his romantic whims. Tuck reluctantly acceded to her wishes, but more than once over the years he had regretted the promise made in the parking lot of Green Airport. He was still very much in love with Juls Whitman.

The past twelve years had been prosperous ones. They'd started with the glass shop, making windows and lamp shades on commission as well as restoring old windows in local churches and the turn of the century Victorian homes of Fall River, Newport and surrounding areas. While the business grew steadily, stained glass was not the booming business on the East coast that it had been out West. After three years, J and T branched out in another direction, becoming J and T Limited in the process.

Most of their business now was caretaking the summer homes, condominiums and multi-million dollar beach houses of Windy Harbor, a wealthy summer enclave fifteen minutes southeast of Fall River. The tiny coastal town had grown by leaps and bounds over the last twelve years as farmers sold out for millions to the affluent New Yorkers and Bostonians voraciously gobbling up the last stretches of virgin coastline. A sleepy little fishing and farming village for many generations, Windy

Harbor had finally been discovered. Like it or not, the locals had had to adapt and many did not do so graciously.

The hostility of Windy Harbor's natives had in fact been largely responsible for the initial success of J and T. Snubbed and shunned by their neighbors, the Harbor's newest residents had had nowhere to turn for help and services until Juls and Tuck appeared on the scene. With open arms and friendly smiles, the partners catered to their clients every whim with efficiency and discretion. J and T looked after clients' properties in winter and summer, handling all rental agreements and arranging to have services—water, phone, electricity, trash collection and so forth—resumed or terminated with the changing seasons.

Having spent the better part of his adult life in the Harbor, Tuck knew the plumbers, electricians, carpenters, painters and various other service oriented people. One room in his weathered shingled beach house served as J and T's office. Thad Potter, Tuck's father had been left the house by a maiden aunt. Since the elder Potter refused to leave the Fall River home where Tuck and his brothers had grown up, when Tuck had approached him about starting the business, he had been only too happy to deed it over. Juls' house was ten miles away in Tiverton, R.I. just outside the Fall River city limits.

The partners took excellent care of their clients, running errands, searching for missing pets, investigating petty thefts—trash barrels and mail boxes were the most frequent targets—arranging for cleaning services, planning parties—or hiring caterers—and helping to arrange for clients' memberships in the area's yacht , golf and beach clubs and Windy Harbor's Ladies Literary Society, the most exclusive and selective of all the 'clubs.' While not always successful in wheedling memberships for the newcomers into the Harbor's closed societies, the partners endeavored, if unsuccessful, to sooth bruised egos by suggesting alternative activities for their wealthy clients, many of whom had never heard the word "no" until they moved to Windy Harbor.

Business had grown so much that J and T now had a waiting list and while there were two rival companies proffering the same type of service, J and T was still the "agency of choice" for those lucky enough to "get on the list". Not a bad way to make a living if you liked people and both partners did. Marcia had not and it showed.

As he turned onto Rosie's street, Tuck spied the Impala and pulled up, parking behind it. Brushing thoughts of Marcia and Karen aside, he wondered what had been important enough to keep Rosie from the game, she lived and died for softball for Christ's sake. Slamming the door, he cursed under his breath, angry at himself for missing Juls at the field, "damn the Willises and their fucked up lawn sprinkler!"

His heart—already in his throat after taking the front steps two at a time— nearly stopped as the first of Juls' screams pierced the stillness of the night.

CHAPTER 3

Racing up the stairs, Bobby puffing along in her wake, Juls reached the third floor in seconds. Rosie's unit was at the end of the hall, number sixteen.

The building was over eighty years old, but Gladys Kenney, the owner kept it in immaculate condition. The plaster walls had recently been white-washed and at the far end of each hallway, window seats had been built in, green and white awning striped cushions inviting passersby to linger. Despite its pristine appearance, the building was still in the heart of the roughest part of the city. In an effort to thwart thieves who continually absconded with her framed prints, Gladys had decoupaged fine arts posters along the corridor's walls. Wall scones bolted to the walls bathed the passageway in soft light, the overall effect one of peaceful serenity.

After several minutes with her finger pressed to the buzzer, Juls went to the window seat, rummaging under the seat cushion to find the key Rosie kept hidden there. "Shit! Why won't this work?" she cried, jabbing the key in, turning to the left and right. The lock refused to budge.

Hand on her shoulder, Bobby reached from behind. "Here, let me try babe."

"I'll get it," she said, shrugging his hand off. "It just... takes a minute to... there, finally!"

She flipped the light switch by the door as they stepped into the living room, into the warm inviting space where they had spent so many evenings drinking, watching movies, playing cards, talking and laughing together. Tonight the room smelled musty, the air close and still and she wondered why all the windows were closed on such a warm summer night.

Rosie collected Native American and Mexican textiles and favored the stark lines of the mission style in her furnishings. All of her pieces were reproductions of Gustaf Stickley designs, well-made, handsome and sturdy like the woman herself. Hanging from the cream colored walls were three Navaho rugs in bold patterns of red, gray and black. The floor was covered in gray wall to wall carpeting, clean and new like the rest of the building, another large Navaho rug lay across its center the same reds and grays slashed through it in a chevron pattern.

The large, comfortable sofa was flanked by two matching armchairs, all three pieces covered in off-white cotton duck; a number bright woven throw pillows echoing the colors of the rugs. Rosie's pride and joy stood in front of the sofa—a massive oak coffee table, also in the mission style, built by Rosie herself in a woodworking class at the local community college.

The morning papers were scattered across the table's polished surface and Rosie's body lay at its far end. She was dead, no question about that. The body sprawled half in the living room, half in the bedroom, legs twisted back at unnatural angles, naked except for gray athletic socks which Juls recognized as her own, loaned to her friend several weeks earlier. Black curls obscured the face and aside from a few scratches here and there, her body appeared untouched, white and smooth in its deathly pallor.

Her good arm lay at her side; the scarred left arm—burned in a child-hood accident—tucked beneath her. There was quite a lot of blood pooled beside the body that appeared to have come from her underside and pieces of a jigsaw puzzle were scattered around the floor, some floating in the blood like tiny amoebae.

Juls screamed, rushing to her friend's side. As she began to claw at the smooth white rope still wrapped around Rosie's neck, Bobby roused himself, leaping forward to yank her back. "Juls, stop it. We can't touch her!"

He pulled her back and Juls let go, the movement causing the body to roll towards them leaving the severed left arm on the floor behind her. Her arm had been amputated at the shoulder.

"Jesus," he whispered. Juls screamed again, beginning to shake violently.

"Oh my God, oh my God," she mumbled over and over as he dragged her towards the kitchen phone.

As she struggled, lunging towards her friend, he tightened his grip. "Cut it out, Juls, come on now for God's sake, we can't touch her. We've gotta call the police, they need to see her just as she is. You can't help her, babe, she's gone, now come on."

He reached the phone just as Tuck burst through the door. Juls crumpled into her partner's arms and Bobby turned away as the police dispatcher answered at the other end of the line.

The next few hours were a blur. The three sat huddled on the sofa as the police went over the apartment, occasionally pausing to ask questions. Cameras flashing, their voices hushed and somber, a small army of men collected samples, searched through drawers and closets going over every inch of the three rooms. Occasionally, neighbors peeked their heads in and were led to the window seat in the hall where an officer waited to take their statements.

"Make them stop," Juls moaned, almost incoherent as the hour approached midnight. "Rosie hated having her picture taken. Please, Tuck, please make them stop." In her Flames uniform covered with grass stains, blood and dirt, she looked like a small child inconsolable after falling off of her bike and skinning her knee.

"Juls, it's okay," Tuck said, drawing her to him. "Hush now, Rosie's past caring. How much longer officer?" he called to Jack Mederois, the homicide detective in charge.

"They'll be taking her out in about five minutes. I have just a couple of questions for Ms. Whitman, then you folks can take off."

True to his word, not five minutes later the photographers packed up their gear and Rosie's draped body was carried out on a stretcher. As his officers began sealing the crime scene, Mederois came to sit beside them.

"Where will they take her?" Juls asked.

"City morgue first. We'll have to keep her a few days, then we'll contact the family and see about the funeral home and all."

"There is no family, just me."

"Well then Ms. Whitman, we'll let you know when you can have her collected and—"

"Oh God, who would do this?"

"We were kinda hopin' you might give us a hint. Someone with a grudge? Ex-boyfriends, disgruntled co-workers, whatever? Or someone new, that she just recently met?"

"There's no one like that. Everyone loved Rosie. No one who knew her would hurt her."

"How 'bout someone she might've met recently? A new boyfriend maybe?"

"None that I know of."

"Do you guys know what Ms. Mikawski was doing today, someone she might've been seeing? Mr. Gagnon says you unlocked the door and there are no signs of forced entry. No broken windows, jimmied locks, what have you. Seems like she must've known the guy. Had to have let him in."

"I don't know what she was doing today except for the game. Softball. We play on a team and we had a game tonight."

"So I see. What time was that?"

"Five."

"She was long gone by then, I'm 'fraid. Preliminary exam puts time of death around one, two somethin' like that."

"Oh, God, the whole time we were playing, Rosie was lying here." Juls crumpled against Tuck, fresh sobs wracking her slender frame.

"Sh, okay now," Tuck whispered, holding her tighter as if his grip might somehow stop the trembling.

"I know this is tough, Ms. Whitman. Just a couple more questions, please. What can you tell me about her arm? Was she able to use it, the scarred one I mean?"

"Yes," she sniffled, regarding him. "Sometimes it stiffened up in the cold, got tingly at unexpected times, things like that, but it was only a scar. It happened when she was four. A kettle of hot water spilled on her. Her family always called it an accident, but her father was a drunk. Rosie had no memory of it, why?"

"Just curious. She's a big woman, strong, I mean. Seems like the type who'd put up a fight, but there's no sign of a struggle and I just wondered if maybe one arm was weaker than—"

"How did she die? I mean, was she—"

"Strangled. That white rope around her neck, guy brought it with him."

"And her arm?" Tuck asked.

"Happened after she was dead. Thank God for that at least." Mederois studied Juls, aware that she was fading fast, withdrawing into herself, unaware of her surroundings. He turned to Tuck. "How 'bout the apartment? Was your friend in the habit of leaving the door unlocked?"

"Never," Juls answered for him. "I'm sorry, but I have to know. Was she? I mean she was naked so was she—"

"Raped? Doesn't look like it, but we won't know for certain until forensics gets through with her."

Juls moaned.

Tuck gripped her tighter. "Look Detective, we're gonna split, okay? She needs to get outta here."

"Sure thing, I'm sorry Ms. Whitman, about your friend and all, and about keepin' you so late. Let's leave it for now and we'll talk in the morning."

He rose, joining his men a few of whom were still collecting their gear. "Oh," he called back over his shoulder. "One more thing—did Ms. Mikawski like jigsaw puzzles? I mean, would she have been working on one do you 'spose?"

"Not that I'm aware of. I didn't even know she owned any jigsaw puzzles," Juls said, looking to Tuck for confirmation. He nodded at Mederois.

"I thought not."

"How's that?" Tuck asked.

"Can't be sure till we check a little further, but, well, we've seen this type of thing before."

"Jesus, a serial killer!" Bobby cried, instantly regretting his words.

Juls' face, red and blotchy from crying, froze in horror.

"We don't know that Mr. Gagnon. There are similarities to other cases, but we'll have to look further. Let's not go spreadin' stuff like that around, okay?"

"Oh God," Juls moaned, as the two men half-carried, half-dragged her from of the apartment, driving her home.

Several shots of brandy and two sleeping pills borrowed from a neighbor and Juls settled down on tear-soaked pillow, a drugged, fretful sleep finally overtaking her. Tuck slept beside her bed in the chaise, Bobby on the living room sofa.

CHAPTER 4

Things were heating up for Brother. With each passing day it was more and more difficult to bury himself under that spineless Other. Mercy, was he sick of him, always whimpering, always remorseful, always clambering to get back to work after an outing when all Brother wanted to do was lie back and savor his triumph. No longer interested in work, Brother was already thinking ahead, planning the next outing, craving the surge of power, the strength and control that came over him the minute he slipped on the gloves. He no longer had the patience for day to day existence—that was the wimp's problem—he wanted the power all the time.

He has plans, big plans. Delicate mousy Beth seemed light years away, overshadowed by his more recent conquests. Poor pathetic little Beth, it had been like strangling a baby bird, a helpless, naked hatchling its eyes still draped in their gossamer veils. Of course Beth had had to die, just as Catherine and Rosie had had to be put out of their misery. What if they'd had children and marked their offspring with one of their dreadful deformities?

Rosie had been fun, fighting, struggling to free herself, refusing to give into the inevitable. In the end, of course, she had screamed for her life, just like the others. If he closed his eyes he could feel her soft body writhing in his arms. Her wrists and ankles tightly bound with Mother's support hose, she had squirmed and wriggled as he reached from behind, running his gloved hands over her ample breasts, along her hard, flat stomach till they reached the soft mound below. Through the gloves, she hardly felt human, but his body—pressed against her back, his face buried in her hair, the soft black curls smelling faintly of coconut. Her all too human flesh had aroused him, making him forget his purpose for several careless seconds and sensing his distraction, Rosie had thrown her head back, slamming him into the wall. Brother had had to come to his senses, fast. Yes, Rosie had given him pleasure beyond his wildest dreams and he must have it again, and soon.

September sixteenth was the date he'd set aside for the next outing, but now he realized how foolish he'd been to think he could wait that long. He'd have to have another, maybe two or three others before then. Less than eight hours after Rosie, he was craving another conquest.

Seven weeks until September sixteenth, plenty of time to kill and kill again. And why not? He had a system now and it was working flawlessly. They'd never catch him unless the wimp, that simpering, mealy-mouthed Mama's boy, gave him away.

There was plenty of time and he had two "works in progress". Perhaps Ellen's time had come, although he did hate to kill Ellen. Her connections might prove useful when the time came for him to flee. There was also the extra element of danger with Ellen and her connections to people who knew him. Her death might put all his plans at risk.

But, Ellen or whomever he selected would only prove a diversion, momentarily deflecting his attention and allowing him to hone his skills for his biggest, most daring conquest. The challenge would come in extracting her from all the meddlesome friends hovering around her like ewes tending a newborn lamb, especially her puppy dog of a partner. First, I will lead her from the flock. A wolf in sheep's clothing, he chuckled. Then, when I have her alone—snap, twist, pop—Julia Whitman will be mine, just like all the others.

CHAPTER 5

August 17, Thursday

"I'm going to see Jack today," Juls announced as the partners—second cup of coffee in hand—went over the day's schedule.

Tuck gave her a sharp look. "It's Jack, now, is it?" Somewhere in the days and weeks following Rosie's death Detective Mederois had become Jack and Tuck wasn't sure he liked the sound of it, nor did he like the idea that his partner, pale and thin, her light blue sundress hanging on her like a sack, was planning yet another visit to the police station. On her first day back at work no less.

Summer was their busiest time of year and he had been swamped the past three weeks. They always hired extra employees, college kids home for the summer, but there were certain things that needed the attention of either J or T, there was no getting around it. The past three weeks had been all T and he needed some relief. Not that he begrudged her the time away, it had been his idea for her to go home and stay with her mom, but now she was back and he needed her. Needed her for the business and needed her for himself. Truth was, Tuck was never the same when Juls was away.

"Want some breakfast?" he asked for the third time. She's dropped twenty pounds at least, he mused, watching her pace back and forth, and she had been too thin to begin with. He wanted to wrap his arms around her, bury his face in her hair and breathe in her earthy sweetness, but he knew she would push him away, the unwanted display of affection leaving her angry and irritable for the rest of the day.

"Thanks, I've had some," she answered a trifle less patiently than she had the previous two times. His concern was smothering her.

"What do you want with Mederois anyhow?"

"I want to check on how the investigation's going. I'd like to help him if I can."

"Do you really think that's a good idea? It'll only dredge things up and get you upset all over again."

"Tuck, this is something I have to do." Period, end of story. "Besides, Gladys wants me to clear out the apartment as soon as possible. She's got a long waiting list for Rosie's unit."

"Juls, that's bullshit and you know it. Gladys couldn't give a shit when the apartment's rented again and she sure as hell doesn't need the money. I know Gladys, remember?" Gladys and Tuck had enjoyed a brief fling just after Rosie had moved into the building. Like most of his relationships, the affair had ended amiably and they remained friends. "Gladys is as broken up about Rosie as we are and she of all people would understand if you needed more time."

"How can you say that!" she cried, eyes shining with angry tears. "How can you compare the way I feel about Rosie with someone who was at best a casual acquaintance? Rosie was such a huge part of my life, I'll never be whole again and you talk about Gladys feeling like me!"

"Stop it Juls—that's not what I meant and you know it."

Realizing he was shouting, Tuck lowered his voice, moving round the desk, pulling up a stool in front of her chair, taking her hands in his. "Juls, I'm sorry. I know you're torn up inside and you want like hell for the cops to find this guy. I do too. But they'll get him, you'll see and I need you here. Look at this place, it's a fucking nightmare. Do you wanna know why? Cause we need you. You think of things that never even occur to me. I can't do this without you. If we hire more people we won't be able to cover expenses and our own salaries."

Extracting her hands from his grasp, she turned away. "I have to do this, Tuck. I'm sorry, I won't draw a paycheck, I have some money saved up, just do whatever you have to do to make ends meet."

"Juls..."

"No, I mean it. I'll do what I can around here, but I will help the police. For starters, they may've missed something in the apartment."

"Doubtful."

Ignoring him, she went on, "I know Rosie's apartment better than my own house, I certainly spent more time there than at home. I can go through things as I pack them up and look for clues."

"I don't believe I'm hearing this, what in the hell do you know about clues?"

"You know what I mean. We've done some investigating."

"Oh yeah, rounding up renegade trash cans and stray dogs. Great preparation for a murder investigator."

"Tuck, you know I hate your sarcasm. I'm not running the investigation, I'm just helping out."

"Oh, terrific, I feel better already!"

"Tuck!"

"You're not gonna change your mind, are you?"

"Nope."

"Fine, how 'bout a compromise then?" He took hold of her hands again. "I'll help you with your investigation and you agree to give J and T a few hours every day."

"Deal," she replied, withdrawing her hands and standing up. He still loved her. She knew it, but would not acknowledge it, especially now.

"And, if we talk to Mederois and he tells us to butt out, we're gonna do what he says, right?"

"Come on. Let's go, if you're coming," she said, ignoring the question. There was no need for a reply. He already knew the answer.

To Tuck's surprise, Jack Mederois seemed happy to see them. "Sure, I got about fifteen minutes, come on up," he called over his shoulder leading them to his second floor office.

Icabod Crane, Juls thought, following the tall, gawky detective. Like the unfortunate school master from the Washington Irving tale, Mederois' clothes hung on his angular frame like they had been tossed there willy-nilly. His hair— or what was left of it—drifted listlessly atop his pointed skull, putting one in mind of a feather duster. His pock-marked face had a long, thin scar running from his right eye to the nape of his neck giving Mederois a somewhat sinister appearance, but it was clear that behind the mask dwelt a kind, gentle spirit. From the deep recesses of their bony sockets, his dark eyes sparkled with mischievous intelligence and his smile transformed the foreboding face into that of an indulgent uncle humoring young relations with a few minutes of his time.

"You two want coffee?"

They both declined.

"I wish I had better news for you, any news for that matter, but we don't have much to go on. He wears gloves, that much we know and somethin' over his head. Never leaves so much as a hair behind, no fingerprints, no fibers, no nothing. He uses some kinda panty hose to tie 'em up, we're pretty sure about that and there's the white cord of course, available in most hardware stores. We've been checking around."

"What about the neighbors? Didn't anyone hear anything?"

"Nope, he gags 'em. Then he kills, takes off the gag, hose, whatever and splits. Clean, neat kinda guy. All three of the women were strangled."

"Three?" they said in unison.

"Yup. Three we know of at least."

Tuck glanced over at his partner who seemed to be holding up pretty well. Before Mederois could go on, she interrupted. "Did he assault them?"

"Nope, no rape. This guy's not in it for the sex. It's some other need he's fulfilling. All three women had been handicapped in some way, physically or in the case of your friend, a cosmetic flaw.

"Then there's these friggin' puzzle pieces—who the the hell knows what they do for him. None of the pieces fit together and they don't come from the same puzzle, different puzzle for each victim."

"May we see them?"

Mederois hesitated, but finally said, "Yea sure, why not? They'll be back from Boston in a couple of days. Stop by and I'll give you a peek. Can't hurt. No prints on 'em, they'd been carefully wiped clean. We still got a few of your friend's things here that you can take too. You're the sole heir I understand."

"Yes."

"Why don't I just get those things and you can look 'em over. Something might stand out."

As they followed him out of the office, down to the evidence room in the basement, Juls asked, "How soon can I clean out the apartment?"

"Anytime Juls. We're all through there."

Now it's Juls, is it, Tuck thought, bringing up the rear.

CHAPTER 6

August 18, Friday

Friday afternoon Ellen Smith readjusted her black velvet headband, straightening the jacket of her impeccably tailored linen suit as she turned to gaze at the clock. It was after four, three hours until her date with Christopher Hurley. Truth be told, she didn't relish the thought of an evening with Chris, but he was taking her to Camilla's overlooking the ocean at Windy Harbor. Camilla's was Ellie's favorite restaurant.

Ellen loved Camilla's and she loved Windy Harbor. Especially the drive, leaving the city, passing through several small towns, finally driving along the river, the road snaking along following the contours of the winding waterway until the turn-off to the restaurant perched on the cliffs at the mouth of the harbor. And Camilla's food was to die for—delicate poached salmon, rich spinach pesto, lobster bisque—piquant and brimming with chunks of fresh lobster meat, dense chocolate torte ringed with raspberries, topped with creme fraiche and luscious salads of baby greens and unusual vegetables. No iceberg lettuce and cardboard tomatoes at Camilla's. She supposed she could tolerate Chris, or just about anyone for that matter, if he took her to Camilla's.

She did hope Chris would be more cheerful tonight, he had been so out of sorts lately. Their first three dates had been wonderful. He'd been charming, witty, even jocular, and Ellen had begun to imagine that he might be the 'one.' While she knew she was not a beauty, like most professional women, Ellen was well put together, her ash blonde hair carefully cut and styled in soft waves that brushed her shoulders. She looked ten years younger than her thirty-one years thanks to hours in the gym each week and her salary allowed her to dress well. Most of the men she dated were crude and ill-mannered so Chris had been a welcome change and she had allowed herself to dream about marriage and children. However, their last two evenings had brought her crashing back to reality. Chris, withdrawn and moody, had acted like a different person. All her attempts to draw him out had only worsened his mood and their most recent date had been so uncomfortable that Ellen had feigned a headache, asking to be driven home halfway through the evening.

They'd gone to Wickford, to see *Othello* the first of three "Shakespeare in the Park" performances. It had been Chris' idea, but he had been so testy and fretful as they ate the picnic supper she prepared that she couldn't wait to get away from him. At the first intermission, she had risen from the blanket, professing to be in severe pain and begged to be taken home. Chris had reluctantly acquiesced and Ellen had vowed never again.

Three weeks had passed and she had endeavored to put Chris from her mind until his call Wednesday evening, contrite and full of apologies for his earlier behavior. Promising to be cheerful next time, he had begged her to give him another chance. Ellen had been civil, but noncommittal until Chris mentioned Camilla's. He knew it was her favorite restaurant and that she'd be hard-pressed to refuse an invitation to dine there and he had been right.

When he popped the question, she heard herself saying, "Yes, I'd love to", afterwards chiding herself for weakening her resolve. She knew it was wrong to lead him on. At the same time, there was no one else in her life so why not? What was the harm in dinner? Perhaps Chris had changed, no harm in giving him one last chance. If things go poorly tonight, she decided, that's it.

And, Chris was good looking. Women noticed him whenever they were out, although he himself seemed completely unaware of his effect on them. How she longed to show him off to co-workers, neighbors, her friends, but that was another thing about Chris, his almost phobic need for privacy. He refused to meet any of her friends, had never introduced her to a single acquaintance of his own and requested that she not "go on and on" about him or their relationship when she was with her friends. He would pick her up and drop her off at her apartment, usually after dark and their one afternoon date, a picnic on the beach, he had insisted on meeting her in the city, claiming his car needed repair, asking if they might take hers instead.

He had never set foot in her home. After a fleeting kiss and a hasty goodnight he would practically sprint run to his car. That was another thing about Chris, his total disinterest in sex. While Ellen had never been one to hop into bed on the first date, she was no prude either. At first, she had found his bashfulness refreshing, a welcome change from the men who groped and pawed at her after only a few hours acquaintance. However, after their third date went by with nothing more than Chris' usual hasty peck on the cheek, she began to feel insulted, worrying that he did not find her desirable.

One evening as they sat in a rustic seafood restaurant forty-five minutes up the coast, platters of boiled lobster in front of them, red and white bibs tied round their necks, she screwed up her courage and said, "Chris, please don't take this the wrong way, but what I mean to say is, do you not find me even the teeniest bit attractive?"

"What kind of a question is that Ellen?" he replied, eyeing her sharply. "Of course I find you attractive, why?"

"You never seem to care about...., well,... when we get home, you never want to stay. You run to your car without so much as a hug."

"Ellen," he hissed, glaring across the table at her. "I cannot believe I'm hearing this. This may be what you're used to, but I was brought up to respect women, not assault them. I wouldn't dream of forcing myself on you at this stage in our relationship, my dear Ellen. Why we hardly know each other."

For a fleeting moment his eyes seemed to draw her in, a queer gaze she had never seen before. Was it a threat she spied? She was never quite certain, but she had apologized, confused and frustrated by his bizarre reaction. The discussion had ended amiably enough, but its aftermath seemed to trigger the first of Chris' moods. While she never raised the subject again, the incident cast a pall over the fledgling relationship, tainting all of their subsequent time together.

Ellen returned to her deskwork, as always piled over every available inch of her desk. Lately, when anything needed doing, the refrain "let Ellie do it" seemed to be the solution. Ellen Smith had been with the Five Cents Savings Bank for nine years, since the summer after her graduation from University of Rhode Island. A biology major, she had toyed with the idea of going on to medical school, but a summer job at the bank after graduation changed her plans and Ellen had never looked back. She pursued an MBA all the while working her way up through the bank's patriarchal ranks to her current position, senior vice president working under Linc Marvell in the trust department. While Linc managed most of the big accounts, families he'd seen through several generations, Ellen was slowly building her own stable of portfolio accounts.

"You take the young ones Ellie," Linc would say. "Up and comers don't want to deal with an old codger like me." Then, he'd add wistfully. "Like it or not, they'll all be yours soon. Can't keep this up much longer, you know how Betsy's at me to retire."

"Don't you dare," Ellen would respond, though secretly she knew Betsy was right. For the past year she had watched the man she adored—the father she'd never had and her best friend—become more and more frail. His mind was still sharp as a tack, but the thinning snowy white hair, his pale skin blotchy with liver spots and his halting, tentative gait made Linc Marvell look every bit of his seventy-eight years. Linc, don't leave me, she often thought, I'm not ready to do this alone.

In a way, Linc had been indirectly responsible for her meeting Chris. For some time Ellen had wondered about the shy, handsome man slipping in and out of Linc's office once a month. Each time he came in, she would think, I must ask Doris, Linc's secretary, his name, but then. it would slip her mind until the next time he passed through. Then, one noon while she was grocery shopping on her lunch hour she had spied him in the next aisle and introduced herself, a rather bold move for her.

Extending her hand, she said, "Hello. I work for Linc, Mr. Marvell at the bank. Ellen Smith, I've seen you going in and out."

"Yes, hello. Chris Hurley, glad to meet you. Of course, I recognize you too, Ms. Smith. Linc has handled my family's accounts for many years."

"He's quite a guy," she said, beginning to feel awkward.

"A very fine man," he said, smiling back at her.

"Well, I didn't mean to interrupt your shopping Mr. Hurley. It was very nice to meet you."

"The pleasure is mine," he replied.

They had separated, each pushing an empty cart down the produce aisle, pretending to be absorbed in selecting fruits and vegetables. The charade lasted until they reached the start of the dairy section when he approached her.

"Excuse me, Miss Smith, but would you like to get a cup of coffee, or tea, maybe a sandwich or something, after you're finished shopping? There's a little diner around the corner, we can walk or—"

Suddenly he'd stopped, aware that she was staring at him, a mixture of disbelief and incredulity written all over her face. Turning red as a beet, he stammered, "Oh, please forgive me. You don't know me, so of course you wouldn't want to—"

"I'd love to," she said and was rewarded by a beautiful smile. A smile that left her weak in the knees.

All thoughts of shopping abandoned, they left their carts in front of the milk cooler, walking out into a cool June drizzle. Sitting in Leo's that afternoon, Chris had asked her not to mention to Linc or anyone else that she had met him. Puzzled by the request, she had nonetheless acceded to his request and had continued throughout their relationship to respect his fanatical need for privacy. After their last date, however, she had decided that privacy or not, she would ask Linc about him. She had been tempted to peek at his portfolio, but had restrained herself. Ellen was a stickler when it came to client confidentiality, Linc was too.

As usual, she had gotten busy and forgotten all about talking to Linc, but as she packed up for the day, her boss popped in, perching himself on the edge of her desk and Ellen decided it was time to bring up the subject of Chris Hurley.

"Ellie, my girl, whatever are you doing still here so late on a Friday? Go on now! Out with you, have some fun! What the blazes do you think yer doin' anyway?"

"Same thing you are."

Smiling up at him, she asked, "Have you got a minute?"

"For you my dear, an eternity." He patted her shoulder affectionately, his kind eyes attentive, concerned. Tiny, gentle Ellie was like a daughter to him.

"It's a personal matter, Linc. It's about someone I'm dating. You know him, he's—"

The phone rang in Linc's office interrupting her.

"Hold on a sec, hon," he said hopping up. "Doris is gone and that's probably Bets calling to give me my orders! I'll be right back."

Ellen sighed as he disappeared, turning her attention once again to her briefcase already stuffed to bursting with file folders.

When Linc returned, his face was ashen, his hands trembling so violently that he had difficulty adjusting his glasses fallen halfway down his nose. "Oh Ellie, she's been in an accident, Bets has! She's at St. Anne's, they've taken her by ambulance."

"Oh, Linc. Come on, I'll drive you over."

"Thanks dear, but Ronnie's downstairs. That was him on the phone."

Ellen accompanied him to the lobby where Ron, the oldest of Linc's three sons, stood waiting at the door, car parked at the curb outside. When he spied his father, Ron moved to his side, trading places with Ellen who had supported him from the elevator.

"She's fine, Dad, really, I told you that on the phone. She's just had a bump on the head. I'm sorry I called like that instead of coming up, but you know Mom, she's screaming for you and it seemed the quickest way."

As they helped Linc into the car, Ellen gave him a look that asked, is she really okay?

"Don't worry Ellie, everything's fine. We'll have her home in an hour and we'll call you, okay?"

Ellen nodded, standing on the sidewalk waving as the two men drove away. They both looked back returning her wave. It was to be the last time they would ever see dear, sweet Ellie. Ellie, the daughter and sister they had never had and never would again.

CHAPTER 7

August 19, Saturday

When Tuck arrived to pick her up, he found Juls in sweat shirt and jeans against the unexpected chill of the morning. The sweat shirt, heather gray like her eyes, had ragged holes at the elbows and paint splotches across its front. Her hair was tied in a loose ponytail, errant strands framing her face.

Greeting him at the front door, she hurled a stack of empty cartons onto the grass, slamming the door behind her. "Hi there," she said, pushing hair from her eyes.

"Hi yourself—how you doin?"

"Great."

"Look Juls, we're not gonna be at this all day, are we? The Callahans are coming in this afternoon and we'll have to get the house opened up, groceries in, not to mention the tenants in the condo on the— "

"Relax partner, I've already arranged everything with Marla. She's gonna do it." Marla was one of their most dependable housekeepers. "Don't worry," she added, noticing his skeptical glance. "She can handle it. Bob and Dottie love her, remember? After she helped cater the Callahans' anniversary party last summer they wanted to adopt her. Besides, you can drop me off and come back later. I only need you for loading the things into the truck, I'll do the packing. I thought you said you were doing errands this morning."

"A few, but then I—" He stopped, regarding her. She stood facing him head on, arms akimbo, challenging him. It was useless to argue. "Forget it, let's go."

"Tuck," she said, squeezing his arm as he backed out of the driveway. "I can handle this. You've been great the past few weeks. I couldn't have gotten through this without you, but I'm okay. Really."

They drove the rest of the way in silence. Mederois had given them plenty to think about the last time they'd been in. No real leads, but he had shared more than he should have. The police psychologist had worked up a profile of the killer—a loner, meticulously clean, nervous, repressed, and of course, sadistic. "Like we needed a shrink to tell us that," the detective had remarked. While Mederois did not elaborate, it was obvious from his accounts of the previous murders that some of the victims had experienced agonizing deaths.

First, there had been the young nursery school teacher, Beth Johnston. Lame from a childhood accident, Beth walked with a decided limp and used a cane. The afflicted leg had been amputated before her death. She had been killed at the start of her school's spring vacation and her body had lain undiscovered for almost ten days. "Blood splatters were fairly contained. He must've drugged her, hacked off the leg, then we don't know, probably finished her off before she regained consciousness," Mederois explained, his voice clinical, detached.

The strangler's second victim, Catherine Foley, died at the end of May, a little over a month before Rosie. Catherine had been the owner of a very successful sporting goods company, *She Runs*, specializing in women's running apparel and shoes. A thalidomide baby, she had been born without fingers on her right hand. The killer had amputated her stump of a hand just above the wrist. The cut was clean, no hacking.

"Drugged before the surgery," Mederois told them, "But Ms. Foley regained consciousness. That much we know. Poor woman tried to escape. Blood trail led to her front door. That's where he caught up with her. She must've woken up, caught him off guard and made a break for it. We found her crumbled up in the front vestibule. Another second or two and she might've made it."

Mederois' eyes had misted over as he recounted the details of Catherine Foley's death and Tuck wondered if there had been a personal relationship between the detective and the businesswoman. It was on the tip of his tongue to ask, but he decided it was none of his business. Besides, no one could remain completely detached in the face of such horror.

"Here we are," Juls said, interrupting his thoughts.

"Sure you're okay about this?"

"Yup, let's go."

Each of them grabbed an armload of boxes and crossed the street. As they approached Rosie's front stoop, they spied a man dressed in stained khakis, a drop leaf table hoisted on his shoulders which he held with one hand, ringing the doorbell with the other.

"Here, let me give you a hand," Tuck called, dropping his load of boxes on the sidewalk.

"Thanks, I'm all set," the other replied, smiling at Juls. "I've got a delivery upstairs. If you could get the door, I can handle it from there. This table's heavier than it looks."

Recognizing the piece," Juls asked, "How did you get that? And where do you think you're going with it?" Her voice, uncharacteristically strident, caused Tuck to turn and stare.

"Excuse me?"

The stranger regarded her curiously as Tuck said, "What my partner means is that that looks like a piece that belongs to a friend of ours. If it's hers, we can take it up if you like?"

"Well, I don't know. It belongs to Ms. Mikawski in number sixteen, but she's very particular about things and she might not like it if I just handed it over. I've been trying to reach her for several weeks, but it appears her phone has been disconnected. Probably needs repair like half the phones in the city. I had another delivery in the area and thought I'd give her a try, see if I could catch her in."

Tuck gave Juls a quick glance before saying, "I'm afraid there's been an accident. Ms. Mikawski died several weeks ago. We're friends of hers, here to clean out her apartment."

"Oh my God, I am sorry. Such a nice person. Seemed the picture of health too, how did she.... Oh, please forgive me, it's none of my business—"

"She was murdered," Juls said. "Where have you been the past three weeks? It's been in all the papers, on the television, radio! You'd have to be deaf, dumb and blind not to have heard about it!"

Realizing she was shouting, Juls noticed that the stranger's face had drained of color and his eyes brimmed with tears. The table was still balanced precariously on his shoulder.

"Juls," Tuck whispered, hand gripping her shoulder.

"Oh God, forgive me," she said, leaning back against her partner. "I'm sorry."

"Please, don't give it a thought, perfectly natural under the circumstances," he replied. "I haven't been under a rock, but away. I just returned from a midwest buying trip on Tuesday. I'm afraid I haven't yet gotten to all the back issues of the newspaper nor have I listened to the news. I'm truly sorry about your friend, shall I carry this up for you before I'm on my way?"

He was in his late thirties, about Tuck's height, six feet, his dark curls flecked with sawdust, a by-product of his livelihood. Soft hazel eyes returned her gaze with interest as well as concern and Juls found herself gazing surreptitiously at his left hand, looking for a wedding band.

Both men were staring, waiting for her reply.

"Oh, no thank you," she stammered, blushing. "We'll just put it in the pick-up across the street. How much do we owe you?"

"Not a thing, I couldn't possibly."

"I insist," she replied, her composure fully restored. "I know that table well and you've done a beautiful job with it. Now, please, how much is it?"

"I wouldn't dream of profiting from your loss," he said, fishing into his pocket and producing a business card. "But, perhaps you'll think of me if you ever need any furniture repaired or refinished? I'm just over the bridge in Somerset."

Juls took the card. It read:

Wilson McCaffrey Studio

128 River View Terrace

Somerset, Mass. 02725

Shaker reproductions   Antique repairs   Furniture restoration

"Thank you Mr. McCaffrey, and I am sorry I lost my temper. These last few weeks have been very hard ones for me."

"Please, say no more Miss?"

"Whitman, Juls Whitman and this is my partner, Dan Potter, Tuck."

"Well, Mr. McCaffrey, we've got a lot of work to do," Tuck interrupted, deciding the conversation had gotten far too friendly. "Thanks again for bringing the table, I'll take it from here."

"I'd be happy to carry it to—"

"Not necessary," Tuck said almost ripping it from the other's grasp. "I'll just toss it into the truck."

"Tuck?" she called, surprised at her partner's abrupt behavior. She watched him cross the street pretending the table was light as a feather even as he struggled under its weight. "Do you think it'll be safe there?"

"I'll watch it," he called, sliding it roughly onto the truck bed, slamming the tailgate behind it.

"Be careful Tuck." Hands on hips, Juls regarded him, knowing exactly what had precipitated this change in behavior.

McCaffrey watched the interplay with bemused expression. When Tuck turned back, glaring, he waved. "Well, I'll be off. Again, I'm sorry for your loss."

"Thank you, Mr. McCaffrey," Juls called, pointedly stopping work to watch his truck pull away.

Sticking his head out the cab, he returned her smile. "My pleasure, stop by the studio anytime."

"Yea right," Tuck mumbled watching the pick-up round the corner out of sight. "We'll be right over."

Juls followed him into the building. "What's the matter with you?"

"Nothing."

"You were just incredibly rude to that man."

"Look who's talking."

"Well, at least I apologized."

"Look Juls, he was coming on to you for Christ's sake. You tell the guy your friend's dead and he's puttin' the moves on you, the creep."

"That's ridiculous and you know it. He was just being friendly. Besides, when have you ever thrown a fit when someone was flirting with me?"

"Just drop it, okay? I don't like the guy, that's all."

"Fine, but I'm gonna keep his card. People are always asking where they can have pieces refinished."

"And we send 'em to Skip."

"Skip does a lousy job and you know it. Mr. McCaffrey will be a valuable contact for us."

"Valuable contact, my ass. Lousy or not my business stays with Skip."

"This is silly, Tuck, can we stop this please?"

They reached the apartment and he ripped the yellow police tape from across the door.

Watching as Juls fumbled in her pocket for the keys, his voice softened. "Yea, we can stop this. I'm an asshole, what can I say?" Before she could pull back, he leaned forward and kissed her forehead.

CHAPTER 8

August 19, Saturday

Mederois got the call right after breakfast.

His assistant, Tim Cottrell caught him just as he was scooping up the last bit of egg yolk on the last bite of english muffin. "We've got another one, Jack."

Mederois needed no explanation. "Jesus, who and where?"

"Name's Ellen Smith. Landlady discovered the body about an hour ago. I'm in her apartment now. It's pretty bad."

Cottrell went on to explain that Ellen's boss, Linc Marvell had been trying to reach her since the previous evening. Alarmed when there was still no answer in the morning—Ellen was apparently one of the last few people in the world to eschew an answering machine—Linc had called her landlady, asking her to deliver a message. When she couldn't rouse her, the landlady, Lois Balboni had used her key.

Heading straight from home to the scene, Mederois arrived in less than fifteen minutes. The street was already clogged with police cars, reporters and hordes of curious onlookers.

"How the hell'd they find out about this already for Christ's sake?" he yelled, fighting his way through the crowd to the apartment building's front door. "Jesus Christ Lewis," he called to one of the officers near the door. "Get someone out here to clear these people away, will you?"

Ellen Smith had lived in a white, three-story, turn-of-the-century Gothic revival at an address hovering along the fringes of the Highlands, Fall River's toniest area. There were nine apartments in the building. Ellen's, number three, was on the first floor at the rear of the building looking out over a small, but well-tended backyard. Mederois whistled, peering out at a verdant oasis of manicured grass, three small fruit trees and a tiny garden, its raised beds bursting with flowers and vegetables in their prime.

"Beautiful isn't it?" said a voice from behind him, echoing his thoughts exactly. "It's all Ellie's doing. She has a green thumb. She's been at it for close to eight years now, she's done it all. Heavenly days, I don't know what I'll do without her, my poor darling Ellie!"

"I'm sorry for your loss," he said, turning to face the plumb woman, her eyes swollen and red from crying. "I'm Detective Mederois and you are?"

"Lois Balboni, Ellie's landlady. I found her, poor dear."

As she broke into fresh sobs, Mederois waited patiently, trying to offer comfort. Mrs. Balboni lived in the apartment adjacent to Ellie's but had heard nothing unusual the previous evening. "I'm deaf as a post without my hearing aid. I take it out after my programs, around nine-thirty and it doesn't go back in till six in the morning. I know, it's foolish. I should keep it on with all the burglaries lately, but the darn thing's so uncomfortable and it keeps me up. Mercy sakes, I'll probably never sleep again after what's happened to poor Ellie! If only I'd been listening, I might've been able to phone for the police!"

Mederois left her settled in a rocker on the back porch weeping softly as he proceeded into Ellen Smith's apartment.

Officers had fanned out questioning the other tenants in the building. The only other first floor resident was an artist, Dick Silvia, whose studio apartment was next to Mrs. Balboni's, but he was away for the summer. Mederois found Tim Cottrell and Otis Booker, the forensic pathologist in the kitchen.

"Jesus Christ," he said, surveying the grisly scene. "What the hell happened here?"

The bright sunny kitchen's white floors and walls were splattered with blood. It was everywhere, even on the ceiling. The table where her body lay was awash in blood and below it on the floor a red river snaked towards the back door.

"Ellen Smith had a heart condition, congenital heart defect, looks like," Booker intoned. "She's had at least two, maybe three open heart surgeries in her life. Hard to tell till we get her back to the lab and get her cleaned up a little. Hole in her heart, that was her handicap. Bastard ripped it right out. My guess is she was heavily sedated and he opened her up and took it out, still beating. That's why there's so goddamn much blood."

"Time?"

"Round midnight."

"We sure it was him?" Mederois asked, willing his mind away from the horror, concentrating on the questions he needed to ask. His stomach was churning viciously as the eggs worked their way up his esophagus.

"Pretty certain," Booker replied, "Sure looks like it. Same cord, same puzzle pieces—more than last time."

"Anything written on 'em?"

"Yup—the word's "love" this time if you can believe it."

"Jesus, Mary and Joseph," Mederois said, wiping sweat from his forehead as he entered the room, stepping carefully to avoid the blood, forcing his eyes to the table where her naked, mutilated body lay, flat on her back, small and white against the dark mahogany wood. "Kind of a fancy table for a kitchen," he said to no one in particular.

"Looks like he fumbled around quite a while gettin' into the chest cavity. Guy's no surgeon, that's for sure. He had to saw through the sternum. Not easy that."

Booker kept talking, but Mederois had ceased listening. He was thinking about the garden and the six foot high sunflowers, the profusion of cosmos, zinnias and snapdragons and the care and attention it took to create something that beautiful.

Finally, he dragged his mind back to Booker who was still droning on about organs and tissues. "Alright, alright, Otis," he snarled. "Just put it in the report, okay? Tim," he beckoned, staggering towards the living room, glimpsing the smirk on Booker's face as he passed by.

"You okay?" Tim asked, as they closed the door behind them.

"No, I feel like puking my guts out, but what else is new? What have you come up with? Anyone hear anything, see anything?"

"Not so far. We found a couple of smudges by the back door. He must've been pretty messed up himself, not his usual clean job. We think he loaded all his things into a garbage bag, or something like that, then went out the back way. They found a board, by the back fence. He may've used it to stand on so he wouldn't leave footprints in the mud."

"Bastard thinks of everything, doesn't he. Have them go over every fuckin' splinter of that wood!"

"They're taking it away now. Probably too rough for prints, but who knows."

Mederois sat down in a chintz covered wing chair, looking around the living furnished in mauves and greens. Large botanical prints lined the walls, their muted colors blending nicely with their surroundings. It was a peaceful room, its serenity belying the chaos of the street and the carnage in the kitchen. Peach linen drapes rustled in the morning breeze as Mederois examined the photographs set on the table beside him. From half dozen frames, the murdered woman stared back at him, surrounded by friends or perhaps family members. There was one shot of her alone, standing on a beach in a green striped sun dress, laughing and waving at the camera. She was lovely—slender, shoulder length ash blonde hair, a broad smile, the dark eyes twinkling with warmth.

"What about her family?" he asked, setting down the frame, his hand trembling.

"We're trying to locate them. We've got—"

"Let me in, please!" a voice called from the front door. "Please! I must see Ellie!"

"Let him in!" Mederois called and the officers stood aside allowing him to pass.

"Who's in charge here?" the elderly gentleman asked, looking as if he'd just risen from his bed after having slept in his clothes.

"I am," Mederois replied, thankful that he'd closed the kitchen door behind him. "Jack Mederois, I'm heading this investigation, this is my assistant, Tim Cottrell and you are?"

"Marvell, Linc Marvell, Ellie's boss. I'm also a dear friend, is she here? She's alright, isn't she? I've been calling you people all morning and no one will give me a straight answer."

Recognizing Marvell from several of the photographs, Mederois motioned him to a chair. "Please, sit down, Mr. Marvell."

"I don't want to sit down. For God's sake son, I want some answers. I'm worried sick about Ellie!"

"Mr. Marvell, please."

Mederois somber tone seemed to do the trick and Marvell collapsed onto the sofa, the fight knocked out of him.

"My officers have not been able to answer your questions because we have been trying to locate Miss Smith's family. We always like to notify family first in cases like this, can you help us out with that?"

"Of course, but what's happened? Ellie's alright, isn't she?"

"I'm sorry, Mr. Marvell, I'm afraid she's not. Miss Smith is dead, she was murdered last night."

"Oh God, no! Not Ellie."

His whole body seemed to cave in and for a moment Mederois was afraid he'd had a heart attack.

"Mr. Marvell, are you alright?" he asked gently.

"How did it happen?"

"She was strangled," he lied. The rope was around Ellen's neck, but in this case, it hadn't killed her. "Happened around midnight last night."

'I don't believe it. Who would want to hurt a kind, gentle soul like Ellie? Was it a break-in?"

"Doesn't look like it sir. We're not absolutely certain yet, but it does appear that Miss Smith knew her killer. There was no sign of forced entry and no one heard anything unusual last night."

"How will I ever tell Betsy?" the other moaned, wiping tears from his eyes.

"Would that be a good friend of Miss Smith's?"

"Betsy's my wife. She's very close to Ellen, we both are. She's like a daughter to us and my sons adore her like she was their own flesh and blood. Ellie's parents live in the Midwest, Betsy could tell you where, oh God, oh God, whatever will we do?"

"Perhaps you'd better let Tim take you home, Mr. Marvell. We'll talk later okay? One of the other officers will drive your car back for you and your wife can give them the information about Ms. Smith's parents."

Marvell nodded mutely, following Cottrell out.

Shortly after Marvell's departure, Mederois returned to the kitchen, forcing himself to go over every inch of the room. After several hours, he cleaned up and assessed the situation, taking notes while things were fresh in his mind.

Finally, glancing at his watch, he found it was already after one. "Damn!" he muttered calling to Cottrell who was sifting through things in the bedroom. It had been Mederois' intention to stop by the Mikawski woman's apartment in the morning when he was sure Juls and Tuck would still be working. He was hoping they might have discovered something unusual in their packing up, but now? Should he go break the news or leave it till later? "What the hell," he said to no one in particular. "They have to know sometime."

He directed Cottrell to drive directly to Willet. Despite the hour, neither man felt like stopping for lunch.

CHAPTER 9

Poor Ellie, Brother mused, shoving the last of the bloodied clothes into the gas-fired incinerator in his basement. Town code prohibited burners of this kind in residences, but he was careful and used it only when absolutely necessary.

He had actually grown to like Ellie and had considered passing her by. After all, she wasn't noticeably flawed like the others, was she? He'd learned about her heart condition from Linc, poor, foolish, unsuspecting Linc. He'd be devastated by Ellie's death, but what would he do if he knew his words had inadvertently signed her death warrant?

Linc's mindless prattling on about his assistant's heart condition had been all the incentive Brother had needed to begin stalking her. How many times had he pushed empty shopping carts up and down in that infernal market, waiting for her to stop in on her lunch break? Enough times so that he feared someone in the store might remember him. On the day that Brother had vowed would be his last, Ellie had walked into the market.

Brother was genuinely sorry for the pain her death would cause the old banker. He liked Linc and Linc understood him, understood what he had endured all those years with Mother. Linc knew Mother had treated him horribly, calling him Brother—when he'd had no siblings—in constant rebuke for the pain he had caused her.

Linc. Brother hoped Ellen had been telling the truth and that she had kept her promise and hadn't mentioned their relationship to her boss. He had asked her one more time as she'd struggled to her feet, realizing she'd been drugged and that he meant to harm her.

"Please," she had cried, begging him to let her go. "I swear to you Chris, I never said a word."

Her words rang sweetly in his memory, transporting him for a brief second back to the restful, attractive apartment, the gleaming white kitchen so like an operating room.

"Ellie, Ellie," he whispered, twisting a length of white cord round his wrists, lost in the ecstasy of the memory.

He would have it again, and soon, that moment of sweet, intoxicating release as he held another's life in his hands and twisted. Of course, with Ellen, he hadn't needed to twist. If he closed his eyes and cupped his hands together he could still feel her beating heart lapping against his palms.

Now, he'd have to focus his energies on Christine. Perky, plump little Christine, just waiting to be put out of her misery. Then there was Julia, beautiful, tragic Julia. Quite the loveliest of all his conquests. Not that the beauty was particularly important, but he did appreciate it. Yes, Julia was lovely, but alas, like the others, tragically flawed.

Brother had work to do, lots of work. He had a date with Christine. Just dinner and dancing, no need for the gloves yet.

Before leaving the basement, he slipped on a fresh pair of gloves. The snap of latex brought hot tears of pleasure to his eyes and a bit of saliva dribbled from the corner of his mouth. Massaging his face, he breathed in the dusty, familiar scent of the powdery latex, releasing a flood of memories.

Half hour later, he glimpsed his reflection in the upstairs mirror and was horrified to see splotches of chalky white residue all over his face. "Idiot!" he screamed aloud, frantically splashing water on his face, scrubbing savagely at his cheeks and forehead.

CHAPTER 10

August 19

Juls had been sorting and sifting through Rosie's things for nearly four hours. After helping her get started, Tuck had cleared out, leaving his beeper behind. "I'm five minutes away, if you need me. I mean it!" had been his parting words. Shooing him out, she had locked the door and turned to her task.

She had already filled several cartons and bags, kitchen things, linens and household items and clothes that she had no use for. These they would drop off at the Salvation Army on their way out of the city. She planned to keep most of the furniture and the rugs as well as items of Rosie's wardrobe she could not bear to part with.

Juls was a saver, but her friend had lived a spartan existence, ridding herself of superfluous possessions on a regular basis. "If more than a year goes by and I don't wear it, it's history" was her motto and she'd stuck to it with only a few exceptions. Juls discovered one of these exceptions at the back of a closet, a peasant blouse she had brought back to Rosie from California. Another treasure was unearthed in a cedar chest—a sweater in soft, blue heather, a Christmas present from Juls. The sweater had been too small for the buxom, full figured Rosie for many years, yet she had kept the gift her best friend had given her, bought with most of Juls' spending money her first semester at boarding school. Juls could still see her friend's face, lit up like the candles they'd smuggled up from the dining room for their own private Christmas celebration in her room. Rosie's family hadn't believed in Christmas.

"Try it on Rosie!" she'd cried.

And Rosie had protested. The gift was too much, she could not accept it. But, Juls had hushed her, helping her dearest friend pull the sweater over her head, declaring it a "perfect fit".

The sweater went into one of Juls' "keep boxes" along with the peasant blouse and Rosie's canvas duck coat.

Almost all of the clothes were sorted, boxed or bagged and she was nearing the end of her work in the bedroom when he knocked at the door. The sudden noise startled her and she took a few seconds to regain her composure before venturing out into the living room. A second, more insistent series of knocks sounded as she inched across the room. She stood stock still in front of the door, afraid to move a muscle.

"Juls! Come on, open up. It's me."

His voice was like an embrace and she pulled back the deadbolt practically throwing herself into Tuck's arms.

"Hey, what's all this? Everything okay?"

Immediately angry at herself, she pulled away. "It's nothing. I'm fine. Just a little jumpy, that's all."

"My fault, we should have arranged a signal. You know—da da da dah, da da."

"Don't be silly, it's broad daylight. You just startled me, that's all. Come on in."

Leave it alone Tuck, he told himself, following her into the room. "Matt and Kerry are downstairs. Matt's got his pick-up. If you're ready I'll give 'em a whistle and we can start loading things into the trucks."

"What about the office?"

"Marvelous Marla's handling everything, remember? Besides, Betty's there and Scott and Pete'll be back in a couple of hours. They're still out weed whacking at the Mays'. We're covered partner, don't sweat it."

"I'm not," she said, giving him a grateful smile. What would she ever do without him, steady, safe, reliable Tuck? The only thing worse than losing Rosie would be to lose Tuck.

"Well, don't just stand there woman, put us to work. You got us all afternoon, you know."

"Come on," she laughed, leading the way to the bedroom. "I've made lots of progress, see. Believe it or not, I'll probably finish today. Rosie traveled light. I'll have to come over tomorrow and give the place a good cleaning, but otherwise we should be able to get it all out today.

"I've marked everything, "J" goes to my house. You can throw most of it in the garage, it's unlocked. Most of the furniture I'm keeping except for the bed, you want it?"

"You sure?"

"Absolutely. In fact, I'm taking most of the rest of the stuff because I can't bear to part with it yet. If you see anything you can use, please take it. Rosie would want you to have it, tables, chairs, whatever."

Spying the keen interest as his eyes scanned the room, she said, "Tuck, I really mean it. Take anything you want, except the armchairs and the rugs."

Tuck's home was a mish mash of junk furniture—moth eaten armchairs, rickety tables, threadbare carpeting, his dish ware an odd assortment of chipped pieces, discards from friends and family. It wasn't that he couldn't afford better furnishings, he just never seemed to get around to buying them. His various live-in girlfriends were always spending his money on china and furniture, but when they moved out they usually took everything with them. His girlfriends were like that.

"Want the couch?"

"Well..."

"It's yours. Coffee table, too, if you want it."

"I don't know Juls, Rosie left this stuff to you and I'm not certain how—"

"Stop it, Tuck. If you don't take it, it's going to the Salvation Army. So, it's your choice. How charitable are you feeling?"

"Not very, I'll take it."

"Good, let's get started. There's a dresser in there, not much to look at, but it's sturdy and the drawers don't stick. Her kitchen table would look nice in your kitchen too, better than that rickety card table. How 'bout the rocker for the office? We could put it in the bay window."

"Yes to all three. We'll take a load out there after we go to your place, then we'll come back for the Salvation Army stuff. You've got quite a bit goin' there by the look of it."

"Oh, you know what, there's a box of Rosie's dishes over there somewhere. You definitely ought to take those. Think you can get all this in one load?"

"With both trucks, sure. Want us to leave somethin' for you to sit on?"

"No, I'm fine."

"You sure?"

"I'm fine," she said, unsuccessfully hiding her irritation. When would he ever stop hovering?

"I'd love a sandwich though, on your way back."

"Already in the works. We'll call in an order to Celia's from the truck. What'dya want?"

"Veggie pocket, chips and a coke, thanks." She turned back to the bedroom as he headed downstairs to retrieve the others.

Seconds later, they appeared in the bedroom door. "Hi Juls," Kerry said, smiling down at her. "How're you doin'?"

"Great, hi Matt.," she said, returning their greetings. Of the five kids they had working for J and T this summer, Matt and Kerry were her favorites. They were dependable, hard workers and Juls was secretly thankful Tuck had brought them instead of loud mouth Marla or clumsy Pete.

Blond, blue-eyed Matt was built like a Mack truck, his neck the size of a tree trunk. He hoisted one of the heavy armchairs onto his shoulder as if it were made of straw instead of massive, heavy oak. Although thin and petite, Kerry's wiry strength was apparent as she lifted the other chair, following Matt out of the apartment. While she didn't look as comfortable as he, she was nevertheless holding up her end of the bargain. Dressed in white cutoffs, sleeveless top and high top red sneakers, her long dark hair fell in two auburn braids halfway down her back. She was cute, Juls mused, watching her. No wonder Tuck was smitten.

The three worked quickly and soon had the apartment cleared of most of its furnishings. Juls then tackled the living room odds and ends, rolling the rugs, clearing off tables of magazines and framed photographs. Wrapping each frame in a dishtowel, she set them one by one in a box. She knew every object, each chronicling a lifetime of friendship. Almost every photograph in the apartment included her.

There was a photo of their first day of school, both of them dressed in jumpers and saddle shoes, and others of the friends in Juls' backyard treehouse, at the beach, in the apartment, even a shot of the Flames taken at the end of the previous summer's season. Then there was a shot of Juls and Tuck, taken ten years ago, right after Juls' knees operations. She was on crutches, her knees bandaged up, her partner's arm round her waist supporting her. Standing on the beach, Tuck's house in the background, they were laughing, Rosie egging them on as she snapped the picture.

So many times during the early years of the partnership, Juls had wanted to relent and tell him she loved him, tell him she wanted to try and make it work—the business and their relationship, but, something had always stopped her. Rosie knew how she felt and supported her. Rosie always knew what she was thinking and feeling, sometimes before she did herself. As she wrapped this last frame, Juls' eyes filled with tears and she ran to the kitchen to splash water on her face, not wanting the others, especially Tuck, to glimpse her distress.

When she returned, she set to work on the drawers of the lowboy which Tuck and Matt had already carried out to the truck. She'd asked that they leave the drawers long enough for her to go through the photographs piled inside them, a process that took longer than she had anticipated. She found old strip candids of her and Rosie taken in the machine at Woolworth's and many college and high school snapshots, each picture unleashing a flood of memories. The pictures were thrown together with other small mementos from the same time period. She started to sort through the drawers, but after her eyes filled up several times in the first drawer alone, she called to Tuck. "Think drawers are alright like this? Unemptied, I mean."

"No sweat, just leave 'em there. We'll cover 'em with towels and they'll be fine. Lowboy's goin' to your house anyway so you'll have plenty of time to go through them." He recognized her distress, but said nothing, knowing she would bite his head off. "After we get this last bit, I'll carry 'em down and that'll probably be it for this trip."

"Wow," she exclaimed, looking around her. "You guys work fast. Put the lowboy in my living room, okay? You know where the key is, right?"

"Any special place?"

"Just leave it by the front door, I'll move it later, thanks."

The last piece to go was the sofa. With Matt on one end, Tuck on the other, they lifted the heavy couch. "Jesus," Tuck said, fumbling with the slip cover. Juls reached over, smoothing it back out of his way. As she did so, two jigsaw puzzle pieces fell from its folds to the floor.

She stooped to pick them up as the two men wended their way out of the apartment and down the hall. Tuck had seen them fall, but said nothing as he followed Matt's lead, Kerry trailing behind with two of the lowboy's drawers draped across her arms.

Juls stared down at the pieces in her hand. On the back of one, printed in neat block letters, was the word "far". Reading the cryptic message she shivered, knowing with certainty who had written it.

"Are those what I think they are?" She jumped, but didn't answer. "Juls?" he said softly, coming to stand beside her.

"How could the police've missed them?"

"Same way we did, they're tiny little suckers. Looks like they came from a thousand piecer. Besides, we were sitting on the couch most of the time that night, remember? They were probably right underneath us."

"What do you think it means?"

"The guy's a sicko."

"No! I mean, the word, "far", what could that have to do with Rosie? Jack never mentioned that the pieces had writing on them. Maybe this will help us find him."

"You mean the police don't you? Help the police find him, that's what you meant to say, right?"

"They already have a bunch of puzzle pieces and they haven't managed to come up with a thing, so what makes you think two more will help?"

"Well, for one thing there's the word. Maybe it links up with somethin' they already have? And there might've been a clean finger print if you'd left 'em alone. You're not thinking of holding onto these, are you?"

"Maybe for a little while. I'll turn 'em in eventually, but I don't think it'll hurt to keep them for a couple of days."

"Well I do, Jesus Juls, this is crazy."

"No it isn't," she snapped, glaring at him.

He knew that look, there was no use arguing. "Look," he said finally, his eyes pleading with her to be reasonable. "I've got an idea. In fact, I don't know why I didn't think of this sooner. A friend of mine, of my older brother's really, is a private investigator. She's good, she might be able to help us."

"Tuck, I want to do this. I have to be involved."

"Fine, but let me finish, okay? This PI's name is Ricky Steele. She's into jigsaws, does 'em all the time. She lives in Swansea and she's always got a puzzle goin' on her dining room table."

"I've heard of her. She's a friend of Rosie's running buddy, Phil Rubin, isn't she? He was at the funeral."

"Why don't I give Ricky a call? It can't hurt to have her take a look at 'em, can it?"

"Alright," she said, slipping the pieces into a small ziplock bag and handing them to him. "But tell her to be careful with them."

"Look, I gotta go, Matt and Kerry are waiting outside. We'll be back in an hour or so. You should be about done by then, huh?" She nodded. "Lock the door behind us, okay?" he leaned over, kissing the top of her head, running out before she could protest.

About forty-five minutes later as she swept the kitchen, she heard another knock. Not the code they'd practiced, but three short raps. Carrying the broom into the living room with her, she jumped as three more knocks echoed through the room. Then a familiar voice called, "Juls, Potter? You guys in there? It's Jack Mederois."

Relieved, she set down the broom and unlocked the door.

"Everything okay?" he asked, stepping into the room.

"Yes, fine. Why didn't you use your key? You have one, don't you?"

"Not on me. I stopped by on my way back to the station on the off chance I might catch you. Got a minute?" His dark eyes seemed to be asking for more than a minute of her time.

"Of course," she said, blushing unexpectedly. "I'm afraid there's no place for us to sit."

"Not necessary, I can only stay a minute. I didn't want you to hear this on the radio, wanted you to know before it hits the street." Her face paled instantly at the somberness of his tone and her hands began shaking uncontrollably. "There's been another murder."

CHAPTER 11

August 19

Christine Barboza loved the beach, especially on hot, hazy days. Christine, or Teeny to her friends owing to her diminutive size—she was four foot, eleven inches in heels—had spent the day at Horseneck Beach with two girlfriends. They had gone home early, leaving Teeny to enjoy a solitary nap in the afternoon sun.

As the air grew cooler she slipped on her sweat shirt wrapping her legs in a towel. Before long she'd have to pack up and head home, too. She had a date with David and needed time to shower, set her hair and iron her dress. She wondered why she had accepted his stupid invitation.

"Shit," she muttered glancing at her watch a short time later. "Get your ass in gear, Teeny."

David was a dork, but hey, he was taking her to Lucky's for dinner and dancing, so what the hell? That's why she'd accepted—Christine loved to dance. The faster and louder the music, the more she liked it. She knew Lucky's wasn't David's kind of place, but screw him. She'd endured enough of his boring plays and chamber music recitals. It was her turn to choose where they would go tonight and she had chosen Lucky's.

"Fine, Christine," he'd replied when she announced where she wanted to go. "Just remember, next time it's my turn."

"Sure David, sure," she'd replied, thinking that if he didn't choose wisely, there wasn't going to be a next time. Truth was, David Simms was starting to give her the creeps, always keeping his distance, barely touching her even though she'd given him plenty of encouragement. He was cute and she had been attracted to him from the start, but she'd thrown herself at him the last few times they'd been out and all he could say was, "it's too soon, let's get to know each other better before we hop into bed."

"I'm not asking you to fuck me," she had told him as they sat in the stands at the dog track. The track had been her choice and David was, as usual, out of sorts. When she had slipped her hand up his thigh, he had gripped it tightly, placing it back in her lap. After her retort, he had insisted they leave.

"No way," she had replied, pointing her nose in the air. "I've got a sure thing in the seventh so you'll just have to cool your jets."

His face a mask of fury, he had seized her elbow, squeezing so hard that she cried out.

"David, stop, you're hurting me," she had cried.

"That's the idea, now come along quickly. Please." His voice sounded like that of a stranger. "I will not be made a spectacle of in public."

The creep, she thought starting up her Mustang. The parking lot was nearly empty now, the last of the beach goers trundling back to their cars with coolers and umbrellas.

It's not natural, no sex, Christine mused. He had better be a decent dancer or I'm outta there with someone else.

On the way home she stopped in to see her mother. Mary Barboza was bedridden, crotchety to everyone except her favorite daughter. "Teeny," she croaked, smiling, she reached her hand out to her youngest daughter.

"Hi, Mama, how you doin'?" Teeny whispered, bending over, kissing her forehead, the skin dry and paper thin.

Teeny stayed long enough to heat some soup and feed her mother dinner, waiting until Madeline, her older sister arrived to sit with her until the night nurse came. After saying her goodnights, Christine passed by the hall mirror on her way out of the house, pausing to stare at her reflection. She ran her hand down the crimson birth mark running from the back of her ear, along the side of her neck until it snaked its way to the top of her right breast. Unless she wore something low cut or sleeveless, her shoulder length black hair hid most of the angry redness.

That was the nicest thing about David, Christine mused, turning away from the mirror. Of all the men she had ever dated, he was the one most comfortable with her birthmark, neither recoiling nor looking away when she had showed it to him.

"I look for beauty on the inside," he had told her on that first date and Teeny had believed him.

CHAPTER 12

August 21, Monday

Juls was in the office by seven making calls, paying bills and getting caught up. Without the distraction of Betty's gabbing and Tuck's mother-henning, she had accomplished most of what she needed to do by nine. She dearly loved Tuck, but if he asked one more time how she was doing, she was going to explode.

As was his habit most mornings, Tuck was out fishing. Rising before the sun was up, he would hike down to fish off the breakwater, or take the whaler out. When things slowed down, he would sometimes hitch a ride with one of the local fishermen and spend half the day fishing and catching up on local gossip. Monday was typically a busy morning—renters checking out, service people checking in and maid service to be lined up—but she had encouraged Tuck to stay out as long as he wanted after the past month he had spent in overdrive. She pinned several notes on the board for Betty and Tuck and was packing up, intending to begin her investigations when the back door slammed.

"Damn," she muttered. She hadn't escaped in time.

"You're here early partner," he said, throwing his wet pack and rain gear on the chair by the door. "How you doin'?"

She smiled through gritted teeth, "Fine. We're all caught up on billing, there've been a couple of calls, the messages on the board. For a Monday, it's actually been pretty quiet. Kerry, Matt or Pete can handle the jobs on the board. Mrs. Crandall's got a broken screen that needs to be taken off and brought to Harbor Hardware. Jim promised to do it this morning if we get it right over to him. Better tell whoever goes to just wait, they're speedier that way and we need to make an order for—"

"Hey, whoa there, Nellie-Belle, slow down, will ya? Why do I get the feeling you're just about to fly outta here?"

"Cause I am. I've got a lot to do and there's nothing here you all can't handle."

"What's this about? Not more investigating, I hope."

"Tuck, please don't start, and will you please take those wet things out of here."

"Yesterday was pretty rough, doncha think? Why don't you give yourself a little distance from this murder business, okay?"

"No, it's not okay. We discussed this, remember?"

"That was before they found Ellen Smith. For Christ's sake, Juls, you go poking around and maybe this maniac sees you and—"

"I'll be careful. I'm not going out with any of these people, I just want to ask a few questions, that's all."

"What people? Where're you going?"

"Please lower your voice, or I'm not discussing this."

"Fine, is this better? Now, please tell me where you're going?"

"Well, I thought I'd go over and talk to Rosie's co-workers at Arnold Graphics, then I'm going to the gym. Did you know that Ellen Smith belonged to the same gym as Rosie? The second woman too, Catherine?"

"Foley."

"Yes. And don't bother giving me that look. It's a pretty interesting coincidence, don't you think?"

"And don't you think the police have explored this interesting coincidence already?"

"If you're going to be sarcastic, I'm not discussing this with you."

"Great, well, this is just great. If the killer's at the gym, he probably weighs in at three fifty, bench presses nine thousand pounds and would love to add another pretty little gal to his collection."

"Stop it, Tuck."

"Jesus Christ, Juls, I'm worried about you. What if the Sportside is the connection? You go pokin' around, askin' a lot of pointed questions and—"

"The other woman didn't belong to the Sportside."

"And, how do you know that?"

"Jack told me this morning."

There it was, Jack again. "I'm coming with you."

"No you're not. You have things to do here. What's happened about the puzzle pieces anyway?"

"Oh didn't I tell you?" he said, knowing damn well he had not. He was sick of the case and what it was doing to her and he'd be damned if he got her all excited over nothing. "Ricky recognized the pieces right off. They're made a special way, somethin' about the paper. Anyway, they're only sold through a subscription company called *Puzzle It Out*, kinda like a Book of the Month club only with jigsaw puzzles. Subscribers get a new puzzle every month and the puzzles get harder and harder the longer you subscribe. I called Jack, but they already knew about it."

"So I heard."

"Look Juls, that's what responsible citizens do when they uncover a piece of information, they phone the police. They don't go traipsing around following up leads themselves."

"Just tell me about what Ricky said, please Tuck."

"They've faxed her a list of subscribers in the area. The list goes back almost thirty years, maybe a name'll pop out."

"Well, I guess I'll take off. Would you please get Kerry to water the window boxes, the petunias are drooping, and if she has time, the hedges need trimming and the office could use straightening up. Tell Betty to do it if she can stay off the phone long enough."

"And what about me? What're my orders?"

"Very funny."

"I'm dead serious, you've got everything figured out, don't you?"

"Tuck, please. I know you're concerned, and I'm grateful, really I am, but I'll be fine. All the victims have been handicapped or scarred in some way and look at me. I may be an emotional wreck, but otherwise I'm visibly unscathed."

"Nothing says the guy can't change his M.O. if he gets the urge, or if you get too close?"

"Tuck, I'll be fine."

"Great, I can rest easy now," he called, but she was gone, slamming the screen door behind her. Tuck threw an appointment calendar across the room. "If it had been a few years ago, you would have been a sitting duck," he muttered under his breath thinking back to her two knee replacements when she'd been on crutches for months following each operation. Thank God, she didn't limp anymore. Not much anyway.

The Arnold Graphics staff was taking a mid-morning coffee break when Juls pulled into the parking lot. Denny's Donut Wagon was still making the rounds through the small industrial park. Arnold occupied three bays of a small strip mall on Route 6 in Swansea. Behind this building, an office park stretched for almost a mile.

Rosie had worked at Arnold for twelve years. She had not been crazy about some of the people, but she liked the work. In the months preceding her death she had done a fair bit of grumbling to Juls and Tuck about certain staff members' abusing disability pay and collecting bogus unemployment payments. The owner, Danny Moniz, paid some of his staff, not Rosie, under the table, making out like a bandit. His three full-time employees had been Rosie, Sarah Bursin, the type setter and Larry Bigalow who did most of the printing, packing and shipping. The bookkeeper, "a sleaze bag" according to Rosie, was paid under the table during periods when he was supposedly "laid off" and all the while collecting unemployment benefits as well.

Rosie had done most of the art work—the computer graphics, the mock-ups, the silk-screening, the prints and drawing. Without her, Danny knew the company would fold so he worked hard to keep her happy. He'd fallen all over her at Rosie's funeral, crying and moaning about "his wonderful Rose", but Juls had attributed most of his histrionics to self-pity rather than genuine grief over her friend's death. "I've lost my little Rembrandt" he told the partners. As he wandered off, Tuck had muttered, "Wouldn't know a Rembrandt from a Ralph, the little weasel."

Danny paid her well, so Rosie had stayed on. "They'll get caught eventually," she'd tell her friend, "then the fun'll be over."

As she crossed the parking lot, Juls wondered if someone was doing well enough to kill in order to keep the fraud going. Not likely, of course, because there was no connection to the other women.

"Julia, how nice." Danny Moniz called, swinging the door open with a flourish. With a marvelously affected show of gallantry, he ushered her in to the stark front office. It stank of stale cigarette smoke and copier fluid and Juls swallowed hard to keep from gagging.

"How are you bearing up, my dear?"

"Okay," she lied, not about to bare her soul to Mr. Phoney Baloney. "Have you got a few minutes?"

"For you honey, I've got hours. Come back to my inner sanctum."

Rolling her eyes, she followed him down a hallway crowded with boxes, file cabinets, paper tubes and packing supplies sweeping her into a cubbyhole furnished in Naugahyde and chrome sorely in need of polishing. "Command Central," he pronounced, sweeping a stack of paper tubes off the nearest chair. "Sit, please."

Jim Arnold must be rolling in his grave, she thought, remembering the old friend of her father's who had started the company over forty years ago. Then it had been both an office supply store and a print shop. With the arrival of office supply superstores and the explosion of the computer graphics technology, small shops like Arnold simply couldn't keep pace. In poor health and tired of the struggle, Jim had sold the company to Danny Moniz. Mercifully, he had died before he could witness its gradual decline to its present sorry state.

First, Danny had liquidated the office supply division, then he'd sold the factory, extremely valuable property in Fall River's industrial park. If Rosie hadn't come along when she had, he would have gone under for sure. It was she who had prodded him into purchasing the computers that kept them apace in the swiftly changing world of graphic design. She was the artist, talented, creative, driving them all to explore new technologies, and she was a people person. Clients came back again and again because of her, not because of Arnold Graphics' name and certainly not because of Danny Moniz.

Several other companies had tried to lure her away, but she would always decline. "Danny's a weasel and a shitbird," she would say. "But at least he's up front about it, and I know who I'm dealing with."

"So what can I do for you Miz Whitman? Coffee, tea or me?"

Ignoring his attempt at humor, she said, "Do you have a membership at the Sportside Gym?"

"Whoa where'd that come from? You taking some kinda fitness survey?"

"Sorry," she mumbled. "It's just on my mind 'cause I'm headed there after this to pick up some of Rosie's things. I'm not sure exactly how to get there."

"So, you came here to ask me for directions to the Sportside?"

"No," she laughed, batting her eyelashes at him. "My mind's always drifting off lately. It's been so hard." Her voice drifted off and Juls sniffled, looking out the window.

"'Course it has honey. Must've been an awful blow for ya. Rosie never stopped talking about you. I know you two were closer than sisters."

"I don't want to take up your time, Danny, I just wanted to ask about Rosie's last few days at work. Did anything funny happen? Any visitors, anything out of the ordinary? Did she mention someone new she'd met, even possibly dated?"

"Nope, but then I'd be the last person she'd confide in, Julie. In fact, I'd expect you to know more about that kinda stuff."

"How 'bout phone calls? Any that might've upset her?"

"None that I know of, but you really oughta check with Sarah. She'd know if anyone would, she and the Rose were pretty tight. Trouble is, she's out sick today, third time this month. A real pain in the butt, I'll tell you, I got deadlines that aren't being met and no artist. This is the time we gotta all pull together, not sit home pretendin' to be sick. Know what I mean? Probably at the beach."

"Have you found a replacement for Rosie yet?"

"Hell no, and we aren't likely to. No one with her talent's gonna want to work in this dump. I got my feelers out though. Don't 'spose you got any talent in that direction?"

"Sorry," she replied, eyeing him. Why did she get the feeling that Danny was purposefully butchering the language? That the folksy, grammatically flawed speech was all a big act? "Well, I'd better get going. If you think of anything, I'd appreciate you letting me know, okay?"

"Sure thing. And, hon, I did have a membership at the Sportside, for your information. Gave it up last year to join Gold's. Larry belongs there too."

"Thanks," she said, noticing Danny's bulging biceps straining the linen of his sports coat. "Is Larry in?"

"Across the hall."

Larry proved to be no more help than his boss and Juls left Arnold disappointed. Investigating wasn't all it was cracked up to be.

CHAPTER 13

August 21, Monday

The voices hounded Brother.

"Oh, do stop your sniveling, you miserable boy. Bring me an iced tea then get out of my sight.

"Once again I see that I will have to take over.

"Three hours you've been working on this and you've only managed to work in five pieces.

"Idiot!

"How did I ever sire such a simpleton.

"A destructive, useless simpleton."

The sound of rubber wheels screeching over the waxed parquet floors competed with the ringing of the telephone. Persistence won out and Brother answered, his voice measured and calm, the very essence of normalcy. "Why of course, Mrs. Higgins. I can surely fit that in some time this week. Yes, yes, I'll be in touch."

Shaking himself, Brother rose from his stool, angry and peevish from the recent intrusion of the past. Try as he might, he could not rid himself of the incessant harping; the hateful recriminations unleashed from the recesses of the spinning, squeaking chair haunted him day and night. He thought about the loathsome chair, the needlepoint back stitched by his own hands moving ahead of him through the dark corridors, his beautifully wrought stitches staring back at him in silent rebuke for his role in putting her there.

"Oh, so you think your pretty stitchery will make up for what you've done, do you? Never, you horrid, deceitful child. You put me here and I will never forget it."

Brother pressed his hands against his temples desperately trying to shut her out, but it was no use. His power had ebbed away and there would be no fighting her off until he killed again. Christine would help to banish Mother for a few days at least. Ellen had been almost too easy. Thin, weak Ellen, lonely and scared with nowhere to go on a Saturday night. Her poor little heart had given out only seconds after he'd taken it up in his hands.

Christine would be different, more feisty like Rosie. Perky, chubby little Christine, with that ridiculous nickname. Christine's death would bring him strength. Then, there'd be Julia. Julia's death would almost certainly banish the specter of the woman in the chair, dying as she would on the anniversary of Mother's death. He'd feel so powerful and fulfilled after that.

He would give Christine a little more time, she wasn't quite ready for the gloves. Then, Christine would squeal like a stuck pig. And, didn't she deserve it, after dragging him to that horrid Lucky's. He shuddered thinking back to the overcrowded, smoke filled bar, all the whores and greenhorns. Brother wished he had the means to do away with them all.

Time to get back to work, he said pushing aside his now cold, congealing plate of steak and onions. Sharpen the ax, he thought, passing the woodbox near the back door; I will need it for Julia. Julia and her pathetic, crippled knees. The photograph in Rosie's apartment had tipped him off. A snapshot, taken less than a week after her first operation with Julia on crutches, supported by that buffoon of a partner of hers, had been the answer to Brother's prayers. Here was a person, well-loved and beautiful, yet seriously flawed. Would her death finally succeed in silencing the voices forever?

Even without the photo, Brother felt certain he would have discerned her deformity. His powers of observation were extraordinary after years spent slaving over the most intricate of puzzles.

Perhaps I'll allow Julia to be awake for the operation, he mused, grinning to himself. Then she can appreciate my gift to her, ridding her of those hopelessly crippled knees. She should have the opportunity to thank me for all the trouble I've gone to before I tighten the noose and put her out of her misery.

Alas, Julia must be the last. Then I must go away, far away with all my money. Linc will arrange things, Linc always arranges things.

CHAPTER 14

August 21, Monday

The afternoon sun stretched its languid, lingering fingers over the dust streaked windshield as Juls drew into the parking lot of the Sportside. The Sportside was not in the best part of town, so she locked the car, proceeding through the awning-covered entryway into the building. Just as she stepped inside, her beeper sounded and the beefy attendant behind the desk directed her to the phone. Tuck carried a cell phone, but Juls refused and it had taken months of pleading on his part to finally persuade her to have a beeper.

"Round the corner, next to the can. Take a right after the treadmills, can't miss it."

She dialed the office.

"J and T, this is Betty speaking, how may I help you?"

"It's me Betty, what's up?"

"Oh Juls, great, thanks for getting back so quickly. Tuck's out and Mrs. Beaman called. They just got in, loved the flowers by the way, said to be sure and thank you. She also couldn't get over what a terrific job the painters did and the window washers were—"

"Betty, I'm really busy. This isn't what you beeped me for, is it?"

"Oh gee, no. Sorry, where are you anyway?"

"Not important Betty, what's up?"

"Sorry, it's just that when Tuck gets back, he'll want to know and I catch hell if I haven't found out."

"Betty, I'm hanging up now. If you've got something to say, you'd damn well better spit it out!"

It would have been simple enough to tell their nosy receptionist where she was, but Juls refused to satisfy Betty's curiosity. Besides, Betty was on Tuck's side. They were both trying to babysit her.

"Well," Betty sniffed, affecting her most wounded tone. Juls could almost see the other's florid face reddening as she shook a head full of tightly curled, dyed black ringlets. "I was getting to it. It is about the Beamans, you know. Seems that when they were bringin' their stuff in, Mr. Beaman set a heavy suitcase on her favorite table in the front hall way and—"

"Betty!"

"Hold your horses, I'm getting there! Anyway, the table, some kinda valuable antique or something, it just collapsed. Two of the legs broke, the top's scratched and Mr. Beaman's in deep shit."

"This is why you beeped me?"

"Juls, the woman was hysterical. Screamed into the phone for a good ten minutes, almost incoherent, she was. Says she has to have it fixed right away. I told her you guys were both out and she started ranting and raving about how much they pay J and T and when there's a problem, look what happens."

"Call Skip Trembley. He'll go over and pick it up right away if you ask him nice."

"That's why I'm calling," Betty snapped, her tone implying I'm not stupid, you know. "Skip's away. When I told Mrs. Beaman, she practically had a coronary. I'm supposed to get back to her right away, as soon as I managed to locate you."

Damn the woman, Juls thought picturing tight-lipped, demanding Mitty Beaman, her graying page boy tucked under a hair net, wizened face flushed with indignation. Tuck might be able to fix it, but no, he probably wouldn't dare with Mitty looking over his shoulder with her beady, critical eye. Wilson McCaffrey suddenly popped into her head. She knew Tuck would be angry if she used McCaffrey, but it was either that or face Mitty Beaman's wrath, so he'd just have to lump it.

"Betty, take a look on the left bulletin board, just above the calendar in the corner. There should be a business card there for the McCaffrey Studio, do you see it?"

"Let's see now. Yup, I got it, who's he?"

"Just someone Tuck and I met recently. He does good work. Call him and see if he can fit the table in this week, then get back to me, okay? I'll wait right here for your call," she added, giving her the number of the pay phone. "I'll check through my book and see if I can come up with another idea in case he can't do it. Remember, call me back either way."

While she waited, Juls gazed around. Directly across from the phone was the entrance to the weight room with three more treadmills, a row of bicycles, a couple of stair steppers, at least twenty stations of Nautilus type equipment and a large open free weight area with six benches and matted floor. A tall, thin man with stooped posture was busy working up a sweat on one of the treadmills and another was stretched out on a bench, his beefy partner standing behind his head, spotting him. A young couple were in the midst of their circuit training, moving in tandem from one machine to the next.

Finally the phone rang. "Juls, it's me, he'll take it, Mr. McCaffrey, I mean. Real nice guy, he couldn't have been more accommodating. Said he remembered you guys and all. Said if it wasn't too bad, he could probably have it back in a couple of days. Wants to know if he should pick it up."

"No, have Matt or Kerry take it over, Mitty won't like it if we send a stranger to the house. Get directions from Mr. McCaffrey and then get someone right over to Beaman's."

"Kerry's out with Tuck, hon."

Figures, Juls thought. Tuck had been fixing the schedule for weeks always arranging for Kerry to be out on jobs with him. Here we go again, she had thought only a week ago, remembering his reaction to her inquiry about what was going on with Kerry. "Jesus Juls, she's only a kid," he had replied. They'd all been kids—Susie, Rachael, Kin, Pammie—all the lovestruck coeds returning to school in the fall after a wild, summer fling with gorgeous Tuck Potter.

"How 'bout Matt?" she asked Betty.

"He's at the Forresters, doin' somethin' with their boats, I think."

"Well call him and tell him to get over there now. The Forresters are away, they won't know the difference. And Betty, if you can't get Matt, go over and get the table yourself and bring it to Matt. Tell him to get it to McCaffrey before he closes so we can shut Mitty up."

"So, I should leave the office unattended if I can't get Matt?"

"Yes, put the machine on and go. I should be back soon, okay?"

Juls hung up, not waiting for Betty's long-winded reply, walking back to the desk where the same, blond hulk sat behind the gleaming white counter reading a magazine. "Find the phone?" he said, looking up from the latest issue of *Pumping Iron*.

"Yes, thanks. I'm Julia Whitman. Rosie Mikawski was a close friend of mine. I believe she used to be a member here?"

"Sure, yea, Rosie. We were all pretty broken up about her. Rosie was like family. Everybody loved her."

"Me too," she murmured. "I wonder if you could tell me who she was particularly friendly with?"

"Hey, wait a minute, you're not with the cops, are you? They've been down our necks for weeks about this already. You don't think any of the guys here would hurt her, do you? Look, you're a pretty lady, and a friend of Rosie's besides, but I ain't helpin' out no cop."

"I'm just a friend, really, Mr.?"

"Arruda, Doug Arruda." The dark brown eyes stared back at her, hooded and wary, all of easy friendliness vanished. Thinking back to Tuck's words, Juls thought again how ridiculous she had been thinking she could investigate anything.

"Mr. Arruda—"

"Doug, please." He said it as a challenge, daring her to say Mr. Arruda again.

"Doug, listen, I'm not a cop or anything like that. I'm just a person who misses her friend terribly and I'm wondering how she spent her last few weeks, that's all. I'm sorry if I upset you."

"Hey, no sweat, Julie, I getcha. Don't 'spose it'd hurt if I told you a few things, but trouble is, like I told the cops, Rosie was friendly to everyone. There's Irene, over there on the biceps curl, then Kevin next to her. They knew her pretty well. Then, there's Linda Murphy, she's a teacher away for the summer. She and Rosie were pretty tight. And then of course there's Billy."

"Billy?"

"Yea, Billy Correira, didn't she ever mention him?" Juls shook her head. "Funny, I'd a thought she'd mention him."

"Is he here now?"

"Nah."

"How about a number where I can reach him?"

"No can do, Julie. Our membership list is strictly confidential, just like doctors. 'Fraid I can't make an exception even for a gorgeous babe like yourself. You work out?"

"I jog a little, but I don't belong to a gym or anything. Rosie was always trying to drag me over here, but I never quite made it."

"Until now," he grinned. "Always a first time Julie, we give three free visits. You look like you're in pretty good shape, but those skinny little arms could use some toning—"

"About Mr. Correira," she interrupted. "When does he usually come in?"

"Tuesday, Thursday, Saturday, four to six, like clock work. Don't miss a day 'less he's outta town or straight out at work. Which, pretty Julia," he drawled, drawing out the a into a long, extended ah. "He is at the moment, out straight I mean. He was in this morning for a quick workout, but said he wouldn't get back again until Saturday at the earliest. You oughta stop back, I guarantee he'd wanna meet you."

"Where's he work?"

"Now that'd be telling, wouldn't it? He'll be here Saturday, that's all I can tell you. He's got a hot date so he'll definitely be in. Always comes in before a date. Pumps up, sweats like a fuckin' pig—excuse my French—then showers, shaves and walks outta here lookin' like a million bucks."

Rosie had never mentioned Billy Correira and referred to everyone at the Sportside as the gang. "Come down and meet the gang," she'd plead with her. "They're all good people."

"Rosie and Billy didn't date, did they?"

"Nah, wasn't his type. He likes 'em long and lean, like yourself. He and Rosie were just buddies. Spotted each other with the weights, worked out together, challenged each other. He was stronger, sure, but she could keep up with him, that's for sure. They mighta gone out for a beer together now and then but I doubt there was any hot romance there."

"Well, thanks Doug."

"My pleasure."

"Maybe I'll stop in Saturday."

"Sure thing. Come early and get in a work-out. Take me fifteen minutes to get you squared away on the machines. Or Ray or Lucy'll fix you up if I'm not here. Just say you want a free three day trial and they'll get you started."

"I'll think about it, thanks."

"Billy'll be foamin' at the mouth when he gets a load of you. You even look a little like one of his old girlfriends, poor little Ellie."

"Excuse me," she said, her blood running cold.

"Yea, Ellen Smith, slim and pretty like you. Too young to die."

Arruda continued talking, his voice smooth, taunting, but Juls heard nothing. Excusing herself, she ran blindly towards her car, stumbling several times as her knees betrayed her. Finally, after several minutes of frantic grappling, the key turned in the lock and she flung herself into the car, slamming the door and locking it behind her. Her limping flight had not been lost on Doug Arruda who had observed it all from his perch at the front window. As her car rounded the corner out of sight, he shrugged turning back to his magazine.

CHAPTER 15

August 24, Thursday

Jack Mederois wiped his brow for the hundredth time. The temperature had been hovering at around a hundred degrees for the past two days and midway through the morning, the station house thermometer read ninety-eight. In accordance with Murphy's Law, the station's air conditioner had promptly broken down, no sign of a repairman in sight.

"Jesus, Mary and Joseph it's hot," he said, to Tim Cottrell who poked his head in with an armload of paperwork.

"Jack, Juls Whitman's on line two. Want talk to her?"

"'Course I do, what're you crazy?" he laughed, winking at his assistant. "Not only is the lady a knockout, but who knows, maybe she and Potter'll get lucky, Christ knows we need some luck."

"Yo, Ms. Whitman, Jack Mederois here."

"Hi, I'm just checking in to see if there's anything new?"

"Fraid not, how 'bout at your end?"

"Nope. What about the puzzle company?"

"We've checked into that, but so far it's taken us nowhere. Haven't been able to connect a name on the list to any of the victims."

"I see, well, thanks anyway."

"Everything okay?"

"Fine, except for the heat."

"Yeah, tell me about it! It's like an oven in here, city threatening to explode at any minute. Between the strangler and the gangs tryin' their darndest to kill each other every night we're havin' trouble keepin' the lid on. Heat brings out the worst in people."

Juls rang off, failing to mention her planned visit to the Sportside on Saturday. Something told her Mederois would disapprove even more strenuously than Tuck. As she returned to her paperwork, her partner walked in dressed in a blue oxford shirt and tie, a beige linen sport jacket slung over his shoulder looking cool as a cucumber.

"Hey," she whistled. "Where are you off to, Mr. Gorgeous?" And, he was gorgeous. No wonder Kerry and every other female within a fifty-mile radius couldn't keep their hands off him. Juls felt instantly frumpy in her wrinkled sundress.

"I gotta be at Fergusons', remember?" he replied, referring to elderly clients who had hired him to chauffeur them to a garden party in East Providence.

"You don't have to be there for a couple of hours. Why, you'll be dripping with sweat by then."

"Thanks for caring, but in five minutes a pretty lady's pickin' me up in her convertible so I'll stay nice and cool."

"Let me guess, Kerry's got Daddy's car?"

"Close, it's her brother's. She just dropped him off at the airport and she has it till Tuesday, Caddy, sixty-eight, lemon yellow. Watch out world, here we come."

"Isn't it a little early for a date?" she observed, rolling her eyes as she shuffled papers around the desk.

"Don't think so. You aren't jealous, are you?"

"Hardly," she lied. "Now, get out of here. Some of us have work to do."

"I am working, we're doin' the rounds, then we're making a quick trip into the city to see Ricky."

"What about the Fergusons?"

"We'll be back in plenty of time, don't worry."

Rounds indeed, Juls thought. When had Tuck ever done rounds in the summer? Since early June, Pete or one of the other kids had handled all the rounds. Walk-throughs or rounds consisted of a J and T employee walking through any unoccupied properties, clipboard in hand, checking appliances, plumbing, alarms systems and overall condition of the homes, noting down if yard work or other maintenance work needed doing. Juls hated rounds and so did Tuck. He just wanted to get Kerry alone. Probably wanted to try out the new king-sized bed J and T had arranged to have delivered to the Kervins two days earlier.

Shaking herself, she asked, "Has Ricky found out anything?"

"Nope, I'm just picking up a copy of the list. I gave mine to Mederois. Cops didn't find shit, but maybe we'll get lucky."

"Tuck?"

"Yo?"

"After Saturday I'm gonna drop this and you better too. We're so far behind around here and if you're going to be taking off every five minutes on joy rides with Kerry, we have to—"

"Whoa, Nelly Belle. It's me you're talking to, remember? You know, the guy who's been workin' overtime all summer?"

"I know Tuck, I'm sorry. This investigation has got me churned up all the time, you know?"

"I noticed. The sooner you drop it the better. And you know I've wanted to can the whole thing from the start. Listen, I'll get the list from Ricky, we'll file it and be done with it, okay?"

A beeping horn sounded from the driveway.

"There she is. Better hurry, Tuckie-poo!"

"You're bad. Wait'll you bring home your next honey, partner."

"At least he'll be legal." she called, but Tuck was gone.

A honey, what a joke. When had she had a honey in recent memory? Since Greg, she hadn't dated at all, and how long had that been, two years? Tuck was always trying to fix her up with someone, but after too many disastrous blind dates, she had declined his offers, telling him that he did not hang around "her type." She suspected that Tuck deliberately fixed her up with people he knew she wouldn't like.

Who is my type, anyway? she mused, waiting for Betty's arrival so that she could take off. Betty thought a nine to five job started at eleven and ended at three, with an hour for lunch. Greg had not been her type although they'd had fun for a while. They certainly shared many of the same interests—hiking, running, tennis, and others. They also enjoyed quiet afternoons reading in the shade on her backyard swing and had had many lively dinner conversations about everything from politics to the Brontes.

And, Greg had been a gentle, considerate lover. Perhaps it was that consideration and the almost total lack of passion in their relationship in and out of the bedroom that had ultimately led to their break-up. Tuck had disliked Greg and that had not helped the situation. For a while, Tuck had tried to hide his dislike, attempting to befriend his partner's shy lover. However, Greg had been immune to the famous Potter charm and barely spoke to Tuck most of the time. He also resisted any plan Juls suggested involving her friends. He claimed her friends were "loud and boisterous." The one person he tolerated was Rosie. Greg and Rosie had hit it off from day one.

"A complete nerd" had been Tuck's candid assessment the day after they broke up. "Never liked the guy, you're much better off without him." He had been right, of course, but his flippant dismissal of Greg had irritated her and Juls had slammed out of the office, refusing to return for five days. Just as he had done this summer, Tuck quietly did her job as well as his own until she was ready to return.

Who was her type? Tuck was her type, she thought morosely continuing to shuffle papers. No one else would ever measure up to Tuck, and that was the truth. It was too bad, but there was no help for it because a relationship with Tuck was completely out of the question. Period, end of story.

Betty finally strolled in dressed in floral print muumuu and matching neon green sandals. Barely five feet tall and the shape of a beach ball, the outfit was not flattering. She received a barking hello.

"Glad you could make it!"

"Sorry, I got tied up at the—"

"Beauty parlor by the look of that tint and perm!"

"Well, I…"

"Skip it, Betty, I'm in a foul mood so don't pay any attention to me. Listen, I've gotta run, I've got a million errands, but I should be back around two."

"Did you see the note about the Beaman's table?"

"No."

"It's ready. That nice Mr. McCaffrey called last night. Should I have Matt run over and get it this morning? He knows the way, cause he took it over there. Mrs. Beaman calls about ten times a day to check on it."

"That's okay," she replied, recalling the rather nice looking woodworker. My luck, he'll probably turn out to be married with ten kids. "I've gotta be in Somerset, I'll pick it up, just jot down the address for me. And, call over to tell him I'm on my way. If it's not convenient or you can't reach him, buzz me, okay?"

"Sure thing. Should I tell Mrs. Beaman that you'll deliver it?"

"Yup, tell her I'll bring it over a little after two. See ya."

After whirling around the city taking care of her errands in record time, Juls pulled up in front of the McCaffrey Studio just after noon. The studio occupied the south end of handsome, reproduction saltbox, extending into an attached three car garage. The shingled facade was stained a deep, weathered brown, a small sign—colonial beige, lettered in black— was attached to the side of the garage, the only indication that the residence housed a place of business.

As she waited on the stoop, strains of Vivaldi's *Four Seasons* reached her from within. Finally, the door opened and he stepped out, "Why Miss Whitman, I'd almost given up on you. Your assistant called and said you'd be right over and when you didn't come, I thought perhaps, I'd misunderstood and was meant to deliver it after all."

"No, sorry, my fault," she blushed.

"No problem, I'm glad you're here. Come in." His warm, friendly smile put her at ease and Juls followed him through a small office area into the huge workshop space. Saws, sanders, lathes, planers and all manner of power tools large and small populated the well-organized work space, the pungent smell of sawdust mingled with varnish and paint thinner surrounded her. It was a pleasant space, reminding Juls of her own father's woodshop where she had spent many hours working alongside him, constructing tiny wooden projects from the scraps of his carving and furniture making.

From the looks of things, McCaffrey was extremely busy—chairs, tables, dressers and several heavy armoires stood all around them, in various stages of restoration. "My," she exclaimed. "You were awfully good to fit us in with all this to do. And lucky for us, because this particular client is very demanding."

"It was my pleasure. Smaller things, like your table are never a problem, although I hope your client will not be disappointed. I can patch things up, but I'm not God. There is a difference, you know."

Laughing, she said, "Don't worry, Mitty's blind as a bat! Oh, I mean, I didn't mean to imply that your work would be—"

"That's quite alright," he said, laughing. "And don't worry about calling on short notice. I can always squeeze things in. This is all a bit deceiving, actually. You see, I own some of these pieces. I have a small antiques business on the side. Now, let's see, ah, here it is, your Queen Anne side table, back in one piece and largely unscathed considering its ill treatment. Who would think of putting a heavy suitcase on such a delicate piece?"

"Well, you can bet Ralph Beaman won't get the idea again in a hurry. It looks wonderful. I will give you the Beamans' address and you can send the bill directly to them, if that's acceptable, Mr. McCaffrey?"

"Wilson, please. Of course, that's fine." He took the slip of paper from her hand, tucking it in his breast pocket. "Now, I'll just carry this out and load it in the car for you."

"Thanks, but I can manage."

"It's my pleasure," he said, lifting the table, holding the pedestal in one hand, lifting the garage door with the other.

"Well, thanks again," she said as he closed the trunk on the table.

There was an awkward silence and Juls made no move to go. "This is a really nice spot you have here."

"Thanks, I feel very fortunate. It's been in my family for many years. I'd never be able to afford it with today's waterfront prices."

"It's great." Her voice trailed off as she gazed towards the river behind the house.

"Have you had lunch? I mean, it's after twelve and I thought, there's a great sandwich shop just around the corner, if you're hungry we could—"

"I'm starved and I'd love to," she interrupted, startling both herself and her companion.

"Great. Let me close up the shop and we'll be off."

True to his word the sandwiches were great and the pair sat for over an hour talking. Not a word was mentioned about the first time they had met, on the sidewalk outside Rosie's building. He asked about her business and she regaled him with stories of their twelve years of dealing with "people too used to getting their own way."

Wilson told her how he'd started the shop. "My father was a woodworker, first as a hobby, then later in life, he managed to make it his livelihood, mostly reproduction stuff, commissioned pieces. He specialized in bureaus and Windsor chairs. Worked almost exclusively in cherry."

"He must have been a wonderful teacher."

"Perhaps he would have been, but he died when I was very young. I never knew him."

"But I thought?"

"My father married in his late fifties, my mother was much younger, early twenties. They were very much in love, or so I'm told, but they were to have only six years together."

"How sad."

"Yes, but he left a wonderful legacy, and his tools of course."

"Did you grow up in that house?"

"The studio has always been here, but the house is only ten years old. I used to rent it out, but then, a few years ago I decided, what the heck. Why keep an apartment in the city when I could live here myself."

"So you've been in this business since—"

"My early twenties, don't worry Miss Whitman. I'm not a total illiterate. I went to college, four years at Amherst and then some post grad at URI."

"I'm not the slightest bit worried," she laughed, "And, please, call me Juls."

"Short for?"

"Julia."

"A pretty name, I had an aunt named Julia."

"Another thing we have in common. I was named for my aunt Julia and my father was a woodworker, too."

"I'll bet we'd find lots more common ground if we kept talking." He laughed, reaching for the check as the waitress laid it on the table. "My treat, you can get the next one."

"Thanks, I've got to run. If I don't get that table delivered soon, I'll be wearing it on my head when I do."

They walked back to the house in companionable silence. When she reached her car, Juls extended her hand, saying, "Thanks again, this was fun."

"My pleasure. I hope someone else's accident will bring you back again."

"Excuse me?"

"The table, I mean the table," he stammered, blushing. Then, out of the blue, he asked, "Are you free Saturday?"

She stared at him, mouth agape.

"Oh, I am sorry. You barely know me, God, what's gotten into me today?" He laughed, smacking his forehead in mock rebuke.

"No, it's okay. It's just been a while. And, unfortunately I'm busy Saturday. Perhaps another time?"

"Do you mean that?"

"Yes, yes I do."

"I'll hold you to it then," he called as she pulled away. "Take care."

Waving, she drove off, feeling happier than she had for many months.

CHAPTER 16

August 25, Friday

Christine woke with a headache dreading the day ahead. First she must drive her mother to St. Anne's outpatient department for her check-up, then, after settling her mother back in bed, she must go right on to work, second shift, her least favorite. She hated coming home in the middle of the night to an empty house.

An operating room nurse, Christine had been on staff at Charleton Memorial since her graduation from nursing school twelve years earlier. She seldom worked weekends, but her day shifts varied from week to week. She didn't mind the midnight to eight a.m. shift, but four to midnight was the pits and it was Friday night to boot.

"Just think Teeny," her supervisor Vivian would say. "You're the most popular nurse in the OR. Why I get more requests for you than all my other nurses combined."

"Small comfort, when I'm falling asleep standing up," Christine replied, deflecting the compliment as usual.

Vivian was not easily put off however. "You give your patients something no one else does, hon. They know it, the docs know it, so don't sell yourself short girl, you're one in a million."

Vivian was right, Christine was loved and respected by physicians and patients alike. Over the years, several doctors had begged her to come to work for them.

An internationally known eye specialist had, in fact, offered to double her salary if she would sign on as his nurse on call, but Christine declined. People like mama needed her care and she refused to join the growing cadre of medical specialists devoting the major portion of their time to catering to a wealthy few.

So, here she was, stuck on second shift, and whose fault was that? Her room-mate, Maisie was away for the week, camping and hiking with her boyfriend in the White Mountains of New Hampshire. Christine almost never took a vacation and at the moment she almost hated Maisie whom she pictured curled up in a sleeping bag, snuggling with Eddie, breathing in the cool mountain air. Far from the hot, humid confines of Fall River.

The phone rang and she ignored it. After five rings, she grabbed the receiver, barking hello.

"Christine?"

Just what she needed right now, a conversation with David the dork.

"Christine, are you there?"

"Yes," she answered wearily, wondering if she dared hang up.

"How are you?"

"Shitty, if you want to know the truth. Look David, I'm in kind of a hurry, you know?"

"Oh, I'm sorry. I wanted to apologize for being so out of sorts at Lucky's the other night. And, I wanted to make it up to you. Are you free tonight?"

Out of sorts, that was the understatement of the year. "No, I can't, I'm working. Listen David, I think we should cool it for a while. I'm just not up for this right now."

"How 'bout tomorrow night?"

"David, I don't know how to say this nicely, but—"

"Look, it's just dinner, Christine, please? We could try out that new Italian place down by the water, what's it called? Capettis? It's supposed to be great. Then maybe take in a movie—your choice, of course. What do you say?"

Silence.

"Christine?"

"Oh, what the hell," she said aloud. "Sure, I'll go." At least she wouldn't have to spend Saturday night alone. Even David was better than an empty house and a B movie on the VCR. Besides, he said she could pick the movie so how bad could it be?

"I'll pick you up then?"

"Fine."

Around seven thirty?"

Aren't we daring, she thought, seven thirty it wouldn't even be dark yet. After they rang off, Christine chided herself for giving in. She had sworn after the fiasco at Lucky's that she would not see him again. What was the matter with her?

"You're really hard up girl," she said to her reflection in the mirror.

Tomorrow night is definitely it, she vowed. There was something very odd about David. He was so secretive and standoffish. First, there was the unpleasantness at the dog track when she had tried to touch him. And, he had barely kissed her in all the time they spent together. In fact, when she had tried to kiss him, David had recoiled as if she were a leper. He was definitely not normal.

CHAPTER 17

Tuck let out a wolf whistle as Juls walked through the door dressed in a pale blue summer sheath that caressed her body in all the right places. "Well, if you don't look good enough to eat, partner." And, she did, her long hair, loose and flowing, a single strand of pearls her only adornment. Barefoot, she carried white, heeled sandals and a small woven evening bag.

Smiling, she tapped him on the head as she passed. "You look pretty good yourself. And, you better watch it. You know how I hate expressions like 'good enough to eat'." Her partner wore a beige linen suit, white dress shirt and brightly patterned tie in blues, greens and yellows. He, too, looked 'good enough to eat,' but she was not about to tell him so. "You ready?"

"Yup. I'll drive." He held the door and as she passed by, Tuck reached out, touching her arm.

"Tuck…"

"Sorry, can't help myself. Old habits die slowly."

"Hmmm." She rushed to the car, opening the door before he could do the honors. They were on their way to a client's cocktail party at the Colsons two miles farther down the beach road. While the partners ordinarily refrained from socializing with clients, Janet and Hank Colson were among their first clients and the four had become friends. Once or twice each summer they shared a casual dinner and Tuck and Juls always attended their annual cocktail party, a huge catered affair, which relied on a great deal of behind the scenes help from J and T.

They parked at the end of a line of cars already a quarter mile away from the Colsons' driveway. Juls took his arm and they walked along the grassy shoulder in companionable silence. Since this was definitely not a date, Juls dared take his arm without encouraging further advances. She drew strength and warmth from him, his nearness enormously comforting. For his part, Tuck hardly dared take a breath. He knew if he returned the embrace she would pull away and he would do nothing to jeopardize these rare moments of intimacy.

Making their way up the driveway, they headed for the backyard, passing through an arbor blanketed with pale pink roses. "You ready?" he asked, patting her hand.

"Not really, but I could use a drink."

"Sit tight and I'll be right back."

"But, Tuck, wait." Juls watched him head for the bar at the far end of the garden, three bartenders working overtime to serve the large crowd of thirsty revelers. The Colsons' was last big party of the summer and almost everyone in Windy Harbor seemed to be present.

As Juls scanned the crowd, looking for a friendly face, a tall, slender man in gray linen suit approached. Handsome, tan and athletic, his dark brown hair brushed his collar, his gray blue eyes the color of the sky. He was a stranger. "Juls Whitman, isn't it?" he asked, extending his hand.

"Yes," she replied, puzzled. "Do I know you…have we met?"

He laughed. "Oh, I'm sorry, Ben Colson. I have an advantage, I'm afraid. My aunt and uncle have been talking about you and your partner continually and how we should meet while I'm here. And, we have a mutual connection, I believe, or did. I'm a veterinarian in Fall River. I treated Rosie Mikawski's cat, Wicky."

Juls realized he had been holding her hand for over a minute, and she slowly withdrew it. "Oh, yes. Wicky is with me now. She and my cat are having some adjustment problems."

"It just takes time. They'll get used to each other. I'm very sorry for your loss."

"Thank you. Did you know Rosie well?" she asked, wondering why her friend had never mentioned Dr. Colson.

"Not really. She called me several months ago when the cat had a seizure. I make house calls, do inoculations and routine check-ups with the Animal Rescue League Mobile Vet Van. I went back a couple of times to check on the cat, that's all. Your friend seemed like a terrific person."

"She was." Juls said, spying Tuck approaching with two gin and tonics.

Noticing his partner's expression, he asked, "Everything okay?"

"Just fine. Tuck, this is Ben Colson, Janet and Hank's nephew. He's a vet in Fall River and treated Wicky."

"Tuck Potter. Nice to meet you."

Tuck's body language told a different story, Juls mused, watching her partner's shoulders stiffen, his eyes wary, expression guarded. "How long are you here for, Ben?" Juls smiled, taking her drink from Tuck with barely a nod.

"Till after Labor Day. I'm desperately seeking tennis partners under 65. Do either of you play?" He looked directly at Juls, making no attempt to hide his interest.

Tuck shook his head.

"I do," she said. "I'm not very good, but I love to play."

"Then, please, let's play tomorrow. What time suits you?"

"Early morning is best since we get busy in the office on the weekends. Is seven too early?"

"Ouch," he grimaced, taking a swallow of what appeared to be straight Scotch. "For a pretty lady like you, I guess I can drag myself out of bed. Seven it is."

"Great."

"Why there you are!" Janet Colson, their hostess bore down on them, waving her drink from which dangled a bright, shredded cocktail napkin. Every silver hair in place, Janet was trim and tan like her nephew, her dress a riot of purple and pink flowers, synched at the waist with a scarlet sash. She looked lovely, every bit the perfect hostess. "I see you've already met. I've been telling Benny for two weeks to give you two a ring. He's so sick of us two old codgers and he has wanted to meet many of the younger crowd."

He laughed. "You make me sound completely pathetic, Aunt Jan."

"We're playing tennis in the morning," Juls said. "That'll be a change of scene even if the play is only mediocre."

"Don't believe a word she says," Tuck said. "She's a much better player than she's letting on."

"Sandbagging me, huh?"

Tuck nodded, as Juls poked him in the ribs. 'That is a complete lie, spoken by a man who never plays tennis yet can usually beat me anyway."

"True, Potter? Then, why not join us?"

"Thanks, but my tennis whites are in the laundry. Besides, someone's got to mind the store if my player's playing hooky."

"Listen you two. I'm going to steal Bennie for a few minutes to meet some friends. So glad you've connected. Have fun."

Ben waved over his shoulder. "If I get lost in the crowd, I'll see you on the court at seven, okay? I don't expect we'll need to reserve at that hour."

"What a fop," Tuck muttered under his breath, watching the Colsons disappear into the crowd.

"I think he's kinda cute."

"Typical."

"What's that supposed to mean?"

"You like pretty boys. Bennie kind of reminds me of Greg."

"Does not. He doesn't look anything like Greg."

"It's the affect."

"You're a fine one to talk. What was that about tennis whites?"

"Sarcasm, m'dear, and you know it. Can we get out of here pretty soon? I'll take you to dinner at Salty's, what'dya say?"

"Not till we've seen Hank and thanked him. Oh, God, there're the Fitzgeralds. Let's go this way so we don't run into them. They're still waiting for us to repair the porch."

They arrived at Salty's shortly after eight. Both had eaten so much at the Colsons' that they decided to share a salad and one large order of steamers. They spent most of the dinner organizing business for the coming week. It was the first time they had sat down to plan and talk for what seemed like months. It felt good.

When they parted company outside the office, Tuck kissed her on the forehead and for an instant, she returned the embrace, allowing him to draw her close. An instant later, she was pulling away, "Night, partner."

"Wanta come in for a nightcap?"

"No, thanks. And, that was a friendly hug. Nothing more."

"Saving yourself for Bennie, huh?"

"Very funny." She hopped into her car, calling that she would be in right after tennis.

Tuck stood watching until her headlights disappeared from sight.

CHAPTER 18

August 26, Saturday

From the minute Tuck walked into the office, the phone had not stopped ringing. The Labor Day rush was on and, as usual, they were short-handed. Last night had been fun, but he had drunk too much wine and now Juls was off with her new tennis buddy. Christ!

The heat wave had finally broken and the temperature was a dry eighty-five, with a decent ocean breeze too, definitely not a day to be tied to the phone. Where the hell was Betty, anyway? And Kerry for that matter?

Kerry, cute little Kerry, she'd be leaving a week from Tuesday. He'd already planned a special farewell dinner for her, at the Lobster Pot, one of his favorite restaurants. Juls had tried to excuse herself from that evening, but he had insisted she come along.

Juls, Juls, Juls, he thought. Whatever am I going to do about you? She knew how he felt about her, yet she kept him firmly at arm's length. How many years had they wasted? He had been crazy about her from the moment he had laid eyes on her at their first glass workshop. She had been stooped over, working on a difficult glass cut, her beautiful eyes hidden behind her scratched safety goggles. The time they spent camping along the west coast had been the happiest weeks of his life. He had fully expected that they would marry soon after they got home, assuming they would have a houseful of children by now.

It had been her wish to end the intimate relationship and it gnawed at him more and more with each passing year. If only he had been less forthright about his past. Maybe he wouldn't have scared her off. They told friends the split had been mutual but they had never fooled Rosie. Several years ago, Rosie had confronted him. "You're crazy in love with her, aren't you?" she had whispered, watching them both after a softball game, sitting side by side at Archie's.

"Juls is my best friend."

"That's not what I mean and you know it." Her eyes challenged him.

"It's a dead issue," had been his only reply.

"What's that supposed to mean? I've watched you guys flit from one relationship to the next like two lost souls. You're both crazy about each other, it's insane."

"Tell it to your friend, not me" was all he could think of to say.

Rosie had talked to Juls, but had gotten nowhere. Now, she was dead and Juls was running around playing tennis with Ben Colson and having lunches with that McCaffrey bozo. Jesus, Skip steps outta town for two days and a perfect stranger's stealing his business. Screw, Mitty Beaman. The old bat could've waited two days for her goddamn table.

His thoughts were interrupted by a knock at the door and an elderly man with snowy white hair peeked his head in. He wore new khakis, ironed with precise, even creases down the middle and a short sleeved madras shirt.

"May I help you?" Tuck asked, rising to greet the newcomer.

"Hello, yes. I'm looking for Julia Whitman or Dan Potter."

"You found him, she's not in yet."

"Mr. Potter, I'm Linc Marvell," he said, extending his hand. The name rung a bell but Tuck couldn't quite place it. "I was Ellen Smith's boss at the bank. Ellen Smith was one of the women who was killed. I heard one of your friends was also a victim?"

"Yes, Rosie Mikawski. She and my partner were like sisters. It's been a rough summer."

"Believe me, I understand, Mr. Potter."

"Tuck, please."

"Ellie was like a daughter to my wife and me," he said, sinking into a chair, his body collapsing as if getting there and introducing himself had sapped all of his strength.

"I'm sorry, Mr. Marvell."

"Thank you, son… I understand from Detective Mederois that you two have been helping out with the investigation?"

"Not really. We've done a little poking around, therapy for Juls mostly. It's been impossible for her to sit idly by and do nothing. I've been tryin' to get her to leave it alone if you wanna know the truth."

"I'd like to help."

"Like I said, we're tryin' to wind things down. Juls is 'sposed to be meeting some guy at the Sportside this afternoon. That's the gym where Rosie and some of the others belonged, and then she's promised me she'll back off."

"Yes, I remember Ellie talking about that place."

"Juls is meeting a guy named Billy Correira, ever hear of him?"

"No."

"Ellen dated him apparently."

"She never mentioned him to me. Actually, she hasn't mentioned a beau since she broke off her engagement last year."

"Oh?"

"His name was Harry Dickinson. He was horrible to Ellie, he hurt her terribly."

"Where's he now?"

"I haven't any idea. I heard that he married someone else soon after he broke it off with Ellie. I can't imagine she'd have had any further contact with him."

"So, was she dating anyone else recently?"

"As I said, she hadn't mentioned anyone, but now that you ask, I believe she might have been."

"How's that?"

"Well, she seemed happier the last month before her death. More animated and lively, more relaxed. Ellie was a kind, friendly soul, but there were times I know when she was desperately lonely. Recently she just seemed perkier, like she was looking forward to her weekends, instead of dreading them. That might mean a new man in her life don't you think?

"She also declined several dinner invitations. We thought that was a little odd as Ellie always jumped at the chance to spend the evening with us. She's very close to our sons and their wives also. To be honest, Betsy, that's my wife and I were a little hurt that she hadn't confided in us, hadn't brought her new man around. But, of course, I'm not even certain there was a new man, just a hunch. You know, I believe she intended to tell me about him the day she died," he added, speaking more to himself than Tuck.

"How so?"

"Well, she started to say something, but you see, we were interrupted, by an emergency. My wife had been in a minor car accident and so I rushed out before Ellie could say whatever it was she'd wanted to tell me. My son came to fetch me, she wished us well and we just drove away." His eyes filled with tears and Linc Marvell aged twenty years, his grief taking cruel measure over his rugged, yet distinguished features.

"Mr. Potter, I've thought about that night so many times over the past week, you have no idea. If I'd only sent Ron to sit with Betsy, then perhaps Ellie would have confided in me. And of course, Betsy feels responsible, too. If she hadn't called and I hadn't rushed away, we might have changed the whole course of Ellie's evening. She offered to drive me to the hospital. Oh, God why didn't I ask her to come along?"

"Don't blame yourself, Mr. Marvell. For all you know she might've had something entirely different on her mind."

"Perhaps," said the other, rising to go. "I won't take anymore of your time son, but please don't hesitate to call if I can be of help. My wife and I go away, to my sister's in Vermont over Labor Day week. We'll be leaving the day after tomorrow, be back the eleventh so please call me. I'm prepared to offer financial assistance too, if it will help. Anything to bring this monster to justice before he harms another young woman."

"Thanks. You take care now and have a good trip," Tuck said, walking him to his car, waving as Marvell drove off.

Three minutes later, Juls breezed in wearing white shorts and a sleeveless blue top. She did have great legs, bronze and muscular after long runs in the summer sun. "Who was that?"

"Linc Marvell, Ellen Smith's boss at the bank. How was your game?"

"Great. What'd Mr. Marvell want?"

"You gonna play again?"

"Yes, tomorrow morning, if it's any of your business. Now, can we drop the subject of tennis so you can tell me what Mr. Marvell wanted."

"Same thing we do, to catch this asshole. Wants to help out 'our investigation.' Got our name from Mederois, can you believe it? Says he'll bankroll us too," he smiled mischievously. Then remembering the man's anguish, he added more soberly, "Real nice guy. Pretty broken up about Ellen Smith, was more than an employee to him."

"Did you ask him about Billy Correira?"

"Yes I asked him about Billy Correira," he said, echoing her. "Never heard of him and I wish you hadn't either. He said he thinks Ellen was dating someone, but hasn't any idea who."

"Did you show him the list?"

"What list?"

"The jigsaw company subscribers."

"Shit, I didn't even think about it. I'll stick it in the mail. He's goin' away Tuesday, but he should get it if I put it in this morning's mail. What're you up to?"

"I'm doin' rounds, it's my turn. Then I'll check back. I've got a hair appointment at two, then I'm heading over to the Sportside."

"This place is hoppin' today and I gotta go out. Do you think you can hang around at least until Betty gets in?"

"Maybe. Where's Kerry?"

"She'll be in soon. I just talked to her."

"I'll bet, Kerry, you in there, Kerry?" she called in the direction of his living quarters.

"Cut it out, she's not in there. Now, listen, be very careful this afternoon, comprende? No gettin' in a car goin' anywhere with the guy, no givin' out your phone number. Just a quick chat and you're outta there, right?"

"Tuck, I can take care of myself."

"Yea, right. Call me tonight, will you?"

"What about Kerry?" she asked, still teasing.

"Just shut up and do it, okay?"

She made a face which he returned before slamming out the door. Sometimes she could be a real pain in the butt.

CHAPTER 19

August 26, Saturday

"Doug don't work Saturdays," was the reply Juls received from the gum-snapping desk attendant. About eighteen, she guessed, and in fabulous shape, but who wasn't at eighteen?

"Would you be Lucy?"

"Yea?" A flicker of interest in the violet eyes.

"Doug told me that you could get me started on the machines. I'm interested in joining and I thought I'd have my first free visit this afternoon."

"Yea, sure, hold on a sec while I get you a card. I'm the only one here so we may be interrupted by the phone and stuff. Why don't you get changed and I'll meet you in there? Ladies locker room just past the phone, look for the blue door. Weigh yourself while you're in there and we'll mark it on your chart, okay? See you in a bit."

The weight room was empty as she passed by. At least I'll get some exercise, she thought, disappointed.

A few minutes later, Lucy was calculating, measuring and setting up a training regimen. "What'cha wanna work on, Julie?"

"It's Julia, or Juls... probably my upper body. My legs are fairly strong from jogging, but my arms are wet noodles."

"Very common. Okay, we'll start there, but you should work on your legs a little, even if you jog, for strength and endurance. Come on, I'll show ya."

They'd gotten through four machines, Lucy adjusting each for her, marking the setting on the chart, when a young couple strolled in. "Hey, Jim, hey Suz," she called, as the pair mounted bicycles at the far end of the room. "Jim, there's a message for you at the desk. Some guy called 'bout twenty minutes ago."

"Thanks Luce, where's Billy?"

"Haven't seen him."

"Me and Suz are goin' out with him and Marsha, so he better show. We was gonna meet him here to make all the arrangements."

"He'll probably be here then. Hardly ever misses a Saturday unless he's outta town. Doug says he's been workin' over at Montauk like a maniac the past few weeks tryin' to finish up some job."

"My brother works at Montauk," Juls lied. "What does your friend do there?"

"Billy? He ain't no frienda mine honey. Jesus, he's a... well, anyway, I dunno what he does out there, some kinda construction, right Suz?"

Suz shrugged, clearly disinterested in the speculation about Correira's livelihood.

"Better keep goin' Julie," Lucy said, returning to the task at hand. "If we wanna get through this today."

It took another half hour to complete the circuit and Lucy felt confident that she "knew what she was doin." At each station, Lucy demonstrated the correct curl, flex, pull or stretch, her firm, lithe body in metallic blue spandex rhythmically performing each exercise with fluency and precision. Then, she'd hop off and watch Juls, critiquing her every move until she was satisfied. Several times she excused herself to answer the phone or to dole out towels or other supplies from behind the desk. By the time they finished the workout, a half dozen others had joined them in the weight room.

They were on the last machine, the shoulder press and Juls' arms were beginning to feel like jelly, when a short, burly figure waltzed in. Everything about the man screamed "look at me" and he was not disappointed. All eyes turned to watch his entrance, a smattering of "hellos" falling over him like a warm spring rain.

"Hey Billy, long time no see," called a man on the rowing machine.

Jim stopped pedaling, leaning over his handlebars. "Bout time Correira, me and Suz had almost given up on you. Still bringin' Marsha out wit ya?"

"Whatd'you think bozo? 'Course she's comin'," Mr. Important grunted, swatting Lucy's behind as he strutted peacock-like towards the men's locker room.

"Billy always likes to let us know he's here," Lucy whispered handing Juls the pink chart with all her measurements and machine adjustments.

"I'll say," Juls said, mouth agape as her eyes followed Billy Correira across the room, his rippling back muscles defining his thin cotton shirt. If he had been six or seven inches taller, Billy Correia would have given Arnold Schwartzenagger a run for his money.

"See what I mean," Lucy whispered. "He's a fuckin' pig, but they worship him. They'd fuckin' kiss his feet if he'd let 'em. And for what? The guy's a—well, never mind, just remember, he's no friend of mine."

"Thanks so much Lucy. Is there somewhere we can go to talk privately? Just for a few minutes?"

"Well, I guess so. Yeah sure, come on back. We can go in the office, but only for a few minutes. Ray'll be pissed if I'm not out front when he gets back."

She led the way behind the desk and down the hall to a small, cramped office. The desk was covered with papers, brochures and unpaid bills. Shelving along two walls was crammed with towels, tee shirts, leotards and socks. There were three chairs two of which were piled high with freshly laundered towels.

Lucy threw one of the piles on the floor in the corner. "Sit down Juls, you earned it.

"Doug's gonna really give Ray hell when he sees this mess. He was 'sposed to put all this away this morning. What'cha wanna talk about anyway?"

"Did you know Rosie Mikawski?"

"Yea, sure, Rosie. She was good people. Sucks about her bein' dead and all. Why you askin'?"

"I'm a friend of hers."

"Yea?"

"I'm trying to find out about how Rosie spent her last few weeks?"

Lucy regarded her suspiciously. "You a cop or somethin'? Christ, have I been wastin' my time with a cop?"

"No," Juls answered, wondering why everyone in the place was so paranoid about the police.

"You know the cops were crawling all over us for weeks after Rosie died."

"Lucy, I'm not a cop. I just... Rosie was my dearest friend in the world and I just have to know what happened to her. She talked about the gym all the time and I thought maybe she'd met someone here who'd know something about her last few days."

"Look, I really can't help you, Julie. I knew Rosie, sure, but only from here. We never did nothin' on the outside together. She was strong. Probably one of our strongest women body builders, but you probably know that."

Didn't help her fend off her killer, Juls thought.

"Now I know why you wanted to know about Billy," Lucy whispered conspiratorially. "Doug must've told you they were friendly. God knows why, I mean him bein' such a prick and Rosie bein' so nice. She could handle him, though, she never took any shit. They worked out together."

"Yes, that's what Doug said. Lucy, if you don't mind me asking, why is it that you dislike Billy so much?"

"Wait'll you see him undressed. Go out and take a good look. He's a fucking monster, built like a brick shit house, hands like iron. That's all well and good 'cept he likes to beat on people with those iron hands of his. Last summer he beat up a friend of mine so bad she had to spend two nights in the hospital. Her nose was broke, shoulder dislocated, both eyes swollen shut. She has permanent nerve damage to her neck and it took her six months of workin' out before she could hold her head up straight again. The bastard didn't even go to see her." Lucy was trembling violently, her face ashy white. There was no need to state the obvious, 'the friend' she described was herself.

"Why didn't she press charges?"

"She wanted to live," she replied turning away, but not before Juls saw the tears in her eyes.

"I'm sorry, Lucy."

"Don't go near him, Julie. That's all I gotta say. He's—" The door behind them opened a crack and Lucy froze, terror written all over her face.

"Towels, Luce. I need four, if you can leave off your gossiping for a few seconds."

"Sure, Billy, sure. I'll be right out." Lucy sprang up. "Do you think he…?"

"No, he didn't hear anything. He'd only just gotten to the door. Don't worry."

"Easy for you to say."

"Lucy," she said, barring the door for an instant. "I know you're scared and I won't keep you, but I have just one more question."

"I gotta go, please! He won't hurt me no more, but he could get me fired."

"It's about Ellen Smith. Do you remember her?"

"Sure, nice lady."

"Doug told me that Billy went out with Ellen."

"Yea, so?

"Do you know if he hit her?"

"No way. Ellie was smarter than me," she replied, dropping the pretense as she grabbed a handful of towels. "After two dates she dumped him. He mighta tried somethin', I dunno, but Ellie dropped him like a bad habit's all I know. Billy was pissed too. He didn't show his face in here for about a month. She had class Ellie, not like me. Look, I gotta go." Lucy pushed by her and Juls followed.

As they reached the desk the phone rang. Lucy hesitated and she interceded. "You answer it, I'll take them in to him, okay?"

Reluctantly, Lucy handed her the towels, turning to the phone as Juls made her way to the weight room. It wasn't difficult to spot him. An amazing expanse of red and black spandex covered the lower half of his bulging form. He lay face up on the bench, two hundred and eighty pounds of barbell raised above his shoulders. Every leg muscle strained at the shiny fabric, his upper body naked and glistening with sweat. Another man half his size stood behind his head spotting him.

Not wishing to upset the delicate balancing act, she approached slowly. He spotted her out of the corner of his eye. "Hey, Jesse, this is our lucky day. We got us a new towel girl, not too hard on the eyes either." Even as he strained to hold the weights, his thick lips puckered emitting a wolf whistle that traveled the length of the room and back again.

"Hi," she said, hoping her smile adequately masked her revulsion.

"Hi yourself, hon. What's your name gorgeous?"

"Julia Whitman, and you are?"

With Jesse's help the barbells were lowered and Billy heaved his bulk to a sitting position, grabbing one of the towels. His hand grazed her side in unmistakable caress. "Hey, honey, I wasn't born yesterday. You know my name, fact is you wanted to meet me so you conned Lucy into lettin' you hand me my towels. That's a privilege you know, bringin' ole Billy his towels. Now 'spose you just set 'em down and tell me what you want."

"I'd like to talk to you, for a few minutes, that's all."

"Oh, we can talk alright, talk's cheap enough." He wiped sweat from his face and chest, draping the drenched towel across his knees.

"In private."

"Get lost Jesse," he said and the other man disappeared. Everyone else in the room seemed to have somewhere else to go too and in less than a minute they were alone.

"Some trick."

"Take a load off, Julia," he said, patting the bench beside him. "And make it quick. I gotta date tonight and I'm runnin' late."

"I am a friend of Rosie's."

"So who wasn't? The lady was a saint in my book. I ever get my hands on the bastard that did her, I'll break his fuckin' neck."

"I know how you feel Mr. Correira, that's why I'm trying to find out what happened to her."

"Hey honey, no offense, but doncha think you oughta leave that to the cops? Pretty little thing like you, be a shame if you was to get hurt."

"I can take care of myself, Mr. Correira."

"Billy, sweetheart, 'Mr. Correira' sounds like a fuckin' mortician or something. With all due respect, Julia, you dunno shit about these kinda sickos. Nice girl like you. You're gonna take care of yourself, yea right. Rosie was as strong as an ox and look where it got her. You're pretty and all that, but a bit on the weak and scrawny side so the way I see it, you don't got a chance in hell."

"Could we get back to Rosie?"

"Sure sweetie, anything you say, but you'd be more comfortable sittin' here beside ole Billy. I ain't gonna bite ya."

Reluctantly, Juls sat down the far end of the bench. He slid up beside her. "Now that's better."

Leaning as far away from him as she could without falling off, she asked, "Do you know anything about the last few days before Rosie died? Did you see her at all?"

"Hey, hon, that was a month ago. I don't even remember what I was doin' this morning."

"Well, could you try, please? You must remember hearing about Rosie's death and thinking back to the last time you saw her, people usually do that when tragedy strikes."

"That what they teach you at amateur detective school?"

Ignoring his sarcasm, she continued, "How did you hear about Rosie?"

"Dougie told me. He read it in the paper."

"Well? Had you seen her that week?"

"Maybe, once or twice. Yea, we probably got a work-out in a couple days before she died. She didn't show Thursday night, but that's not uncommon during the summer.   She plays on some softball team."

"Yes, I do, too."

"Hey, I've been missing out. When's your next game?"

Ignoring the question, she asked, "Did she say anything unusual when you saw her Tuesday? Was she going out with anyone? Upset about anything?"

"Listen, Julia, this is a gym, not a coffee klatch. We're here to work out not pour out our personal lives like we was talkin' to Ann Fucking Landers or somethin'."

"I know, but you must remember something. Doug said you and Rosie went out a couple of times."

"Whoa, slow down, Sherlock. We're talkin' a couple of beers round the corner after we're done here, that's it. Rosie was good people, no doubt about it, but not exactly my type, if you get my drift?"

She did, but chose to ignore it. "Well? What did you guys talk about over those beers?"

"Just chit chat, you know, the weather, the price of beans, the Red Sox. Nothin' personal, if that's what you're getting' at." His eyes undressed her, smugness radiating from every pore. "She did talk about work sometimes. Hated her boss. A real prick. I know him, he comes around once and a while, a real slime ball."

Takes one to know one, she thought. "What do you have against Danny Moniz?"

"He's a freeloading sleaze, that's all. A crook on the job and no better in public. Never pays his bill here and is always bringin' his candy ass friends in for free workouts, buys 'em drinks, clothes, what have you and he charges everything, never settles up with Doug. I don't like that kinda shit, know what I mean? Look sweetheart, why don't you and I have dinner some night?"

"Thanks, but I don't think so."

"Why, you got a boyfriend?"

"Yes."

"Well, dump 'em. I'll show you a much better time."

"What about Ellen Smith? I understand you went out with her?"

"No comment."

His voice spoke volumes, but she decided to press on nonetheless. "Excuse me?"

"Ellie's ancient history." His gaze softened, but he still white-knuckled the side of the bench.

"But Ellie's death and Rosie's may be related."

"So what? You think I whacked both of 'em? Think again, sweetheart. I love women, I don't kill 'em. Believe me, I can think of much better things to do with broads than kill 'em. Why a pretty lady like yourself," he said, stroking her arm, sending shivers through her body. "Hey, Julia, you cold? Let me warm you up."

Hopping up, she stammered, "I have to go. Thanks for your time."

"Oh now I've done it, I've scared you off, just when we were getting friendly. Look Julia, I'd like to see you. Come around the gym again soon, will ya? And let me know if you change your mind about dinner. Maybe a few glasses of Chianti and I'd remember something important. I'd show you a good time, better than Greg the dregs ever did."

"How did you…?"

"Rosie and I talked, remember? You don't think she'd leave her oldest and dearest friend out of our little heart to hearts, do you? I know a damned sight more about you than you know about me, honey. That's how come I know we'd make such beautiful music together."

His laugh echoed through the room, chasing her into the hallway as Juls gathered her things and fled from the building. Still dressed in her leotard, she threw her bag in the back of the car and tore out of the parking lot.

He knew her, had known all about her for years. This loathsome creature knew her past, her old boyfriends and who knew what else. Rosie, how could you, she thought speeding through the city streets heedless of the traffic around her. Miles away heading down the Ocean Avenue, Juls could still hear Billy Correia laughing.

CHAPTER 20

August 26, Saturday

In the lamplight, her hair fell away revealing the angry swath of red. Christine tried to conceal it beneath high necked blouses. Her hair loose and flowing offered an extra measure of subterfuge, but he never forgot its existence. As they reached her door, its throbbing, malevolent presence almost overwhelmed him.

"How 'bout a cup of coffee, Christine?"

"I'm sorry David, but I feel like crashing, do you mind? I had a good time and all, but I really want to go to bed, you know? Mama's been bad lately and between taking her back and forth for the chemo, cleaning her house and cooking all the meals, not to mention work, I'm beat, that's all."

"I don't know how you do it. How 'bout if I make the coffee?"

"David, please, I can't, really. Thanks again for the dinner, movie, everything, good night."

She very nearly slammed the door in his face, but there was no help for it. Peeking through the window, she spied him standing dejected and forlorn on the stoop. Tapping on the glass, she waved, shooing him away, locking the door, turning her back on him. She had meant what she said about the evening. It had been fun and David had made such an effort to be charming. Still, she didn't want to be drinking coffee at midnight and since she felt certain he wasn't interested in anything more, she didn't want him around. She was almost too tired for sex anyway.

It felt good to be home, the lingering odors of garlic and spices from her morning's cooking soothed her frayed nerves as if she had come home to Mama instead of an empty house. She always tried to make a week's worth of meals at once, delivering them to her mother's freezer with cooking instructions. The instructions were largely perfunctory as Christine herself usually warmed and served the meals herself. Mama was too weak to eat, never mind cook, but her favorite daughter could usually coax her into finishing a small dish of pasta with homemade tomato sauce, Mama's own recipe.

Christine and Maisie lived on the ground floor of a three story building, one unit to a floor. The landlady lived on the second floor and an unmarried couple, both boat designers, lived on the third. At the moment, the Pearsons were away at a boat show in Maryland and Mrs. Grady, the landlady, had long since drunken herself into a stupor so Christine turned up the stereo, kicking off her shoes as she danced from room to room switching on the ceiling fans.

The fans' cooling breeze invigorated her as she poured herself a plastic cupful of lime seltzer, dancing her way through the rooms, tidying up and singing along with Sting's *Roxanne*. After starting a load of wash, she tackled the dishes continuing to move to the music as the sink filled with soap. Soon, pots and pans filled the dishrack.

The CD ended as she dried her hands and squeezed a liberal dollop of hand-cream from the bottle perched over the sink. For a second she considered putting in another CD, but the clock's sobering truth drove her towards bed instead.

As she reached for the kitchen light, she gazed absently through the window over the sink. Had something moved outside? Was there someone in the backyard? Rushing to the window she yanked at the yellow curtains, drawing them together shutting out the inky blackness. In her haste she knocked a small cactus into the sink and its clay pot shattered on the white porcelain spraying dirt everywhere.

"Shit!" she cried, tiny needles pricking her skin as she lifted the plant from the sink and searched for a temporary container. Deciding a paper cup would suffice until morning, she gathered as much dirt as possible around the forlorn little prickly pear leaving it and the rest of the mess in the sink.

Satisfied all was secure, she went through the living room turning out the lights. Again she sensed it... an unshakable feeling that someone was watching her. What was it, this nameless terror that lurked in the shadows of her tiny yard?

"Stop it Teeny," she said aloud, switching off lights and the ceiling fan.

As the night terrors of her youth revisited her, Teeny tried to remember the comforting words Mama or Papa had used to drive the goblins of her childhood away. Slipping into bed a few minutes later, she whispered, "Mama, oh Mama, I need you," her fingertips still stinging and sore from the prickly cactus.

CHAPTER 21

August 30, Wednesday

"Brother, brother!

"Where have you gotten to, you miserable wretch!

"Brother! I'm calling you, do you hear me?

"Come here you sniveling fool and bring me a blanket for my legs!

"I'm thirsty—another glass of tea and don't forget the lemon!

"Hurry up!

"I need help with this puzzle you idiot!

"Brother!

"Brother!

"Brother!"

His fingers tore the pieces apart, the brittle glue giving way to his savage fury. This had been one of Mother's supreme achievements, a two thousand piece puzzle, her only one. A magnificent view of the Bavarian Alps with one of the most beautiful of King Ludwig's castles perched high on a mountain top at its center. As he ripped and clawed, the puzzle pieces scattered around his chair.

He laughed, remembering his mother's smug face as she sat back after spraying the fixative, gluing her masterpiece together. "There now, it is preserved for all eternity, you wretched boy. This is my legacy. Your inheritance. Take great care of it always."

"Yes, mother," he sneered, gazing at the destruction surrounding him, a demonic smile distorting his usually placid features. "I'll take very good care of it. Your precious jigsaw puzzle is going to be famous beyond your wildest dreams. Perhaps someday they'll catch me and then your name and the name of your wretched husband will be preserved in infamy forever."

After Julia, perhaps he could give himself up? No. But, perhaps he should send a letter from far away, revealing the details of all his outings. Everyone should know of his cleverness. The police were so incredibly stupid. Those bumbling amateurs, Potter and Julia were probably making more headway than the coppers. The absurdity of it disgusted him. None of them had a prayer of catching him. Julia was so young and innocent, poor Julia with her silly, useless investigating. After September sixteenth she'd be dead just like the rest of them.

First, he'd deal with Christine. Plump, loud-mouthed Christine was becoming tiresome. She had refused him twice already. He had had the gloves and other equipment ready and she had slipped away the little fool. His powers were ebbing and he feared he was growing lax and sloppy.

Julia's death had been on the calendar for over a month and yet Christine lived on. He made no move and had not even made a definite plan about Christine. What was happening to him? He was slowly unraveling and powerless to pull himself back. Get a grip, you fool, he chided himself, but his words failed to rouse his flagging manhood.

He had stood for a long time watching Christine dance around her pathetic apartment. Dancing—after telling him she was too tired to make him a cup of coffee. He should have burst in and taken care of her right then. Why hadn't he? Caution? Fear? He was starting to lose his strength. And, he had forgotten the puzzle pieces. That meant he would have to go and return. What an idiot, without the pieces what was the point?

Soon, Christine, he crooned softly under his breath. Soon.

The phone rang, interrupting his revere.

Tossing the broken puzzle pieces into a box, he answered, his voice friendly, accent perfect, the very model of civility.

CHAPTER 22

August 31, Thursday

"Yo, Miz Whitman." Recognizing the voice, Juls tensed up, holding her breath as he paused, then continued. "Billy C. here, 'member me?"

"Yes." She swung her legs from the desk, needing to have both feet on the floor. She and Tuck had been going over J and T accounts and he watched her, eyes questioning the dramatic change in her body language.

"Listen, Julie, I want to apologize. I can be a real jerk sometimes."

I'll say, she thought.

"I mean, okay, I'm a jerk, that's a given."

"Yes?"

"What I mean to say is, I'd like to make it up to you. Whatd'ya say? So you won't go away thinkin' a friend of Rosie's is a total waste. If you're not busy tomorrow night, I'd like to take you to dinner."

"Thanks, but I don't think so."

"Please Julia, no funny business I promise."

"Listen Mr. Correira."

"Billy, please."

"Billy, thanks for the invitation but I'm swamped here at work." Tuck was now standing in front of her making slashing motions at his neck. She turned away.

"I might have remembered a few things about Rosie and Ellen that could help you."

"Oh, what?"

"Now that'd be telling wouldn't it, Julia? Look, Tortugas is a great spot, do you know it? It's just across the river and I'd love to take you there. Just dinner, that's all."

"I don't think so—"

"I'll pick you up at six, have you home by eight. You can even have your bloodhound, what's his name, Potter, chaperon if you like. Come on, what do you say?"

"You're not going to take no for an answer, are you?"

"Nope."

"Fine, but I'll meet you at Tortuga's, at six-thirty."

"Suit yourself, but my Caddy's very comfortable."

"I'll see you there," she added, ignoring Tuck who was still gesturing futilely. "I'll look for you in the bar. Now, I really have to go." She hung up, bracing herself for the explosion.

"What was that about?"

"Just a dinner invitation, nothing to get excited about."

"What? Are you crazy? Have you completely lost your mind, Jesus Christ, Juls."

"Tuck, calm down. I'm meeting him there, there's absolutely no danger involved. Do you honestly think after what happened to Rosie that I'd take a chance?"

"Don't do this, please. I refuse to let you."

"Since when did you become my babysitter?"

"Since you lost your mind."

"Butt out."

"You're an asshole, you know that?" He slammed out the back door.

"Tuck!" she called, but he was long gone, heading for the beach. She wanted to follow, but the phone stopped her.

"J and T," she answered in the most cheerful voice she could muster.

"Julia?"

"Yes?"

"Hi, it's Wilson McCaffrey, remember me?"

"Of course, hi, how are you?"

"Fine, and yourself?"

"Not great," she answered honestly. "I'm afraid I just had an argument with my partner." Then wondering why she'd confided in a stranger, she added, "He's my best friend, we never fight so it's upsetting, that's all," by way of an explanation.

"I'm sorry, I can call back another time."

"No, it's fine, what was it you needed?"

"I thought maybe you'd have a free night for dinner sometime soon?"

Boy, I'm popular today, she thought. "Well, I can't tonight, but then—" She hesitated, knowing Tuck would be furious. Then, shrugging her shoulders, she said, "My partner and I are taking one of our summer employees out for a farewell dinner."

"Lucky guy! Maybe I'll apply for a job next summer?"

"He is a she," she laughed. "Why don't you come along? You know Tuck, and you'll enjoy Kerry. She's the guest of honor."

"I don't want to impose."

"Nonsense, it'd be fun. We'd love to have you, in fact, I insist. In fact, you'll be helping me out. Kerry and Tuck have been dating so having you along will prevent my feeling like a fifth wheel. Please say you'll come. We're going to the Lobster Pot in Bristol, do you know it?"

"Sure do. I used to go there years ago with my family."

"Me, too. It's changed a lot in recent years, but it's still nice. So, you'll come?"

"If you're absolutely sure I won't be imposing."

"Absolutely," she replied, knowing what Tuck would think of her impulsive invitation. He would hate it, but at this moment she didn't care. If she had to sit and watch him moon over Kerry O'Donnell all evening, at least she could have company doing it.

"Thank you then, I'd be delighted."

"We'll meet you there at seven? Unless you'd rather we come by for you?"

"No, I'm happy to meet you there. See you then."

Juls hung up, whistling to herself as she switched on the answering machine and raced out the back door to find him. Kicking off her sandals when she hit the sand, she began a slow jog towards the familiar figure already a half mile down the beach. Breathless and drenched in sweat as she drew near him, she slowed down, her knees throbbing with pain and growing more wobbly with every step. Some days they balked and the tennis had given them a workout. "Tuck, please slow down," she yelled. He quickened his pace.

"What's the matter?" she cried. "Tuck please." Finally, she gave up and flopped down on the sand, exhausted and close to tears. Since Rosie's death she had lost her endurance. She hadn't jogged or walked more than twice in the past month and until Ben, she hadn't played tennis all summer. Lack of exercise and failure to stretch had taken their toll. Her artificial joints and the surrounding tissue had grown stiff and unforgiving.

Her last desperate cry seemed to do the trick and he slowed down, turning back. When he reached her, he sat down, silently staring out at the ocean.

"That's the first time you've ever called me an asshole," she said.

"Sorry." Silence.

Finally he said, "When Rosie died all I could think about for days and weeks was, what if it had been Juls? Rosie was bad enough, but I don't know what I would have done if it had been you. Then you wanted to investigate, so I said fine. Even though I was scared shitless, I figured this was your way of working through the grief. Then, you poke around, get all upset and come up with zip."

"That's not true, I found out—"

"Juls, I don't want to hear it, okay? I care about you, you know that. I'm crazy in love with you, for Christ's sake. If you hadn't made up all those fucking rules about the business and all we'd be—"

"Tuck."

"Okay, okay, don't get panicky. We're friends, I know my place." The bitterness in his voice cut like a knife.

"That's not fair."

"None of it's fair, if you ask me. But, this is the way you wanted it so fine, we're friends. Just don't expect me to stop caring about you 'cause I can't.'"

"I know," she said, reaching over to touch his cheek, his day old beard rough and scratchy. "I'll be careful, I'm not taking chances. I'm meeting him at the restaurant," she added, neglecting to mention Billy's invitation for Tuck to be her chaperon.

"And what if he's the guy?"

"Well, it's not like he's going to strangle me in the middle of Tortuga's, is he?"

"You don't get it, do you? If he's the guy, you shouldn't be anywhere near him. It's not tomorrow night I'm worried about, Juls. What if he gets fixated on you and decides you'd be a perfect candidate for his next murder? Maybe that's what he does, takes 'em out a few times, then decides to kill 'em?"

"I'm not going on several dates, just one. He might have remembered something really important about Rosie."

"Bullshit. I'm calling Marc Palumbo. He's the maitre de at Tortuga's. I'm gonna tell him to watch you like a hawk."

"Fine, great idea, now can we go back?"

As they walked back slowly arm in arm, Juls leaned against him for support. "Oh, about Saturday night, Kerry's celebration?" she said, suddenly remembering Wilson's call.

"Oh, no, you don't, you're not backin' out. I told you before, Kerry wants you there. She and I already went out alone for our own farewell dinner and this time it's J and T. We want you there."

"I wasn't trying to get out of it, but I'd like to bring a date, if that's okay with you?"

"Fine." Pressed against him, she could feel his body tense, belying the casual response. "Who?"

"Wilson McCaffrey."

"Oh God, not Mr. Fix-it!"

"Stop it! I don't make cracks about your girlfriends."

"The hell you don't, you've been giving me shit all summer about Kerry. Is that what McCaffrey is now, your boyfriend?"

"No, you know what I mean."

"No I don't. Tell me."

"Stop it Tuck. Anyway, Wilson's coming and it'll be fun, you'll see. He's a nice guy and you will be nice too."

"Me? I'm always nice."

"Yeah right, and no going on about him stealing Skip's jobs either. Mitty Beaman couldn't be happier with her table, says it looks better than it did before. At least Wilson's not a hacker like—"

"Oh, Wilson, now is it?"

"Shut up," she said, poking him in the ribs as they climbed the steep path from the beach. "What do you want me to do, call him Mr. McCaffrey all through dinner?"

"Sounds good to me," he laughed, harmony restored. "While you're at it, why not ask Ben Colson to come along, too. The more men mooning over you, the better."

"Ben isn't mooning. He's just looking for a few games of tennis."

"And I'm Albert Einstein."

"Very funny." She grasped his arm, leaning against him as they stepped onto the porch.

As they reached the door, he paused, turning to take her hands. Smiling, she looked up, his brown eyes solemn. "When will it be our turn, Juls?"

"Please, don't."

"I'm serious. You know I'd give up this tomorrow if it meant we could be together."

"We are together."

"You know what I mean."

"It isn't the business," she said, softly, her eyes misting.

"Then what?"

"I don't want to lose you, that's all."

"Never happen."

"Your record with women is pretty dismal."

"This is different and you know it. My record with women is dismal because I'm never with the woman I love."

"Uh, oh," she said, peering over her shoulder to spy Ben Colson strolling up the path.

Tuck followed her gaze, spying Colson. "Great," he muttered, releasing her and slamming into the house.

Ben looked crisp and fresh in his tennis whites.

"Oh, no," she said, having completely forgotten their tennis date. She waited on the porch until he reached her.

"Hi, gorgeous." His eyes scanned her attire, cut-off shorts and sleeveless tee shirt. "I'm a little early. Did I interrupt something?"

"No, but I'm really sorry. I'm going to have to take a rain check on the tennis. I should have called you. My knees are killing me and we're swamped here."

"No problem. Why not let me take you to dinner."

"That's really nice, but I'm going to finish up here then head home to soak in a hot bath."

"What about a drink, then?"

"Another night, okay?"

For a second, Ben's features registered annoyance, his eyes narrow, mouth set. Just as quickly he recovered his suave, debonair exterior, however, smiling. "Of course. And, I'll hold you to that promise of another night, okay?"

"It's a deal," she said, watching as he headed back down the path to his car. Now, I've got two men angry with me, she sighed, going in to make amends with her partner.

CHAPTER 23

August 31, Thursday

"It's okay Mama. I don't mind, really," Christine said for the tenth time. "Just let me throw on some clothes and I'll be right over."

She hung up the phone using all of her willpower to stem the tears. Bone tired after a double shift at work, she wanted nothing more than to soak in a hot bath and then to sleep for two or three days. On top of her fatigue she was battling a summer cold all the while praying she would not give it to her desperately ill mother.

Mama hadn't long. The doctor had told them Monday that it was only a matter of weeks. The treatments were having little or no effect on the tumors that curled like vines round and round her spine, sending their virulent tendrils into the surrounding tissue, their encroachment growing more destructive with each passing day. The sisters had made the decision to stop treatments; Mama had never wanted them in the first place.

Most of the time Mama writhed in pain, crying out for Teeny. It was always Teeny, never Maddie, always Teeny.

Christine knew that she should move in with her mother until the end, but something held her back. She needed the sanctuary of her own home. The time she spent in her own home allowed her to imagine that all the suffering was happening to someone else and not her darling Mama.

Just as she headed out, the phone rang again. She considered ignoring it, but finally grabbed the receiver.

"Christine, David, hi."

"Oh, David, sorry, I'm on my way out the door."

"Oh, well, I won't keep you. Just thought we could go out this week, maybe Monday or Tuesday night?"

"I don't think so, but thanks anyway." She was so desperately weary. Weary of life, weary of Mama, weary of work and at this moment very weary of David.

"Please Christine, I'd like to see you."

"David, look," she said, unable to keep up the pretense of civility another second. "I tried to say this the last time we went out, but you wouldn't let me. We have had some good times, but it's over. I really don't think we should see each other anymore, okay? You're a nice guy and all, but we're not very compatible."

"I think we are."

"Well, I don't, I'm sorry. Please don't call anymore, okay? You were nice to take me out and I do appreciate it, but it's over. Now, I really have to go, Mama needs me."

"Christine wait!" he cried, but she had already slammed down the phone.

"I'm sorry David," she whispered, grabbing her bag and running out the door.

CHAPTER 24

September 1, Friday

"Bitch, bitch, bitch!" he screamed, slamming an empty clay pot against the wall. As he paced back and forth across the damp cement floor of the basement, he pulled on a fresh pair of gloves, the latex snapping and twisting as he shoved his fingers home. He would show her. How dare she refuse to go out with him, the little whore.

"You'll not get far, my plump little Christine. I'll have you one way or the other before the week is out." Unable to stop his relentless pacing, the voices in his head reached a crescendo matched in tempo by the clicking sounds of his footfall.

He had woken that morning with a terrible headache, still furious at Christine's rejection. The others had been so easy, like lambs to the slaughter and now this common little tramp had rebuffed him. After all those horrid places she dragged him to. She'd pay alright, she'd pay.

As always, the pungent scent of the latex had a tranquilizing effect and Brother calmed down, his pacing less frantic, his breathing returning to normal. At length he stopped, ripping off the gloves and throwing them into the trash.

Christine's puzzle pieces were already encased in a plastic bag. He had chosen the blown-up photograph of his own mother, a special puzzle created just for her. Wouldn't Mother die if she knew he was dating a cheap little tramp like Christine,

Brother chuckled. He had decided to save Mother's favorite—Bavaria and mad King Ludwig—for Julia. This time he was giving the idiots thirty pieces, double what he had left with Ellen. It did not matter in the least, he thought. The idiots would have no more luck with these than the others.

Wouldn't Mother be furious if she could see her puzzles now—all broken up and splattered with blood? By September sixteenth not a single one of her treasured masterpieces would be intact. Mother's worst nightmare would finally be realized. Every single one of her precious puzzles would be missing pieces.

"Ha, ha, ha!" His laugh rang out in the empty basement, a hollow, mournful, half sobbing laugh that seemed to choke in his throat tapering off into a retch before ceasing all together.

CHAPTER 25

September 4, Monday

It was only nine a.m. and Jack Mederois had already spent two hours wrestling with staggering glut of paperwork from caseloads neglected in his all-consuming pursuit of the "Jigsaw Strangler", an appellation recently made public by Pat Graeber, a *Providence Journal* reporter who had somehow gotten wind of the puzzle pieces. "God dammit, why don't they fuckin' stay in Rhode Island where they belong!" Mederois had exploded upon reading Graeber's front page account. The puzzle pieces had been a closely guarded secret, yet someone had leaked the information. If Mederois found out who, he'd have their head.

Some Labor Day, he mused, flipping through a file that should have been sent to Records in April.

Tim Cottrell poked his head in. "Excuse me sir, there's someone here to see you." Before Cottrell could continue, he was elbowed out of the way, the visitor, all six feet of her standing in his place.

"Steele, oh great, just what I need this morning! Things aren't bad enough, no, I gotta have you breathin' down my neck!"

"Good to see you too, Jack. What's it been, two weeks at least?" She plunked herself down in the only chair that wasn't piled high with papers, draping a blue jeaned leg over one arm. She was wearing red cowboy boots that matched her sweat shirt, her curly chestnut hair pulled back in a tangly pony tail.

Although never one to fuss with her appearance, Ricky Steele was a handsome woman for her age and stage of life. Had to be in her late fifties, but she looked forty, if a day. Her stature alone commanded attention. Mederois always found women taller than him a bit unnerving, but underneath his banter he had a grudging respect for the independent private investigator though he'd never let her know it. For a newcomer who had been in the field for less than a year, she was a damn sight more professional than most of the male PI's hanging their shingles out all over the city. Useless bunch of freeloaders, most of 'em, in Mederois' opinion. At least Steele did something to earn her keep, even if it invariably meant sticking her nose into his business.

"Look Steele, I'm buried here and I don't have time to play cops and robbers today."

"Jack, I hear you. I'm buried myself, five minutes, that's all I ask, five minutes."

"Bullshit, now what'dya want?"

"Well, okay, if you won't talk to me, at least let me have five minutes with the puzzle pieces."

"What do I look like, Milton Bradley? There's a Kiddy Land Toys just around the corner, try there if you're lookin' for puzzles."

"You know what I mean Jack, quit playing around. I read Pat Graeber you know, and you also know damn well I'm helping Tuck and Juls on this. Who found out about *Puzzle It Out?*"

"News flash—we already had that information. We'd already contacted *Puzzle it Out* after Catherine Foley's murder and we've had the friggin' list for three months, hon."

The blue eyes flashed fire, but she kept her voice calm, coaxing. "Come on Jack, what's the harm. I'll be careful, I'll wear gloves, I won't even touch 'em if you don't want me to. Just let me have a quick peek."

"What the hell business are they of yours anyway?"

"Come on Jack, they've already been tested to death, what's the harm? I'm not gonna slip one in my pocket, you know. I'm here to help you know, not to muck you up."

"Okay, what the hell."

"Thanks Jack," she gushed, leaping from her chair. For a moment, Mederois thought she might actually hug him.

"Five minutes, Steele, that's what you're gettin' and then I'm kickin' you out on your fanny! It's Labor Day you know, I got a neighborhood cook-out. My wife'll kill me if I don't get home."

He ushered her out of the office, following her upstairs to the evidence room. Long legged and slender, her body was firm in all the right places, he mused, thinking of Muriel his wife who had let herself go in recent years. "Here we are," he said, stopping her halfway down the hall, unlocking the door. It took only a few seconds for him to locate the box; he'd been through it a hundred times over the past few weeks. Extracting a large plastic bag that contained four smaller zip lock bags, he closed the box and led her to a table.

"No bending, no fiddling, no scraping. I'd have Cottrell come stand over you, but we're too busy today so no funny business. One of those pieces disappears or looks funny after you're through and I'll have you permanently barred from this station house, got it?"

Completely ignoring him, Ricky already had the first bag unzipped and was examining the pieces slowly, one by one. The bag had been labeled Beth Johnston and contained four pieces, all irregular shapes, no borders, no corners. The backing was a light green color, tiny brown stains flecked over its surface in several spots. The picture appeared to be a marble or alabaster statue against a black background, but she couldn't be sure. On the back of one of the pieces the word "woe" was printed in neat, block letters. "Maybe it's Michaelangelo's *Pieta*," she said more to herself than Mederois, who despite his pronouncements about being too busy seemed in no rush to depart. "That would go with 'woe', wouldn't it? The *Pieta* I mean?"

"Can't get much more woeful, than that," he agreed, sitting down beside her, abandoning all pretense of rushing off. "'Course, there may not be any connection, you know?"

After several futile attempts to fit the pieces together, she lay them aside and reached for the next bag. Mederois reached across her, the empty bag in his hand. "No, wait, please," she said, grabbing hold of his hand. "I'll be careful, I won't mix them up. Please can we leave them out?"

Shrugging, he tossed the bag aside, watching her open the baggie labeled "C. Foley".

"She was a real nice person," Ricky said. "She was a member of my running club, did you know that?"

"Yeah, I believe I heard that somewhere."

"Yeah, I couldn't believe it when I heard she'd been killed. We did Boston together a few years back."

"Boston?"

"The Marathon. 'Course no way we ran together, she was a zillion years younger and twice as fast."

"Didn't help her much in the end, her speed I mean," he said glumly.

"These murders are getting to you aren't they?"

He shrugged. "Have to be in a coma for them not to hit you."

Catherine Foley's puzzle pieces were slightly larger than Beth Johnston's. This time the backing was gray, and the picture seemed to be an Impressionist painting. All pastels and light—perhaps Degas ballerinas? she thought. All eight pieces were spattered with blood front and back and the largest piece which looked like the long fingers of a ballerina's hand had the word 'grace' written on it, the same precise lettering as the other.

"These pieces were all over the crime scene, but in Miss Foley's case there was a fair amount of blood. We believe her hand may have been amputated before she died, poor woman."

"How long before?"

"Maybe a few minutes, maybe half hour."

"Oh God!"

"Wanna stop now?"

Ignoring him, she tried to fit these pieces together. "Don't bother, he interrupted. "None of 'em fit, believe me."

In Rosie's bag there were fourteen pieces, but unlike the other two, they seemed to come from two different puzzles. Six had a reddish backing and the front appeared to be some kind of ornate temple or cathedral. The remaining eight pieces backed with blue, their front a kaleidoscope of colors. "This looks like one of those really hard ones with no borders," she said. "And, the pattern looks like the result of one of those spin paint machines."

Mederois nodded.

"No blood either and no writing."

"Nope."

"Why was that do you suppose?"

"There wasn't much blood in Ms. Mikawski's case, thank God, her friends finding her and all. No, her arm was hacked off after death, maybe a good half hour later. My guess is she worried him, she struggled more than the others and gave him a harder time than he was used to. He drugged her first, then maybe he decided it'd be prudent not to let her wake up again."

"None of these pieces fit either, do they?"

"Nope. This batch doesn't fit the numerical pattern either. First he drops four, then eight. Dropped thirty two pieces over the Smith woman, get it? He doubles them every time, except for Rosie Mikawski. His calculations are two short, but then he compensates on Ellen Smith anyway."

"So?"

"So it's funny. This guy's meticulous. Makes Mr. Clean look like a pig. He plans everything down to the minutest detail, then we get these two funny inconsistencies. Screwy math and—"

"No writing," she said, finishing his thought, feeling guilty because she had the answer to the inconsistencies, Juls' two missing pieces. The missing pieces that had led her to *Puzzle It Out*. When Mederois had asked how she could have come up with the company, Juls and Tuck had explained how they'd described the puzzle pieces to her in detail and that had been all she needed. Never mind the fact that she'd spent hours with a magnifying glass pouring over the contraband evidence. She would insist Juls turn the pieces in as soon as possible, she thought helping him to spread the contents of Ellen Smith's bag.

"All the same puzzle, this one," he said. "And, we got two fits here." He shoved the paired pieces towards her.

"Looks like a Botticelli, doesn't it? One of his early Madonnas I bet. Goes well with the word 'love', she said, reading the back of one of the small pieces. That's a start at least."

"Start my ass. Gives us shit."

"Can I take a picture of these?"

"No, why?"

"I want to send them to the company to see if they can—"

"It's been done, along with tracings, measurements, the whole shebang. They can tell us what the paintings are, but that's about it. You're right on all of them, by the way. You're good."

"It's an art, fragmented thinking." She laughed, as they scooped the pieces up, zipping them into their baggies.

"They're at least ten to fifteen years old. They were all part of the subscription series."

"What about the fixative?"

"It's a spray-on product, specially made for jigsaw puzzles. *Puzzle It Out* carries it, so do most arts and crafts stores."

"Well, thanks Jack, I gotta run."

"You're welcome to stick around and come to the neighborhood barbecue if you want. Your buddy Doug'll be there," he said, referring to Steele's nemesis,

Douglas Roberts a fellow police officer who also happened to be Mederois' brother-in-law.

"Thanks, but no thanks. Something tells me Dougie needs a little more of a cooling off period before we meet again! He's still pretty steamed about my part in the Carvalho case."

Even though he was well aware of the recent fracas between his colleague and the private investigator, Mederois chose not to comment. "Any ideas about the puzzles? Looked like you saw somethin' there when we were openin' up Ellen Smith's bag?"

"No, 'fraid not," she said, irritated that her poker face had betrayed her. "If you've already sent photographs and followed up."

"We're not completely incompetent around here, you know."

"I know," she said, smiling broadly. She had a gorgeous, albeit slightly crooked, smile. "Thanks again, Jack and tell Doug I say hi."

"Will do. He'll be broken hearted!"

Waving she breezed out the door and Mederois called "you're welcome" shoving the box back up on the shelf, relocking the door.

CHAPTER 26

September 4, Monday

Labor Day dawned misty and cool as Tuck and Juls took an early morning jog along the beach. It was a tradition for them on this, the busiest day of their business. No matter what the weather, they always did their ten miles on Labor Day—part walking, part running—finishing it off by a plunge in the ocean, clothes and all. Since Juls' surgeries, they walked more than ran. Both were showered and changed, in the office by nine and neither would stop for a single second until way into the night.... giving rides to the airport, checking people out and meeting with clients concerning winter plans and schedules.

Midmorning, Juls returned from rounds to find Tuck on the phone, employing his most patient voice. "Yes, Mrs. Bower, I'm sorry. I wish I could, but all of our college kids have gone back to school and the cars are booked solid today taking people to the airports. We just can't take the time. I do apologize. Yes, I know, I—" He paused, holding the phone at bay. Juls could hear Aggie Bower's deep, graveley voice from across the room and began making faces at her partner. He swiveled his chair away from her. Laughing would really get Aggie going!

"I realize Mr. Bower has been ill," he continued, "But I think you'll find the limo service very satisfactory and comfortable. They keep their cars in immaculate condition, much better than mine, I can tell you. I'll tell you what, I'll request

Charlie, okay? He sometimes drives for us too, I'll bet you've seen him, am I right? No? Well, no matter, he's a great guy. Tell me the time and I'll have him there. Thanks, Mrs. B., have a great day. Sure, we can get together whenever you're ready to talk about the winter schedule. You'll be around a few weeks, right? Great, talk to you soon." He hung up before she could get another word in.

"Phew, she's something!"

"You're too nice Tuck, that's your problem. You have to be forceful with these people. What'd she want anyway?"

"They wanted a car to take them shopping this afternoon. Apparently only you or I would do."

"Unbelievable. We baby them Tuck, that's our problem! You should have said right off the bat—transportation services stop August thirty first with no exceptions. Period, end of story."

"Yea, right. You're one of the biggest pushovers since Stanley Laurel, why the other day you—"

"Sh! I'm on the phone. Hi, Jack, it's Juls Whitman. I'm fine, how are you?"

"Christ," Tuck mumbled retreating to the back deck. "Just what we need."

"What can I do for you?" the detective asked. He sounded weary and distracted.

"Have you got anything new?"

"Not since five minutes ago when your private eye friend left or hasn't she been in touch?"

"You mean Ricky?"

"The very same."

"She isn't my private eye, she's Tuck's friend and no, we haven't heard from her."

"Well, make her give you the report, okay? I'm too busy to go through it now. I let her take a look at the puzzle pieces, that's all."

"Well, I'm sorry to have bothered you."

"Hey, it's alright kid. I'm just grumpy 'cause I got a shitload of work to do and the wife's waitin' on me. You got anything at your end?"

"No, did Tuck tell you about Friday night and my dinner with Billy Correira?"

"Yea, he told me. Worse than stupid, if you ask me."

"Well, it's alright, 'cause I don't think he did it."

"How's that?"

"Well, a woman in Catherine Foley's office remembers speaking to a man that called the afternoon before she died. They had a date that night."

"I know who you're talkin' about—Richards, wasn't it? Dana Richards, right? So what?"

"So the man Dana remembers had a refined, cultured way of speaking, so I'd say that pretty much rules out Mr. Correira, wouldn't you?"

"Yeah and people who knew Beth Johnston said the guy was a punk, so what's that prove? Maybe the guy's an impersonator? Rich Little gone bad or somethin'?"

"What are you talking about?"

"I'm talkin' about I gotta go. This is a holiday, remember? I'm not supposed to be working and I sure as hell don't wanna prolong my day worrying about cultured voices, okay?"

"I'm sorry, I didn't mean to disturb you," she said, voice shaky. "I'll just let you go and—"

"Look Juls, I'm sorry. I shouldn't have snapped at you, but like I told Potter Saturday, you shouldn't be foolin' around with a scum bag like Correira. Your partner and I apparently think alike in this regard. No matter whether Correira's involved in these murders or not, he's someone I wouldn't fix up with my worst enemy. Bad news with a capital b. You were takin' a big risk just lettin' the prick get to know you.

"As for the voices, the guy's a pro, the strangler I mean. Even if he is off his rocker, he's a fuckin' genius. For all we know, he could be a master of disguise maybe even a female impersonator, so it'd be no trick for him to sound like the Godfather one minute and Laurence Olivier the next. What these broads claim to have heard over the phone means shit."

"But?"

"But nothing! You stay away from Correira, you got me?"

"Fine," she snapped. "I've got to go." Hanging up, she shuddered at the recollection of her date with Billy Correira. From the moment she'd sat down until they said goodnight at the restaurant door, Juls had been subjected to a steady stream of tasteless remarks, crude jokes and lascivious come-ons. Afterwards, she had kicked herself for not bringing a tape recorder. She could never recreate, much less want to repeat, most of what he'd said. No one would believe it anyway.

Initially, he'd attempted to sit beside her at the table, but she'd maneuvered around to face him, a relatively safe distance away with the table a partial buffer against his roving hands. Nevertheless, they were only midway through their antipasto when she was compelled to issue her first warning.

"Mr. Correira, the next time your hand squeezes my leg, I will stab it with my fork." The hand was removed, replaced by his leg rubbing against hers. She then moved her chair so far from the table that diners around them began to stare. This seemed to do the trick, and for the remainder of the meal he confined his advances to verbal ones, delivered in a voice smooth as silk.

As their dinners were served, she managed to steer the conversation to Rosie and Ellen Smith, but unfortunately he offered little of substance.

"Rosie was good people, but I sure wish she'd introduced us sooner babe. Must've been hidin' you from ole Billy, keepin' you for herself. You guys weren't lezzies or anything were you?"

Juls declined to respond, shooting an icy glare in his direction before devoting her attention to her meal, a luscious casserole of scallops and shrimp sauteed in an Ouzo and tarragon butter. It was not on the menu, Billy had ordered it specially prepared. If she hadn't been so disgusted with him, she would have complimented him.

"Yea, like I said," he started, less interested in his food than she. "Rosie was good people. I hope they catch the guy and string him up by his...., well, never mind. I just hope they do. I'd do it myself, if they'd let me. Torture the hell outta the bastard!"

I'll just bet you would, Juls thought, asking, "Had you seen her very much in the weeks before she died?"

"Nope, but hey wait a minute. I did have lunch with her. Yea, the Saturday before she died, come to think of it. Instead of working out in the afternoon, I was in in the morning and we worked out together, then grabbed a bite at Rego's. It's right around the corner from the gym."

"Did she say anything unusual?" she asked, realizing once again how totally inept she was as an investigator.

"What, like I'm goin' off to meet my new boyfriend Bill, he's real good with his hands...somethin' like that maybe?" She blanched, turning away but not before he had spied the unbidden tears. "Geez, I'm sorry babe, you were close, I know."

Regaining her composure, she abruptly changed the subject. "What do you remember about Ellen Smith?"

He stiffened ever so slightly, before answering. "Classy broad. Lonely, pretty quiet. On the surface she was the complete opposite of Rosie, but underneath, well...they were both good people. We went out a couple of times, Ellie and me. You remind me of her a little bit, you know? I exhausted all my charms and never could get that woman to loosen up!"

"Why did you stop seeing her?"

"We weren't exactly an item. Just a few dinners and a couple of concerts, that's it. We weren't what you call simpatico. She didn't move quite as fast as I like 'em and I was a little too...oh what the hell, you probably heard already, she dumped me. Somethin' I don't like to advertise, you know?"

"When did you last see her?"

"A while back, maybe three, four months. She started goin' to the gym on my off days so we weren't likely to run into each other. If I had an ego problem—which I don't—I'd say she was avoiding me, but hey, everyone changes their schedules now and then, don't they?"

Juls said nothing allowing him to continue. "I did catch a glimpse of her from afar, at a restaurant at the beginning of the summer. I didn't bother to go up and say howdy-do 'cause she was with some guy and it looked like they were havin' a hot and heavy."

"What did he look like?"

"Damned if I know. Brown hair, that's about all I remember. Like I said, I kept my distance although I was tempted to stroll by and get a look at the competition. I figured this was probably the guy she dumped me for."

"Where was this?"

"Bayside, you know it? They were chowin' down on lobster, had those silly white bibs on, red pliers in their hands. She was waving hers around, gesturing at him that's how come I remember.

"So Julie, why don't you and I go back to my place for a nightcap? See if we can loosen you up a bit?"

"No thanks," she said, brandishing her fork as his hand slipped under the table again.

"Put the fuckin' fork down," he said, holding both hands above his head in a mock stick-up. "I won't lay another hand on you, promise."

After coffee, he escorted her to the car under the watchful eye of Marc Palumbo and she escaped without further incident. When she got home, Juls headed straight for the shower. Fifteen minutes under the soothing, hot spray couldn't wash away the feeling of violation her date with Billy Correira had left.

The next evening had proven much more pleasant—at least for Juls and Wilson McCaffrey. Tuck and Kerry seemed to be at odds which was mildly embarrassing, but as the evening progressed, Juls and Wilson blocked the others out, lost in their own conversation across the table in the crowded, noisy Lobster Pot. Afterwards, they went to the Beachcomber for dessert and coffee—Kerry's idea—where Tuck's humor went from bad to worse. Juls knew her partner wanted to go home, she could see all the signs. He was angry and jealous of her relationship with Wilson and tired of Kerry. It was a familiar scenario and one that got played out with subtle variations at the close of each summer. Kerry would go back to college, he'd write her a few friendly letters—each one a little less personal—to tide her over till she'd found a new boyfriend then he'd be off the hook while remaining friendly in case she came back to work the following summer. Tuck was good friends with ninety percent of his ex-girlfriends.

When Kerry had suggested the Beachcomber, a bar down the coast with live music and dancing, he'd groaned, looking to his partner for support. Ordinarily, she'd have begged off, but Wilson's response had been, "I'm game" and so she'd replied, "Sure, let's go!" incurring Tuck's wrath for the rest of the evening.

She didn't care. She liked Wilson; he was fun, interesting and easy to talk to and she was not going to let Tuck ruin it for her. He'd complained all the way down to the Seaside Saturday morning where they'd gone to question the help about Ellen Smith, no one remembered seeing her and a strange man at the beginning of the summer. All the way down and all the way back, Juls had had to listen to her partner's teasing and coaxing for her to "call off Gepetto", but she had ignored him.

Now on Labor Day, the busiest day of the year, he was in a foul mood, still miffed about Saturday night and licking his wounds. He'd barely spoken to her all day Sunday and now it seemed she'd have to endure yet another day of his moodiness. It really was too much, she thought, banging the screen door on her way out.

She found him on the back deck, stretched out on a chaise his eyes closed against the glare of the early morning sun. "Well?" she muttered, standing over him, blocking the sun.

"Well what," he said, eyes still closed.

"What's up?"

"That sounds like your department, babe." He never called her babe and knew it drove her up the wall—babe, hon, sweetie, they all made Juls see red. "You're the one just got off the phone with Jackie boy. Shouldn't you be tellin' me what's up?"

"What's wrong, Tuck? This isn't like you at all."

He shrugged, sitting up. "I'm just beat, that's all, forget it, okay?"

"What's going on with you and Kerry?"

"Nada, not a goddamn thing. She's gone back to Middlebury, back to Mitch, all-American, Breadloaf phenom and lover extraordinaire!"

"What?"

"She has a boyfriend Juls."

Suppressing a smile, she sat down at the edge of the chaise. "That's the way you wanted it, isn't it? No strings?"

"Can we just drop it please? What'd Mederois have to say?"

"Nothing, but Ricky was there today."

"Yea, she called Friday and said she was gonna stop in and try and get a look at the puzzle pieces."

"She did. Have you talked to her?"

"Nope."

"I've got to run over to the Thompsons' to go over their winter schedule—relax, their son's taking them to the airport—but I wish you'd call Ricky and see what she found out."

"What about the Crowthers?"

"I haven't heard a thing and I'm not about to call. We have enough to do today without Dolly Crowther thinking up a few dozen odd jobs on the spur of the moment. I'm pretty sure they're staying till next weekend, but if they call, they're all yours partner."

"I'm comin' in," he said rising, grabbing his tee shirt from the back of the chaise. "I'll man the phones, you better get going. If Betty ever decides to drag her indolent ass in I'll get outta here too."

"Betty's off today, remember? She's in Nova Scotia with her family?"

She watched as he pulled the tee shirt over his tanned, muscular chest. His hair still tousled and damp from his shower smelled of coconut oil. He caught her staring and grinned—he knew exactly what she was thinking. I'm crazy, she thought, turning away from him. There'll never be anyone else like him.

"You liked her, didn't you," she said, following him into the office.

"Who?"

"Kerry."

"Sure I liked her. Liked being the key word because 'liked' is about all I can muster up when I'm crazy in love with someone else."

"I'll see you tonight then," she said, grabbing her things and hurrying out, not trusting herself to stay a second longer. Once in the drive a safe distance away, she called back, "Are you coming tonight?"

"What's that?" he called back from behind the screen door.

"The game, are you coming?"

"Jesus, I forgot all about it! I'll never make the start, but I'll try to get there for the last couple of innings. You pitching?"

"Yes, unfortunately. It's our last game before the playoffs!"

"I'll try. Gotta be at my folks for supper—Labor Day cook-out and all, but I'll try. Maybe I can get away by seven. You drivin'?"

"Gladys is picking me up."

"Fine, then, it's settled. I'll be there the last few innings and take you home, okay?"

"You don't have to."

"Yes I do. Besides, Gagnon'd never let me forget it if I miss your last game. I've been a pretty lousy assistant coach this season."

"See ya," she called tossing her clipboard into the car, then hopping in herself.

CHAPTER 27

September 4, Monday

The heat was becoming unbearable, the heat and the excruciating yearning. Poor disfigured Christine still lived and breathed, her life a constant torment from which she would soon be free. If only she knew the risks he took in his heroic efforts to end her suffering. If she knew, she'd never have treated him so shabbily!

In twelve days it would all be over and Brother could finally rest. He would retire the gloves, the whole case of them! Maybe he'd hold on to a pair or two, but the rest would have to be destroyed. After the sixteenth, they'd be looking for him because Julia would not be as easy as the others. In order to get closer enough to kill her, he would have to reveal himself, there was no way to avoid it.

Oh God, why was it so bloody hot?

CHAPTER 28

September 4, Monday

The Flames led eight to five after four innings. Juls was pitching a steady, controlled game and Bobby Gagnon sat silent and hopeful at the far end of the bench. If they pulled this one off, they'd be headed for the playoffs in Taunton starting on the sixteenth of September. If they made the playoffs, it'd be a first for the Flames who usually finished in the cellar, thereby disqualifying them from post season play. Not this year, Gagnon mused, this year "his girls" had played their hearts out, in unspoken tribute to Rosie. Keeping her spirit alive had made them winners.

Top of the fifth, Juls had just taken the mound when Billy Correira drove up in his powder blue Caddy, three of his lackies in tow. "Hey, Julie baby!" he called turning heads all round the field. "Ya didn't tell me you was the pitcher! Go get 'em!"

Juls looked towards the bench where Tuck sat beside Bobby. He'd been in that same spot since the start of the game. "Forget about him," he mouthed, not speaking aloud, giving her the thumbs up. Gagnon was already off the bench glaring in the direction of this obvious distraction to his pitcher.

One of the Bedford Belles' left fielder shouted at the newcomer, "Hey Billy, yoo, hoo, over here!" Juls turned in time to see Correira give his admirer a cursory nod. He was dressed all in black—acid washed jeans, a diaphanous, open-necked shirt, and black and white suede boots. His shirt, open almost to the waist revealed a thick forest of grey-black hair bisected by a heavy gold medallion putting Juls in mind of an Olympic gold medal. Repressing a shudder, she turned away, pitching a slow, arcing curve ball.

Carla Merendez swung and missed as the ump called, "Strike one!"

When the Belles retook the field their shortstop appeared to be missing. Their coach, Ted Guimond started yelling for the missing player, Donna Kowalski but to no avail. He had just about given up and was beginning to shuffle his players around when a car door opened behind the backstop and a bright blue Belles uniform appeared. "Jesus Christ, Kowalski—is that you?"

"My fault Ted!" called a voice behind her and to Juls surprise, Danny Moniz emerged from the white Lexus, smoothing his hair. "I had a little business to discuss with Donna!"

"I'll bet," Guimond growled, watching his shortstop's frantic attempts to straighten her uniform which had somehow become untucked and unbuttoned in the course of their business. "Donna get your goddamn fanny out there on the double and you," he added pointing at Danny Moniz. "You stay outta my face!"

What is going on, Juls thought, too shocked to speak as she sat on the bench waiting her turn at bat. Tuck rose after the first batter, slowly making his way along the bench until he stood behind her. He said nothing, nor did he touch her, but his presence spoke volumes and Juls calmed down feeling safe and protected by his nearness.

One out with two runners on base and Juls stepped up to the plate, slamming a hard drive into left field. She made it to second as two runners scored and was bent over catching her breath when she spied Billy Correira. The Belle who had hailed him looked ready to scale the stone wall at any second, leaving a huge hole in left field which she had all but abandoned. Correira was attempting to ignore her, but it wasn't easy. Finally, Ted Guimond spied the little drama and screamed at his player to get back in the game. All the while, Billy's attention hadn't wavered from the runner on second and Juls felt his eyes bore into her, his wolf whistles finding their mark despite her efforts to block them out.

As she loped home on the next hit, a long drive deep into center field, one of his lackeys ran towards her. "Hey Julie," he called, stopping just short of the field. "Billy's gotta go, but he sends his regards!" He jumped the wall behind the backstop and hopped into the Caddy as it rounded the curve disappearing from sight.

So shaken was she that she didn't notice Danny Moniz until they practically collided in back of the bench. Tuck had failed to intercept him, but he stepped between them now. "Look buddy, we've got a game to play so could you please step back. This area's for players and coaches only so either get up in the bleachers or go back behind the wall, will you?"

"Hey man, chill out, will ya. Julia and I are old friends, aren't we hon?"

"What brings you out here Danny?" she asked, wondering whether she was dreaming.

"Well, Donna and me are goin' out, you know? She's been beggin' me to come to a game and Rosie was always goin' on about your games so, here I am. How you been, anyway?"

"Fine, but I can't talk now, sorry."

"Hey, no problem. Maybe we can grab a beer after the game or have lunch sometime?"

"Don't you get it, pal," Tuck snarled, his eyes blazing. "The lady said she was busy, now back off."

"Thanks, but I don't think so," Juls said, peeking over Tuck's shoulder.

"Well, I thought maybe you'd wanna come out someday and clean out Rosie's desk and things?"

"Oh?"

"Oh sure," he grinned, knowing he'd hooked her now. "Her desk's full of shit and I assumed you'd want to have it?"

"Whitman!" Bobby called. "We're in the field now! Do you suppose you could join us?"

"Think about it," Danny called. "I don't know what's there, but you're welcome to it."

Waving, Juls picked up her glove and trotted out to the mound. By the time the Flames came up to bat again, Moniz had disappeared and Juls forgot about him in the heat of the game. The score narrowed after a four run sixth inning for the Belles. The Flames still led by one run, but Gagnon was chewing his sleeve and Ted Guimond smelled victory.

As she headed towards the bench at the end of the inning, Juls spied Wilson halfway up the bleachers, smiling at her. He'd been at their last three games quietly cheering them on, slipping away at each game's conclusion before she could speak to him. If they won, he called to congratulate her and when they had lost, he'd sent flowers, a small bouquet of delicate purple violets. His presence at the games irritated Tuck to no end, but Juls didn't care and she waved up at him smiling, knowing her partner was watching her every move.

Bottom of the seventh with two outs, the Belles put runners on first and second. Juls had walked two in a row and Bobby was preparing to yank her. Not that it mattered, there was no one that would fare any better. Slow pitch softball was a game of finesse and grace. Surprise and variation were more important than strength and no one did better under pressure than Juls, if she couldn't pitch them out of the jam, no one could.

The score was eleven - ten, Flames ahead and darkness was descending fast. When Kitty Perkins, the Belle's six foot catcher stepped into the batter's box, everyone groaned. Kitty was cagey and a heavy hitter when she connected. With two runners on base she could win the game for the Belles with one swat of her bat; she'd hit seventeen home runs this summer out of this field alone. Bobby made a move towards the mound, but then, thinking better of it, he sat back down.

Tuck called out, "Pitch it right in Juls! You can do it! Nice and easy now, take your time."

"Strike one!" The ump's voice rang out across the field as relief washed over Juls. She'd been certain the pitch had been low and outside.

Two balls followed the strike and Kitty fouled the next pitch over the wall behind third base as the ump called "Strike two!" The count was two and two and she paused, looking back over her shoulder towards the bleachers. Wilson winked, surreptiously flashing her a victory sign and Juls turned back to the plate, throwing a perfect arcing curve. Kitty swung hard, twisting around nearly falling over as the ump called "strike three!"

The bench erupted as Tuck, Bobby and the remaining Flames charged the mound, lifting Juls onto their shoulders, the entire team converging on them in one laughing, cheering mass. As the dust settled, she searched the field afraid Wilson had left again, but there he was, standing at the edge of the field smiling, waving at her. She ran out, giving him a hug which he returned, saying, "Great game!"

"Thanks," she smiled, stepping back, shyly. "That wave really helped."

"I'm glad," he replied, blushing. "Can I give you a ride home?"

She turned back to her teammates celebrating wildly now, drenching each other with foaming beers, as they drifted slowly towards Archie's. "I'd love a ride," she said. "Can you wait a sec?" He nodded and she ran off to find Tuck who was locked in a clutching embrace with Karen Ramos, already three sheets to the wind. The front of her uniform was drenched leaving little to the imagination.

"Tuck?" she called, not sure she was ready to take on Karen.

With difficulty, he extricated himself and trotted over to meet her. "Yo?"

"Wilson's here."

"Yea, I saw him. He comin' to Archie's?"

"No, he's giving me a ride home, okay?"

"You're not coming over to celebrate?"

"I really don't feel like it, do you mind?"

"No, 'course not," he lied, his true feelings only too obvious in his eyes. "Girls'll be disappointed though."

"They'll never know the difference," she said, touching his arm which he pulled away immediately. "I'll be seeing plenty of them anyway. I'm sure Bobby'll have us doing double practices to get ready for the playoffs. See ya then." She turned and ran off, not waiting for his response, unable to gaze into his sad puppy dog eyes another minute. When she dared to glance back, she saw that Karen once again had him in her clutches, their party already halfway across the street on the sidewalk outside of Archies.

"You're lucky," he said as they drove off in his gray pick-up. "That's a great group of people there."

"Yes, they're pretty special. Of course, it's not the same without Rosie," she said, her voice trailing off as she thought about how her friend would be screaming and carrying on. "We've been playing all summer for her, you know, tryin' to make up for losing her."

"Well, your team's really good whatever the reason, much better than the other teams I've watched you play. I mean that and you're talking to a ten year Little League veteran here."

She laughed, thanking him as they pulled up in front of her house. "Would you like to come in for a beer or something?"

"Well..., if you wouldn't rather—"

"I'd rather be with you," she said and meant it. "Actually, why don't you stay for dinner? I have chili I made yesterday and tortillas and beer?"

"Sounds great, I'd love to."

While she showered, Wilson warmed the chili and tortillas and afterwards they took their plates to the back terrace.

"You certainly had some interesting fans there tonight," he said, giving her a sidelong glance. "Who were those men, if you don't mind my asking?"

"Just some people I've met recently. They were acquaintances of Rosie's and I've been asking around a little lately and I met them. Horrible men, both of them. Frankly, I'm amazed that they showed up like that, at the same game too. The whole thing gave me the creeps if you want to know the truth."

"I thought you said you'd given up investigating."

"I have."

"Good. That's one thing Tuck and I agree upon. Especially if your investigating puts you in contact with people like that."

They walked along the river after dinner, the sky reflected in the calm glassy water ablaze with stars. On the way back the talk turned to Tuck and she fell silent, not wanting to discuss her partner.

"I'm sorry, I didn't mean to pry," he said, opening the back door for her.

"You're not and it's okay. I'm just tired, and Tuck and my relationship is complicated, that's all."

"You're in love with Potter, aren't you?"

Surprised, she turned to face him. "To be honest, I really don't know. Of course, I love him as a friend, but—" She broke off, her eyes filling with tears.

"Oh Juls, I'm sorry."

"Please be my friend," she sobbed, leaning against him as they stood in the dimly lit kitchen, her tears catching her completely off guard.

"Come on now," he whispered, helping her into the living room, settling her on the couch.

"Oh Wilson," she said, recovering herself, wiping her eyes as she sat up. "You must think me an awful fool!"

"Nothing of the sort," he said, sitting down beside her.

"Thank you."

"You're beginning to sound like a broken record you know, all this thanking." She laughed, stifling a yawn.

"You're tired and I've gotta get going, if you're sure you're okay?"

"Fine."

Standing up, he bent, kissing her on the forehead. "Take care," he whispered, closing the door softly on his way out.

"Thank you," she said aloud to the empty room, wishing more than anything that she'd asked him to stay.

CHAPTER 29

September 5, Tuesday

Her replacement was late as usual so Christine worked an hour over her shift. Making a mental note to request a change with next month's rotation, she was determined never to work again backed up with Cathy Melman. The woman was hopeless. She had more flimsy excuses than most people use in a lifetime and Teeny was sick to death of her offhand apologies delivered as she strolled onto the floor usually at least forty-five minutes late. "Oh Teeny, you're a doll! The car's done it again, I keep telling Wayne to get it fixed, but he never listens to me, sorreeee!"

"You're a doormat Teeny," her sister, Maddie said as they sat eating dinner that evening. "You're nothing but a doormat to that floozy and as long as you let her, she'll walk all over you, mark my words."

Like the pot calling the kettle black, Christine mused, watching her sister inhale the dinner she'd prepared. Right after dinner, Maddie would make a great show helping to clean up for about five minutes, then she'd wrap up the leftovers and hurry home to feed them to Les and the kids."

"Vivian's aware of the situation," Christine answered patiently, referring to her supervisor. "When Cathy comes up for review, it'll all be there in black and white."

"Lotta good that'll do with her daddy on the hospital Board!"

"Maybe," she replied weary of the conversation. The last thing she wanted to talk about was lazy, inconsiderate Cathy Melman.

"'Course you don't have a family to look after like I do," Maddie continued, unwilling to let the matter die. "So, perhaps you can be a little more free with your time!"

It was all she could do to hold her temper, but Christine did, for Mama's sake. Mama had so little time left, she deserved to spend it without strife.

When her mother had first taken to her bed, Christine had cooked large meals, carefully wrapping the leftovers in individual servings, enough for her mother for several nights. It hadn't taken Maddie long to get wind of this extra bounty, however, and Mama's leftovers were soon disappearing along with her silver, china and linens, whatever Maddie could stuff into her bag each time she came to visit.

When Christine had protested, Maddie made her feel guilty saying, "Don't tell me you're planning on giving Mama the same meal all week?" She had fought back by decreasing the size of the meals, just enough for two and for a while Maddie had been shamed into going home and cooking for her family. Now, as her mother reached the end, Christine had softened and wanted Maddie there for her mother's sake. She wanted desperately for them to be a family for the few short weeks Mama had left. So, she made larger meals again and now Maddie came every night, greedily snapping up the leftovers often without bothering to inquire as to whether her sister or mother wanted second helpings. Neither ever did, Mama's appetite was next to nothing and Teeny was usually too tired to eat so there was plenty left over for "Les and the kids".

"Leave Teeny be," her mother squeaked from under her mountain of blankets. "Goodness knows, she manages as best she can! Better than some people I know."

They took their meals in the bedroom, Maddie and Teeny on rickety plastic television tables, Mama propped up in bed with her supper on the white wicker breakfast tray, a Mother's Day present from Teeny. Tonight they were having Christine's homemade chicken pot pie. As it had been a rather small pie, there was only one piece left. As it was one of their mother's favorite things, Christine insisted it be wrapped for her lunch the next day, receiving a glare from her sister in return.

Maddie complied, giving the pie a wistful glance as she put it into the refrigerator, whining, "Too bad you didn't make a bigger pie. It's Les' favorite too, you know."

"I'll write down the recipe and you can fix it for him!" her sister replied cheerfully.

Maddie shrugged, saying goodnight and Teeny stayed behind to clean up. Mama had barely touched her dinner. Despite efforts to conceal it, her mother's face betrayed the pain that was her constant companion, robbing her of her strength and appetite. Teeny scraped a small portion into the cat's dish and threw the rest of her mother's supper away.

"Night Mama," she whispered, bending to kiss the wizened forehead, nodding to the night nurse who had taken up her seat in the corner of the room. "I'm off tomorrow, so I'll stop by. If it's nice we'll have a sit in the sun, what do you say?"

"That would be lovely dear," she replied, her voice a rasping whisper.

"Call me if there's trouble, won't you Alice?" she said on her way out. The nurse nodded in silent reply.

At the doorway, Christine turned back, blowing her mother a kiss, forcing a smile she didn't feel. Her mother smiled back, keeping up her part of the ritual played out each night without fail. Neither knew then it was to be their last goodbye.

In her final three weeks of life, Mary Barboza was to be cruelly deprived of her only comfort, her beloved daughter Teeny. Once Teeny was gone, there was no one to visit her, no one to cook her special meals, no one to coax her to try "just a little bite". Once Christine was gone, Alice heated frozen dinners left untouched by her patient, until the final week when Mary Barboza lay alone and forgotten in the sterile, white hospital room with no visitors save the sporadic comings and goings of the nursing staff. In her final three weeks of life, Mary saw her oldest daughter once, when Maddie came to the house to collect "a few things". Saw her, yet didn't see because from the moment she was told of Teeny's death, Mary collapsed into a delirium from which she never emerged.

Christine drove home that evening, lost in thought, thankful she had declined David's invitation to go out. A hot bath, a glass of wine and she'd be sleeping like a baby.

She was right about David, she told herself, thinking back over their last few times together. He'd behaved himself on their last date, but still, there was something bizarre about him. Much better to end things now, before he became really impossible. Something told Christine that he could be really impossible if he chose. She shuddered remembering how she almost run into him the previous day. She'd just completed her shift and was passing by the Globe Corners field when she'd spied him in the crowd watching the game. As the field was quite near the hospital, she wondered for an instant if he might be following her, but he seemed engrossed in the game, women's softball.

Maybe he's got a new girl, she mused, praying he wouldn't catch sight of her. "Good luck, honey!" she said aloud as her car rounded the corner out of sight.

CHAPTER 30

September 6, Wednesday

"I'm so glad you dragged me out here," Juls said, leaning over the side of the Sunfish, fingers grazing water as they sailed out of the river into Mount Hope Bay. It was a beautiful day, the gentle breeze just enough to propel the boat over the glassy surface of the bay. "And I sure needed to get out of the office, it was a zoo!"

Wilson laughed, changing course as the sail began to luff. "We're lucky, the Bay's been so choppy lately and then it's not this nice greeny blue, more brown and murky I'm afraid."

"Do you swim in it?"

"Absolutely, but then I've been swimming in it all my life. Except for a few skin rashes along the way, it hasn't hurt me and on days like today when it's almost clear it's easy to forget what lurks below the surface. Probably cleaner now than twenty years ago. We can go out and anchor by Spar Island if you like, swim or whatever?"

"I don't know. Once Labor Day rolls around, it gets a little chilly for me."

"You're kidding? Not here. This water is warmer than the ocean at its warmest summer temperature."

"Well, maybe." She was wearing her suit under her shorts and tee shirt. "I've never been on Spar Island."

"Then let's do it," he declared, setting a course towards the tiny island, a sand bar really, that lay in the shadow of the Mount Hope Bridge. At high tide all but the largest dunes, were underwater, but at low tide the entire stretch of land was visible, scrubby marsh grasses growing along the length of the island's center.

They swam, then picnicked on the food Juls had packed, lying on blankets in the warm September sun. After lunch she closed her eyes, drifting off.

His voice called her back. "Juls, we'd better go," he whispered, his hand on her arm. "The tide's coming in."

Jumping up, she realized she'd been asleep for a good long while. "Oh Wilson, I'm sorry," she began, but soon gave up, realizing that he was busy with the boat and wasn't listening. Silently thanking him for the few moments peace, she hastily gathered her things. Such moments had been almost nonexistent since Rosie's death. Sleep had not come easily since she'd lost her friend and what little she got was punctuated by nightmares and tearful awakenings.

"It's nearly four," she cried, running out to help with the boat. "I had no idea. I'm gonna be in trouble now!"

"I thought you had the whole day off." Just a touch of irritation in his voice. "I was going to ask you to stay for dinner."

"I'd love to but I can't. I promised Tuck I'd be back to check on the office and we've got practice in half an hour! I'll never make it, will I?"

"Probably not, but we can try," he said, throwing the last things to her and shoving off.

They tied up at Wilson's dock just after five. A long expanse of green grass stretched from the house to the dock where a Boston whaler and a small dory were tied up. They dragged the Sunfish onto the grass, storing the sails in a small shed to the left of the dock. "I used to keep this on the dock," he said, as they let go of their burden, allowing the Sunfish's bow to fall to the soft ground. "It was much easier, but I've had two Sunfishes stolen, so what can you do? River's not the same as it was ten years ago."

"I wouldn't know. I'm a city girl."

"I grew up in the city, but we always had a place summers on the river. We always rented till I bought this house. It's been a dream of mine."

"That's nice," she said. "I'm glad for you. I've been on the river, of course, with my uncle Bud. He used to take us across from Fall River to Bristol, to the Fourth of July parade."

"We did that too, neighbors of ours took us. That was great, huh?"

"I'll bet we sat right next to each other and didn't even know it," she said, taking his arm. "How many years did you go?"

"Just till I was six, then—"

Wilson was interrupted by a voice calling from the house. "Juls!"

Looking up, they spied Tuck leaping from the terrace where he'd obviously been waiting, worry and concern evident in his expression. Irritated, Juls looked away as he drew near.

"Jeez, you guys, I'm glad I caught you."

"Everything alright?" Wilson asked. "You look as if you've seen a ghost."

"Not exactly," Tuck answered, suddenly looking awkward and unsure. "Look, I'm sorry. I wouldn't have bothered you guys if it wasn't important. It's not good news I'm afraid."

Juls blanched, her anger seeping away in an instant, replaced by dread.

"Don't worry about bothering us," Wilson said quietly, his hand steadying her. "Juls has practice so we were just coming up. I was going to give her a drink and send her on her way, will you join us?"

Tuck hadn't heard a word the other man had spoken. His eyes were riveted on his partner, his worry almost palpable as she stared back at him, transfixed.

"Juls, I'm sorry, I didn't want you to hear it on the radio."

"Hear what?" she said, moving closer to Wilson, taking his hand.

"There's been another murder, same guy they're pretty sure. Jack called an hour ago. They found her this morning."

"Who?" she croaked, falling back, losing consciousness. Wilson just barely managed to catch her before she fell to the ground.

"Someone she knew?" Wilson asked as they carried her between them up to the house.

"No, but it doesn't matter. Every time it's like Rosie all over again. This one's name is Christine Barboza, I believe. A nurse, no apparent connection to the others so far."

CHAPTER 31

September 6, Wednesday

"Snippy, snappy, aren't I happy," Brother sang as the steaming hot water of his shower washed over him. It had been so easy, after all his fretting, Christine had been ridiculously easy! The old drunken hag upstairs had had the television blaring so loud she'd have missed a train wreck in the next room. No way she heard the few brief minutes of shuffling heralding Christine's final minutes.

He'd been so clever, everything in place ahead of time—the rope, the scalpel, the chloroform soaked washcloth. Of course, he'd been sporting a new pair of gloves, the smell of the Latex filling the tiny closet where he crouched, waiting. When the front door opened he'd slipped into the hallway and Christine had walked straight into his arms!

Then she was sorry! Sorry she hadn't gone out with him, sorry she hadn't been nicer... sorry, sorry, sorry. Not that sorry would have helped her in the end, but he might have shown her a better time. As it was, she hardly knew what hit her. He supposed she had just returned from her mother's... slaving away as usual... he hadn't bothered to ask, there wasn't time.

Now it was over. A hot shower, a good book... he felt peaceful, satisfied. Well-acquainted with the ephemeral nature of his satiety, he nonetheless gave himself over to its spell, however brief it might be. Soon, the restlessness would begin again, along with the voice.

"Brother, come here!"

"Brother, get me some soup!"

"Stop sniveling and help me with this puzzle you imbecile!"

"You can whine and cry for a million years and you'll never make up for what you've done to me!"

"Done to me!"

"Done to me!"

As the sixteenth approached, he was beginning to have doubts, dreadful, creeping doubts. He'd put so much store in this particular killing. What if he were disappointed?

From the moment he'd first laid eyes on Julia's photograph in Rosie's apartment, he'd felt sure that she at last might still the voices. Her death might erase the ceaseless harangues that plagued his sleepless nights. If she were to die on the anniversary of the other, perhaps the peace he so desperately craved might finally be his.

It hadn't been his fault... that's what the shrink had told him over and over and over again. "You mustn't blame yourself son. This type of thing happens sometimes during difficult births. It's rare, but it happens."

Dr, Carmichael didn't hear Mother though, did he? Didn't hear her screaming and the ceaseless screeching wheels of her chair!

"But Mother says—"

"Son, that's understandable under the circumstances. After all, your mother had already lost three other children before you. And, she was a real beauty, the loss of her legs was quite a blow what with her active social life and all. Perhaps as she grows older, she'll come to terms with it, but in the meantime, be patient. Don't worry, you and I know that you are not to blame, that's all that matters!"

"Don't worry." What a fool, Dr. Carmichael was! Brother had begun seeing him after three unsuccessful suicide attempts, but the good doctor's counsel had not helped in the slightest. His mother's harping had continued unabated, its sting unmitigated by the doctor's admonitions about worrying. The sessions had served a purpose, however, they had turned his anger outward. After six months of Dr. Carmichael, Brother no longer wished to hurt himself, 'let others suffer instead' became his credo.

Sometimes he wondered if he should give up the idea of killing Julia. It was so dangerous. With the exception of Rosie, the others had all been loners, with few friends and family hovering around, but not Julia. She was always surrounded by people. How would he ever lure her away from Potter especially? Potter could prove dangerous if Brother wasn't careful.

Where should he do it? Certainly not at her house with all those snoopy neighbors, the houses practically touching each other on either side. Every time he'd driven by her house the old bitch next door was parked on her porch or peeking through the curtains. Probably had a hearing aid too the way his luck was running.

He'd taken an enormous risk with Christine, using mother's special order puzzle, the portrait of herself she'd had blown-up and made into a poster-sized puzzle. There weren't enough pieces to recognize her, but could it be traced? Was he getting sloppy? Did he want to get caught?

He'd saved his favorite puzzle for Julia, Mother's pride and joy, the twelve hundred piecer of mad Ludwig's castle. The castle itself perched high on gray cliffs was almost colorless except for the crimson flag flying from its highest tower, but the foreground of the photograph was riotous palette of color—violets, wild flowers and heather in full bloom that followed the sloping contours of the hills below the mountain.

Yes, he thought, slipping the broken pieces into a baggie, Julia would look lovely covered with violets.

CHAPTER 32

September 7, Friday

"I'm coming, and that's final", Tuck said. "I have a few ideas of my own, and besides, things are pretty quiet around here today."

"Fine," she said, gathering up her things. "But, remember, no solicitous looks, no pats on the shoulder."

"Promise."

Having received permission from Jack Mederois to examine the puzzle pieces, they were paying a visit to the police station. Ricky's examination had yielded little, but as Juls insisted that they go, they were going. She just couldn't let go.

They had just turned the answering machine on when the phone rang. Grabbing it before the recorded message could take over, she sat down, pad in hand.

An unfamiliar woman's voice said, "Miss Whitman, please."

"Speaking."

"Hi, this is Sarah Bursin. You probably don't remember me, but I used to work with Rosie. At Arnold Graphics? I saw you a bunch of times there, pickin' up Rosie. And then, of course, at her funeral. Maybe you didn't notice me."

"I remember you, Sarah. Hi. You've been away. I tried to call a few weeks ago, but they said you were on vacation."

"A permanent one. I quit."

"Any special reason?"

"Without Rosie, Arnold Graphics won't last six months. They're already in deep trouble, Danny doesn't know his ass from his elbow and Larry, the other full time employee blew town too, three days after I quit."

"Danny must be having a hell of a time," Juls smiled in spite of herself, thinking about the oily owner of Arnold Graphics frantically trying to hold things together.

"I wouldn't know, Miss Whitman, but can I see you, when you have a few minutes? There's something I think you oughta know."

"Excuse me?"

"About the company. About Danny... I mean. It's probably nothin', but I'd feel better if I told someone and I hate cops."

"Fine. I'm on my way out, but I could meet you somewhere for lunch?"

"Sure, fine."

"Where's easy for you? We're, I'm going to be in the city, downtown."

"How 'bout Lizzy's, around twelve-thirty?"

"Great, I'll see you there. Oh, Sarah," she said, catching Tuck's questioning look. "Okay if I bring my partner, Tuck Potter? He was a good friend of Rosie's too."

"Sure, fine. See ya at twelve-thirty."

Chapter 33

Jack Mederois was in a foul mood, announcing upon their arrival that he had a "headache that wouldn't quit". He led them back to his office where the baggies were laid across the top of his desk, the reams of paperwork usually covering it piled in a precarious stack in the corner.

"Nothing leaves this room, got it?"

He ushered them into the office then disappeared, returning with three cups of lukewarm coffee.

"These are the new ones," he said, pushing the bag with Christine's pieces towards Juls. "There wasn't any blood 'cause he sprinkled them at her feet, almost as an afterthought. We think he was in a hurry, maybe a little spooked by this one."

"How was she?" Juls' voice wavered only slightly as she looked at the disheveled detective. It was clear he hadn't slept in several days nor had he bothered to wash or change clothes. His rankness filled the closed, airless room.

"Same as the others—strangled, like always, he used gloves. Hard to tell exactly because the mutilation occurred in the neck area and our guy is getting sloppy."

"What's that?" Tuck asked, instantly regretting his question as he saw Juls face pale.

"Miss Barboza had a large, birthmark that ran the length of her neck. That's what he—"

"Never mind," Tuck said, his voice a hoarse whisper.

"She was already dead. Died quickly. First, he subdued her, chloroform, just enough to knock her out. We think he intended to cut her first, but then he panicked and killed her. There was very little blood, except in the neck area."

"The bastard's getting sloppy though," Mederois spit the words out. "We know how he got in. Left a foot print on the window sill. Laundry room window. Appears it was unlocked, something jammed into the lock, so it didn't quite catch.

"We figure he knew Christine, jammed the window earlier, then broke in and waited for her Tuesday night. Poor kid was just coming home from her mother's. The old lady's only got a few weeks left, cancer. Christine did everything for her. Cooked, cleaned, ran errands, drove her around. There's another sister, but according to the neighbors, she's a total waste. Now the poor old lady's wishin' she checked out weeks earlier, I'll wager."

"What about his footprint?"

"Size nine and a half, Saucony trainers. *Men's Shadow* they're called. Pretty popular shoe, from what I hear. That's all we know so far. Anyway, let's get started, see what you can find."

"Jack," Juls said, reaching into her bag. "I have something for you. Something I should've given you weeks ago." She pulled out the Baggie holding the two puzzle pieces she'd found at Rosie's. "I'm sorry. We handled them very carefully, never touched the surface, only the rims. This one has a word on it, see it says 'far'."

"Well, that clears up some inconsistencies," Mederois sighed too weary to react to the deception. "But don't worry about prints, he hasn't left one yet. Wears gloves, disposable Latex ones. We ain't gonna find no print."

"Your buddy Steele went through these pretty carefully and didn't find much. This latest puzzle is interesting though."

"Does it have a word?"

"Yup, 'fair', although I'm not sure it fits Ms. Barboza as far as looks go anyway. Nice kid and all but nothing much to look at. Anyway, it's the front that interested us more. We faxed a picture to the company, to see if they recognized it."

"Did they?"

"Nope. Ain't one of theirs. Seems this particular item was made to order, from a photograph. Looks like a woman, but we can't be sure. Wearing some kinda red thing, like a tent."

"You mean, this may be a picture of someone the killer knew?"

"More than likely. She's got brown hair, longish."

They worked at the puzzle for nearly an hour, but none of the pieces fit together. He'd chosen carefully; most of the pieces were background, in varying shades of green. It appeared that the photograph had been taken outside, perhaps in the shade of a tree or on the grass beside a garden or hedge row.

After they wrestled with the puzzle labeled Christine Barboza, they made their way back through the baggies till they held the four pieces that had been found with the body of Beth Johnston.

"Now that we've checked 'em all we'd like to try something Jack." Tuck said, stretching, taking a sip of his now ice cold coffee.

"Yes....."

"Ricky claims *Puzzle It Out* told her that most of the subscription puzzles have interchangeable pieces."

"Oh no you don't."

"Why not, we'll be careful," Juls piped in, suddenly alert and too excited to be angry at Tuck for not telling her about the interchangeable puzzle pieces. "They all appear to have different colored backings, so we can easily separate them later."

"Oh, what the heck. Go ahead," he shrugged. "Can't hurt and God knows we don't have any other ideas."

They quickly put aside the pieces found with Catherine Foley as they clearly came from a different size puzzle and as Christina Barboza's puzzle had not come from *Puzzle It Out,* these too were set aside. Then, turning all the pieces upside down, they worked slowly and carefully, attempting to match pieces.

After an hour of work, they'd made no progress and Juls sighed, "Another dead end. Too bad, it was a good idea."

"Whoa partner," Tuck said, gazing down at his watch. "It's twenty after twelve!"

"Uh oh, we gotta go."

"What's your hurry?"

"Meeting a friend for lunch," she lied, not wanting to tell him about Sarah Bursin.

"Once again I'm left picking up the pieces," Mederois mumbled.

"Oh, hold on, Jack."

"What is it now?"

"Can I take a picture of this last puzzle? I promised Ricky I would. It's just one photo, okay?"

"Go ahead, why not. And no more poking around, you understand? This maniac's still out there and we don't want him gettin' pissed off at you." He fixed a hard look at Juls before stepping aside so she could open the door.

"Thanks Jack," she said, kissing him lightly on the cheek as she passed by, Tuck right behind her.

Almost makes the job worth it, Mederois, thought, closing the door. Almost, but not quite.

CHAPTER 34

September 7, Friday

Linc Marvell paced the length of his sister's family room. Laura's home was usually a place where Linc could really relax. His favorite spot was the wood paneled room where he was now pacing with its soaring cathedral ceiling and ten foot windows overlooking the Vermont woods, the mountains just visible through the trees. It was the perfect retreat from the pressures and stresses of everyday life and goodness knew, he needed the respite after the horror of Ellie's death, still raw and festering in the not so distant past.

They always drove up to spend Labor Day weekend with Laurie and Stu and if Betsy worked hard enough, she could sometimes coax him into staying longer; this year she had succeeded. In Vermont, he really rested, often spending entire days in one of the overstuffed chairs wrapped in one of Laurie's quilts reading and dozing. Today rest was eluding him, however, due to a recent phone call from Doris, his secretary.

She had phoned an hour earlier to inform him that one of his largest trust accounts, a client whose portfolio of investments he had managed for many years, wished to liquidate his assets immediately. He had tried to call the client, but had thus far been unsuccessful in reaching him. What could he be thinking of, Linc wondered.

Thank goodness Betsy had gone off with Stu and Laurie and wasn't here to see him fretting. She'd start right in again about his retiring and he wasn't up to that just now. The three had gone into town to shop and plan their dinner party, collaborators in what Betsy referred to as "a gourmet feast". They had invited three other couples to join them. Linc had no interest in gourmet feasts and wished he could slip away and drive home to meet with his client in person, but of course, that was out of the question. Betsy would never agree to it, nor would she brook any suggestion of abbreviating the visit. They planned to stay through Wednesday and stay they would.

Betsy.... Betsy.... Betsy. In the past he'd been the strong one, the one making decisions, taking charge. Lately however, their roles had been reversed and meek, frail, delicate little Betsy had come to the fore. Since Ellie's death, Betsy had had to run things; Linc no longer seemed able to cope.

Resigned to the inevitable, Linc had already called Doris back, instructing her to proceed with the client's request. If only Ellie had been in the office he thought sadly. Ellie would have known just what to do. Instead, he gave his instructions from afar, with a heavy heart. "Anything he wants, Dottie. After all, his mother left it to him and God knows the poor man deserves it after the way that woman treated him. Didn't say what he wanted with so much money, did he? No? Well, hopefully it'll give him a bit of fun."

The shoppers appeared in the drive and Linc left off his pacing, going out to greet them, helping with the bags laden with "gourmet delights". Smiling, as he grabbed two bags from the back of the jeep, Linc feigned a festive spirit he neither felt nor wished to be a part of.

Clients made large withdrawals from time to time; it wasn't all that unusual, but not this one. He rarely touched the money bequeathed to him and if asked, Linc would not have been able to explain why the situation worried him, but it did. It wasn't the bank's loss that worried him, but rather an inexplicable unease he couldn't quite seem to shake.

The episode cast a pall over his remaining days in Vermont and Linc was moody, detached and edgy. Each of his companions remarked about it on different occasions until Betsy finally erupted. "Lincoln Marvell, snap out of it! You are making us all very depressed! Whatever is the matter?"

"Nothing dear," he replied, knowing better than to mention the bank; Betsy had left strict orders with Doris not to disturb him "no matter what!" It was nothing, he told himself over and over again. So why does it bother me so?

CHAPTER 35

September 7, Friday

Sarah Bursin walked into Lizzy's Cafe on the dot of twelve-thirty, scanning the room for Juls Whitman. Her eyes, furtive and restless, took in the tables of business men a few women scattered in their midst, her heavily made-up face registering disappointment at not finding Rosie's friend among the lunch crowd. Although she'd barely spoken a word to her beyond a quick hello, Sarah knew Juls from her occasional visits to the office and from several of Rosie's parties over the years. The tall, slender beauty, such a contrast to stocky, rugged Rosie, fascinated Sarah and she had found herself wishing on more than one occasion for the body and grace of Juls Whitman. She'd often asked Rosie about her friend, but Rosie's accounts were usually of things the friends did together. What she really wanted to hear was what Juls ate, who cut her hair, what she thought about, who she went out with— subjects that Rosie rarely touched upon.

To a casual observer, Sarah Bursin would be considered mousy. Mousy, drab and ordinary. Danny had told her often enough during their brief, pathetic little romance. Sarah believed him, that was the worst of it. Truth was she'd always been a plain Jane. She wasn't ordinarily the type of person who lived vicariously through others, but somehow she found herself inexplicably drawn to Juls.

Flustered, she followed the waitress to a table in the dark recesses of the restaurant, the table closest to the kitchen. She ordered a coke, sipping nervously, her eyes on the door, irritated at herself for leaving the latest issue of *Vanity Fair* on the seat of her car.

As she waited, Sarah pondered the reason she'd asked to meet with Juls. Was it just an excuse to get close to her idol or did she really have something useful to share with her? She could tell some stories about Danny and the way the company had been run, that was for damn sure! She didn't really believe Danny's scheming had anything to do with Rosie's death, but how could she be sure? Her boss didn't give a shit about the company from what she could see and God knows he didn't need the money. One night she'd found a bank book open on his desk; the red Five Cents Saving passbook was just like her own on the outside, but not inside! The guy was loaded. She dropped the book like a hot potato afraid Danny'd catch her snooping, but she'd seen enough to know that Arnold Graphics could go belly up the next day and Danny'd never feel a thing.

Still, there was the business of all the phony unemployment claims; she had to tell someone. Perhaps Rosie had already told Juls before she died, but Sarah wanted to be sure. Someone ought to know about Danny Moniz before she washed her hands of the sleazeball forever.

Suddenly spying Juls at the restaurant's front door, Sarah waved, her eyes riveted on the other's handsome companion. Sarah waited feeling awkward and unsure at her dark, cramped little table. Juls had brought the infamous Tuck Potter with her and, Sarah, mousy little plain Jane that she was, was about to have lunch with him. Maybe this was her lucky day after all.

CHAPTER 36

September 8, Friday

"Fool, idiot, imbecile!" Brother paced, his face distorted in anger. Anger at Doris Kittery! "I understand, dear," she'd said, her voice dripping with condescension. "But that large a sum, I simply must check with Mr. Marvell."

Calmly, he'd explained that Mr. Marvell really had nothing to do with it. "It's my money! There are no restrictions whatsoever on the account."

"Of course, dear, but ordinarily with such a large transaction we like to move cautiously. After all...."

"Excuse me Mrs. Kittery, but with all due respect, I wish you to begin the paperwork immediately. I will be in early Friday morning, the fifteenth, around nine. At that time, I would like the full amount ready, in cash. Oh, and see that it's in twenties and fifties, nothing larger please."

"But—"

"As for what remains in the account, I'll discuss that with Linc at a later date."

"Of course, but I will still need to call Mr. Marvell."

"Look—" he started, fighting to remain civil, the white hot rage surging higher with each passing second. "I'll call back in exactly one hour. Go ahead and phone Linc, but I expect a response immediately. If you do not have a satisfactory answer for me within the hour, I will come today, before closing and begin proceedings to close all my accounts with the bank. Do I make myself clear?"

"Perfectly," she sniffed, hanging up.

The conversation had left him shaken and weary unable to do a lick of work. She sounded just like Mother, thwarting his every move, not trusting him, not giving him the freedom he so desperately craved. Wouldn't he love to put the gloves on Doris Kittery!

The phone had rung several times—Linc Marvell's voice on his answering machine, desperately pleading with him to be in touch—but Brother hadn't answered. Exactly fifty-five minutes later, she called back.

"Hello, it's Doris Kittery. We're in luck. I was able to reach Mr. Marvell and of course he gave his approval. Said to send his regards. After all you are one of his most valued customers."

Thanking her, he hung up, vindicated at last. Her voice had been saccharine sweet, the old bitch. She'd never liked him, he knew that. He'd never been good enough for snooty, prim and proper Doris Kittery. He'd caught the sidelong glances, disgust and disapproval clearly evident in her eyes. Well, fuck her, fuck all of them. Soon he'd be gone and would never again have to endure Doris Kittery's disdain.

Of course he couldn't tell the old bag why he needed the money. Couldn't tell her that after next Friday he'd never be allowed to touch another cent of it. "Take the money and run," he chuckled. "And you, my fat, old Dottie, can go fuck yourself!"

CHAPTER 37

September 8, Friday

"What'dya got for us, Sarah," Tuck asked, midway through their lunch. All three had ordered soup and sandwich combinations, the women half sandwiches, Sarah following Juls' lead with tuna on rye while Tuck requested a "monster turkey club" on whole wheat. The soup, a thick seafood chowder, complimented the sandwiches perfectly and for several minutes they had given themselves over to the meal, conversation taking a backseat.

Unattractive, was Tuck's private assessment of Sarah Bursin. In skin tight black lycra mini skirt, a mustard-colored tunic sweater stretched over it, she reminded him of a turnip, the frizzy mass of bleached blond hair the plant's foliage. An enormous human root, that's what she looked like, he decided. Her thick, unevenly applied pancake make-up failed to mask the pitted and rough complexion and her mascara, eye shadow, rouge and lipstick appeared to have been applied with the finesse of a two-year-old. The entire effect, just short of macabre, was made all the more ghoulish by industrial strength eyelashes furiously batting whenever he looked in her direction. While he guessed the eyelash deployment was intended to be alluring, it had quite the opposite effect; he was having difficulty finishing his lunch.

They'd exchanged pleasantries, reminiscing about Rosie and how they missed her, but now it was time to get down to business. Juls had been quiet both because talking about Rosie was still painful and because Sarah Bursin made her feel slightly uncomfortable. The way she stared, it was unnerving. Sensing his partner's discomfort, Tuck had taken charge of the conversation, moving them from one subject to the next, turning on the charm as only he could do. Gratefully, she sat back and listened.

"Well, it's a little awkward," Sarah began. "But I feel I have to tell someone. It probably means nothing, but I wanted someone to know before I left the company. There's no one connected with Arnold Graphics I trust."

Spit it out, Juls thought watching Sarah's eyelashes, fearful that one might drop off at any moment, kerplunk right into her soup.

Ignoring the hand Sarah kept resting on his arm—her touch anything but casual—he said, "Sure, we understand. Talk away, we're all ears."

"It's about Danny. I don't know if Rosie ever told you about the scams he was pulling?"

"A little," Juls volunteered.

"Well, there was the benefits stuff."

"How did that work?"

"He had five or six guys workin' there all the time, besides those of us on payroll, but he paid 'em under the table. First year they'd declare they were makin' megabucks—I don't know how he fixed the books to show that, but anyway. Then he laid 'em off—on paper—and they'd start to collect.

"They're still workin' every day, see? And collecting and gettin' paid. Danny got a cut of everything. It wasn't the money, like I said, he sure didn't need it. It was just the thrill of gettin' away with something I think.

"Danny comes from a lot of money. Doesn't need a dime. That's why he doesn't give a shit whether Arnold Graphics survives."

"Family money?" Tuck asked.

"Must've been, I mean, he rarely talks about his family, but I got the feeling his dad hadn't ever been in the picture much, you know? Raised by Mommy. Never talked about her, but I heard him on the phone talkin' about 'my mother's house',or 'my mother's estate', stuff like that."

"You mentioned other scams?"

"I think he was dealin'. Coke, maybe grass."

Juls sat up, "Rosie never mentioned drugs."

"No one knew 'cept me, and maybe Larry. I may be wrong, but there was a time back about six months ago when every sleazeball in the city was holdin' little pow wows in Danny's back office.

"I knew 'cause I worked later than Rosie. She came at seven, left at three. Me, I don't like to get up early, kind of a night owl," she purred, leaning her ample chest in Tuck's direction. "I'd kinda coast in around ten, ten-thirty. Us regular salaried folks were expected to put in eight hours. I never left before six."

Repressing a wave of embarrassment at the other woman's behavior, Juls asked, "Do you have any proof? Do you think Rosie might have found out? I mean, do you think he might've had a reason to kill her? Is this what you're telling us?" Her voice had risen to a shrill, half-scream and all conversation at neighboring tables had ceased. Tuck leaned over, placing his hand on her shoulder.

"So what exactly are you trying to say, Ms. Bursin?"

"I don't know. Juls, I'm sorry if I upset you. I wouldn't have done that for anything. Rosie talked about you constantly. I always used to wonder what it'd be like to be loved like you. To have a girl friend as close as you and Rosie. I…" her eyes filled up and Sarah rummaged in her enormous purse for a Kleenex.

"It's me that should apologize, Sarah. I don't do very well when Rosie's death is mentioned… it still hurts so much. I'm sorry, really I am. I'm not even sure why we've been asking all these questions anyway. We're not investigators, we don't know what we're doing and, Detective Mederois says more than likely the killer is someone who only just met the women. And there's absolutely no connection between Danny and the other girls."

"That's true," Tuck interrupted. "Juls is right. Danny Moniz probably has nothing to do with Rosie's death."

"I'm sure you're right," Sarah said. "On top of everything else, Danny was crazy about Rosie. Not romantically that I know of—"

"Definitely not," Juls stated, emphatically.

"But, he did like her. And, as you probably know, she ran the company. After she died, there was nothing left."

"Well, we got to get going," Tuck said, picking up the check as he stood stretching. "You two stay here and I'll settle up."

"He's great," Sarah sighed, as Tuck headed for the cashier. "You're really lucky. I wish I had a boyfriend like him."

"He's not my boyfriend, Sarah, we're business partners."

"Yeah, sure," Sarah said, a knowing look accompanying her toothy grin.

"Really," Juls said, gathering her things, suddenly eager to be gone.

CHAPTER 38

September 15, Thursday

Two cartons held all of Rosie's personal things from her office at Arnold Graphics. There hadn't been much to clean out, just two desk drawers and a small file cabinet. Juls sat looking around the stripped, bare cubicle and her eyes filled with tears as she thought about Rosie, bigger than life Rosie, maneuvering in the tiny, cluttered space.

"Want these posters?" His voice startled her and she jumped up, a cascade of papers spilling from her lap to the floor. "Hey, sorry, don't get up hon. Didn't mean to scare you." She turned away too late, he had spotted the tears. "You okay? Can I get you a cup of coffee or somethin'?"

"No, thanks. I'm fine. I'm all set. I think that's everything."
"Okay, if you're sure. Anyway, these were hers," he said, holding up two prints of whaling scenes. The original paintings hung in the New Bedford Whaling Museum, a favorite haunt of Rosie's.

"She let me hang 'em in the front office. You want 'em?"
"Thanks, but I don't think so." Juls had never shared her friend's interest in whaling.

"Okay if I hang onto them then, sweetcakes? Somethin' to remember Rosie by?"

"Fine, they're yours," she said, forcing a smile. Sweetcakes indeed!

"Look, it's almost noon, why don't I take you to lunch?"

"Thanks, but I've got to get back to the office."

"Hey, what's half an hour. Come on, what'dya say? There's a great deli right around the corner, soups, salads, whatever."

"I can't really," she said, squeezing past him.

He grabbed the other carton, following her, cajoling and coaxing all the way to her car. "Just a quick bite, what do ya say, Julie?"

"Bye Danny," she said, ramming the car into gear.

"You owe me one Julie! I'm callin' you! For dinner and I won't take no for an answer, you know! Didn't Rosie tell you how persistent I am?"

Despite the warmth of the day, Juls rolled up her window silencing the voice still calling to her as her car swung onto Route 6.

CHAPTER 39

September 15, Friday

He had it, the money was finally his! Linc had put up an awful fuss, but in the end, he had had no choice. It was Brother's money and he could do what he wanted with it. Money, money. money, enough money to live comfortably for the rest of his life if he lived frugally and reinvested wisely.

Brother was still unsure of his final destination. First, he must leave the city. He would fly to England and tour the countryside, then decide. As a college student, he'd spent the happiest summer of his life living out of a backpack traipsing through the British countryside. Yes, after Julia he'd begin his new life's journey in London and take it from there.

Sweet Julia, your time has come! Will you go gently or should I take you by surprise like Christine? So much easier when one went willingly to death, rather than fighting as Rosie had done. Such a beast that Rosie!

"They're all dead, Mother," he said aloud, a choking laugh echoing in the empty house. "All except one."

Last night the voices had been terrible. Brother supposed it had been trepidation about the trip to the bank and the excitement about the weekend ahead. Whatever the reason, the voices had screamed and carried on until dawn, his head throbbing in agony as he vainly tried to silence them.

"If you'd only been a girl!

"Why couldn't my one child have been a girl?

"A girl would never cripple me!

"Cripple me!

"Cripple me!"

CHAPTER 40

September 15, Friday

"We're missing something Tuck, I just know it. Let's go through it all again."

"Juls, you wanna know what I think? And don't give me that look either."

"Oh, what the hell, I give up, one more shot, but then we're doin' J. & T. stuff. Deal?"

She nodded. A cold Sam Adams in hand, Tuck leaned back, waiting for the familiar recitation of their assembled clues.

The remains of a lobster dinner, courtesy of Tuck's lobsterman brother, were pushed aside as they spread photographs and other assorted bits of evidence across his dining room table, Rosie's table. They were alone in the house, the office door ajar so they could listen for the phone. Ordinarily, their business day ended at five, but they were waiting for a call from a client needing airport transportation.

"First we've got Beth Johnston. Killed April twelfth, Sunday. She was lame, walked with a cane. The puzzle appears to be a photograph of a marble sculpture, Michaelangelo's *Pieta*, isn't that what Ricky said?"

"And the word is "woe". What do you 'spose that means? We don't know a thing about Beth Johnston, beyond the fact of her disability, that could certainly be considered woeful, I'd say, wouldn't you?" He shrugged.

"That's our problem," he said finally, preparing to launch into his 'we don't know shit about investigating' speech but Juls pulled out the next folder, ignoring him. "Catherine Foley, killed May thirtieth, Tuesday. Birth defect, no fingers on her right hand, or was it left? Her word was "grace". The ballerinas on her puzzle fit that description. Catherine was a runner, runners might also be considered graceful."

"Not the way I run."

"Be serious Tuck! The words might simply refer to the subject of the puzzle and not the women at all. They were all glued together, right? He had to work with what he had."

"Okay, so what's the connection? Why's he pick the women? To fit the puzzles he's got squirreled away or is it random selection?"

"Well, he appears to choose them because of handicaps or physical anomalies. Lame's his game and—"

"Tuck!"

"Juls, calm down. I'm not being factitious. He can't scour the world for the perfect match between puzzle, handicap, whatever, can he? So, he makes the women fit his vision, however warped or perverted it might be."

"Let's keep going," she said, seeming not to have heard a word he said. "Next came Rosie." She swallowed hard, composing herself before continuing. "Killed July twenty-seventh, Thursday. The scars on her arm—"

"Let's take a break, whatdya say?"

Juls shook her head vehemently.

"Okay, fine," he snapped, picking up one of the pieces they'd found in the folds of the sofa. "The word was "far" and her puzzle's some kind of artwork, spin painting."

"And there's no connection between any of the women except for the Sportside. Rosie, Ellen and Catherine Foley were all members, right?"

"When'd you hear that about Catherine Foley?" she cried, jumping up, her tear streaked face all attention.

"I dunno, I thought you told me. Maybe Ricky."

"How long have you known about this?"

"Since the beginning, I mean I knew about it before you went on your date with Correira. We talked about it, I'm pretty sure."

"No we didn't!" Her eyes flashed anger, her fists clenching and unclenching in an effort to control her temper.

"Juls, now hold on."

"Never mind."

"Look, I'm sorry."

They sat in silence for several minutes until she finally picked up the next folder, "Ellen Smith," she started in, giving him a look that said, 'I don't want to talk about it'. "Killed August eighteenth, Friday. She had a heart condition, her word was "love". Love definitely goes with the heart or he might've been in love with her?"

"If he was he's got a funny way of showing it. Okay, okay, I'm serious and no, I don't think the bastard's capable of love, do you?"

She shrugged. "Puzzle seems to be a Madonna and child, Botticelli?"

"Ellen had no kids, no family. So the puzzle probably wasn't directly connected to her, beyond the word "love". Unless of course, she had a passion for Italian Renaissance painters. We wouldn't know about that though, would we? 'Cause we didn't search her house, interview her friends, fact is we don't know shit about her and—"

"Stop it."

He shoved the last folder towards her.

"The last woman was Christine Barboza. Killed September fourth, Monday. Large, red birthmark running down her face and neck, her word is "fair"."

"No disrespect for the dead, but Ms. Barboza wasn't what I'd call a real looker."

"Maybe 'fair' doesn't refer to physical beauty, some people can see beyond that you know. Maybe it means 'fair' as in equitable or accommodating?"

"Maybe, her puzzle was a picture of a woman, right?"

"Custom made according to Jack."

"So what have we got?"

"Not much."

"He's still got Sunday and Saturday."

"What do you mean?"

"Days of the week. Maybe the bastard takes a rest on the weekends, only kills during the week, and..."

"That's something new, doncha see? We haven't ever made that connection before, now we're getting somewhere. Do you think he's deliberately choosing the days?"

"Maybe," he replied absently. "Do you hear something?"

"Sounds like a car, are you expecting someone? Somebody just drove in," she said, rising to peek out the window. "Tall woman, just got out of a battered jeep."

"Sounds like Ricky," he said, coming to stand behind her, resting his chin on her shoulder. "Yup, that's her alright."

Dressed in faded jeans and a light blue tee shirt—Spindle City Athletic Club in white, peeling letters splayed across its front—Ricky carried a huge, leather shoulder bag that made Juls wonder if she was planning on an overnight.

The woman filled the room as soon as she stepped over the threshold. Juls felt like a midget.

"Juls, Ricky Steele. Ricky, Juls Whitman, my partner," Tuck said, stepping aside as the women shook hands.

"Hi," Juls said. "I've heard a lot about you and thanks for all your help on this."

"No problem." She smiled, the angular features softening. "Anything for little Danny-boy."

"Okay, okay. Let's not dredge up horrid childhood memories," Tuck said. "What's up, Rick?"

"Sorry to barge in, but I stumbled across something I thought might interest you. Actually, a friend who lives up in the Berkshires stumbled across it. He's someone I met last year on a case, he's a private investigator, too. Real nice guy, low key, not your usual over inflated ego. Cute too.

"Anyway, I got a call from him this morning, asking about a native Fall Riverite who's involved in a case he's workin' on and we get to shootin' the breeze and he asks what I've been up to. I tell him about the strangler cases and he says yeah he's been reading about them wondering if they were near to an arrest. Then he says, 'bet it's the same guy'. When I asked what he meant he told me about a murder thirteen years ago in Amherst. No puzzle pieces, but the guy left a word, and the girl had a disability. She'd lost part of her foot, all her toes, some kinda frostbite she picked up hiking Mount Washington. Walked with a limp."

"Name was Blythe Leeming. That was her word too, "blithe" with an "i" instead of a "y"."

"I can't believe Mederois didn't know about this," Juls said, scribbling on a legal pad.

"Oh, he knew."

"How do you know?" Tuck said.

"I asked him, stopped by the station an hour ago. He's known all along. Amherst made contact right after Beth Johnston was killed."

"I can't believe Jack wouldn't tell us. Wouldn't....."

"Take it easy, Juls. Mederois has gone above and beyond in letting us in on this. Showing us the puzzles, telling us stuff we never should've heard."

"Tuck's right," Ricky added. "I've never managed to pry as much out of him as you two have and I'm in there all the time. 'Course, he's not crazy about me and—"

"We've been going over things," Juls interrupted. Going through each murder and what we know. Are they really sure this old case is connected?"

"Sounds like it. What've you got?"

"When was this Blythe killed?" Tuck asked.

"I'm not sure of the exact date, sometime in January."

"Know what day of the week?"

Staring at him for an instant, she replied, "Must have been Sunday 'cause I think he said she'd just come from church."

"That takes care of Sunday," Tuck said. "Leaving us with Saturday."

"Say what?" Ricky looked from one to the other.

"He's killed someone on each day of the week except Saturday,",Juls said. "Listen to this. Monday, Christine- 'fair', Tuesday, Catherine- 'grace', Wednesday, Beth- 'woe', Thursday, Rosie- 'far', Friday, Ellen-'love' and Sunday, Blythe- 'blithe'."

Ricky listened, saying, "Sounds like some kind of chant or maybe a—"

"That's it," Juls screamed. "Blythe started it all!"

Tuck and Ricky stared at her, Tuck convinced that she'd finally snapped.

"Don't you see? He's following the children's rhyme. You know,

Monday's child is fair of face,

Tuesday's child is full of grace,

Wednesday's child is full of woe,

Thursday's child has far to go,

Friday's child is loving and giving,

Saturday's child works hard for a living,

But the child that is born on the Sabbath day is bonny and blithe and good and gay!

"That's it! That's what the words mean."

"Sounds good to me," he said. "Wish we knew if Miss Saturday was already dead or if he's stalking her right now. What else did your friend say, Rick? Did they have any suspects in the old case? Anyone Blythe was hangin' out with?"

"He couldn't remember, but he's gonna check it out and call me tomorrow. Police didn't uncover much, at least not that was ever made public."

"Want a beer Rick?"

"Thanks Tuck, but I've gotta run. Just checkin' in. I'll be in touch tomorrow."

"Thanks," Juls said. "It's great to finally meet you. I wish it was under happier circumstances."

"Me too,",the other said, kissing Tuck on the cheek and grabbing her bag. "Take care, both of you. I'll let you know what I find out tomorrow."

"She's a trip, isn't she?" Tuck said as the jeep sputtered down the road. "I like her. I hope she's careful. I mean, we dragged her into this. And we're not paying her, are we? "

"Nope, but don't go worrying about Ricky, Juls. First of all, she loves it, and second, she can take care of herself. She's some kind of martial arts expert. Plus, I've heard she carries a gun now."

"Before this happened, I'd have said that Rosie could take care of herself," she answered quietly, clearing the table.

It was nearly eleven when Juls drove into her driveway, a darkened house awaiting her. Tuck had begged her to stay as she sometimes did when they worked late, sleeping in the cottage's spare bedroom, but Juls wanted to be home in her own bed. Or so she thought until she'd parked in the drive. The stillness of a moonless night hovered around her, alive with menace and unseen goblins, the thought of walking from her car to the back door inexplicably terrifying.

CHAPTER 41

September 16, Saturday

Saturday morning found Linc Marvell at the office catching up on his paper-work, memos, correspondence and Doris' detailed notes covering each day of his absence. It was a rainy day, otherwise Betsy would never have allowed him to come in. "Oh go ahead," she'd said, when he'd broached the subject. "What else is there to do."

Vacations made for so much work upon one's return, he mused, leafing through the stacks of paper. Better to have stayed home, now I'll be behind for weeks.

Scanning the mail, he came upon the letter from Tuck, with the *Puzzle It Out* subscriber list enclosed. Glad of a chance to escape Doris' missives if only for a few minutes, he scanned the list, searching for a name he recognized. "Now there's an interesting coincidence," he said aloud, stopping at the name Raines, Editha M. Raines.

How odd that Editha's name should be the only one he recognized given his recent run-in with the son. Several times he'd looked heavenward, silently apologizing to Editha for allowing the boy to decimate the trust, but what could he do? It was his money and he could do what he liked with it.

Linc sat back, thinking about Editha and the many times he'd gone out to the house to consult with her. How she did love her puzzles! One was always going, laid out on a velvet covered card table in her front parlor. How many times had he sat in the dark, curtain-shrouded parlor over the years? In the early days, it had been next to impossible for Editha to come to the bank when wheelchair access was still a thing of the future. So Linc had gone to her, with deposits, withdrawals, investments, whatever she needed.

While they talked, the boy would sit working the puzzles, never daring to slip away for fear of his mother's wrath. Once, Linc had glimpsed Editha Raines wrath and it had not been a pretty sight. He'd watched the boy cringe in fear at his mother's harsh, spiteful words, even as he hurried to fulfill her wishes.

"Idiot boy you've spilled the tea!

"You are the most useless good for nothing boy!

"Hurry, get a rag and wipe this up!"

When he hadn't moved fast enough punishment had been swift and terrible. The knobby, wooden cane always at her side struck home again and again. What Linc most remembered about the episode was the quiet, the absolute stillness, each crack of the cane resonating through the house, the boy silently enduring his abuse, not a whimper, not a gasp, not a cry. When the beating ceased, he retreated, mopping up the droplets of tea before disappearing. The mother had then turned back to Linc with, "now then dear, where were we?" as if the scene he had just witnessed was a perfectly natural interaction between mother and son.

The poor boy, Linc thought, what a life. God knows, if he wants to spend the money to have a bit of fun, why not? Perhaps it will bring him a little happiness after such a dismal, lonely childhood.

Slowly, his thoughts returned to the present and the list. Could Editha's son possibly be involved in all this dreadful business? He was a strange man, but murder? Linc thought about Ellie and the dull ache of sorrow settled in his chest. Could the boy have actually killed Ellie?

To his knowledge, Ellie had never met his client, but perhaps that was what she had been intending to tell him on their last evening together. Perhaps, he should at least call Potter and tell him about Editha though he prayed with all his heart that the boy was not involved.

The J. & T. line was busy and Linc set the list aside, resolving to try again later.

CHAPTER 42

September 16, Saturday

"What's on tap for you today?" Tuck asked, watching his partner rifle through files scattered over the desk.

"I've got a bunch of errands to run in the city that I'm hoping to finish up by early afternoon. My garden's completely overrun and if I don't start freezing tomatoes they're going to rot and I'll lose 'em all. What about you?"

"I'll hang around for a while, then I'll be in the vicinity. Forresters need a walk through and some decorator from Boston's coming in. Then I'll probably roust Bobby from the store, shoot some hoops. We're going out tonight, wanna come?"

"Where?" she asked, knowing where they'd end up.

"Who knows, dinner, maybe the Tavern maybe Archie's, shoot some pool."

"Thanks, but I don't think so."

"Why not? You got a date with Willie boy or the Doggie Doc?"

"No," she said, giving him an icy glare.

"Why not?"

"I'm tired, that's why. I feel like crawling into bed and reading a trashy romance novel, maybe I'll stop by the library and pick up a whole stack of them."

"You okay?"

"Yup. I'm off then. If Mrs. Nadeau calls, I'm checking on her mums this afternoon."

"What's that about? Can't I do it on my way to Forresters?"

"No, she's very fussy and wants them 'carefully pruned'. You know what a butcher you are with the pruning shears. Do you really want to risk Joanie's fury?"

"As always, you're right, carry on, m'lady!"

"And call me if you hear from Ricky."

After Juls' departure, Tuck returned to his own kitchen leaving the office door ajar. He'd barely sat down when he heard her back in the office bustling around again. He looked at the clock. Eight-fifteen. She's gonna burn herself out, he thought dismally as she slammed out again.

As he sat back down with his plate of eggs and home fries, the phone rang.

"Mr. Potter?"

"Speaking."

"This is Linc Marvell, from the Five Cents Savings. I've just gotten back from my vacation and I've had a chance to look at your list."

"Recognize anyone?"

"I'd like to talk with you about it, in person if that's possible. Are you free today?"

"I'm tied up this morning, but what about this afternoon?"

"How 'bout six-thirty? I live on the Neck, do you know it? Could you come by the house?"

"I know it well and I'd be glad to stop by."

Linc gave directions, his address and home telephone number and they rung off.

CHAPTER 43

September 16, Saturday

"Well, if it isn't little Miss Investigator."

She recognized the voice immediately and considered walking on, without acknowledging him. She'd just finished the last of her errands and he'd caught her in the bank parking lot off Rock Street. Deciding it'd be better to face him than run, she finally turned, facing him head on. "Hello Mr. Correira."

For an instant, she thought she was staring at a stranger. He looked almost handsome, his light gray, exquisitely-tailored linen suit hung perfectly over the broad shoulders and his sandy hair, free of the thick pomade he'd worn at their last meeting, was slightly tousled giving him a totally different look.

"Nice to see you again."

She didn't return the compliment.

"Look Julia, since you're right here have lunch with me. Lizzie's is just around the corner or the Q Club? What do you say? For old times' sake?"

"Thanks, but I have an appointment."

"Bullshit. You haven't eaten yet have you?"

"No, but I'm—"

"Come on, what have you got to lose? Half an hour. I won't lay a hand on you, promise. No funny stuff under the table. Kinda scared you off at our dinner, didn't I?"

Unbelievable, the arrogance of the man, she thought. "I can't, Billy, really. It has nothing to do with the last time. I just have to—"

"I'm not taking no for an answer. We'll go to Corky's. I'll get us in and out in fifteen minutes. It's only two blocks away. Come on Julie."

Finally, caving in, she accompanied him down the street, his chest puffed out to double its size. The noon rush was over and Corky's lunch crowd had thinned out. They had no trouble finding a seat sparing her the spectacle of Billy throwing his weight around.

The waitress, *Mary Lou* emblazoned on her breast pocket, swept over at once. They both ordered salads, Juls a small seafood, Billy a large chef's special.

Mary Lou, reappeared in record time with their iced teas. "Thanks doll," he said, waving her away and turning his full attention to his companion. "So what have you been up to since our date? I've wanted to call, but I've been afraid you'd hang up. I hate rejection you know."

What had happened to his voice? she wondered. Where were the rough edges, the butchered grammar?

"Hello? Julia, anybody home?" he teased, and she realized he'd asked her a question.

Blushing, she replied, "Nothing really. Just working. Labor Day's our busiest time, people moving out and closing up their houses and all."

"So now what?"

"Same thing, it's just a slower pace. We can finally catch up on bills, paperwork, repairs, all kinds of stuff in September."

"I know your partner, did I tell you that? Potter went to school with my cousin, Jimmy, at SMU, 'cuse me, U. Mass Dartmouth now. Nice guy, used to come over the house sometimes."

"I think you must be thinking of one of Tuck's brothers. He's never mentioned you."

"It's the name. Used to be Collins. Ask him if he knows Will Collins. You look surprised. Shocked that someone would trade a waspish name like Collins for Correira, but hey, it suits me better that's all. Suits my line of work. I mean, I can't go round calling myself Will Collins, know what I mean? Sounds like a fucking twerp or some kinda wimpy cocktail." The coarse vernacular was back and Juls wondered which was the real Billy, or Will, or whoever he was.

"Where'd you go to college?"

"So, now you're interested in my life history? That's a start anyway. Getting curious about me, I like it. U. Mass. Majored in anthropology, if you can believe it."

She couldn't. "How 'bout brothers and sisters? I mean did you have any?"

"Now you wanna meet the family. This is progress Julia." Impossible, she thought, chuckling in spite of herself. .

Their salads arrived and conversation tapered off for several minutes until he finally deigned to answer her question. "No brothers or sisters, just adorable little me, Julia. How 'bout you?"

"I have three brothers and one sister, all older."

"The baby of the family, that fits. So you grew up right here in old Fall Reve?"

"Yes and you?"

"Sure did."

"Do your parents still live here?"

"No, look, let's drop this family shit, okay?"

"I'm sorry," she said, frightened by the sudden change. His eyes blazed for an instant, but he quickly recovered himself. The mood remained somber, however and for a while Billy seemed unable to keep up his end of the conversation.

Back on the street, she prepared to make her escape, "Thanks for lunch. It really wasn't necessary for you to pay, but the salad was delicious."

"Have dinner with me, I promise I'll behave." It came out of the blue, catching her off guard. "Don't look so surprised. If you haven't noticed already, I'm crazy about you. That first day I saw you in the Sportside, I knew you were the one. I'd like a chance to show you how I—"

"Billy, I can't. I'm sorry. Look, I really have to go. Thanks again!" She broke away, almost running down the sidewalk.

"Jesus Christ, I only want to have dinner with you! I'm not asking to fuckin' marry you!"

Several people stopped to stare as she wended her way up the street, round the corner. Shaken and queasy, she started the car, praying he hadn't followed. Fool, she thought, as she made her way out of the city. What a stupid fool to have accepted another one of his invitations. Had he been following her? Jack Mederois' words, "Don't get too close, or he might fix on you" came back to her.

First, the irrational terror of the night before and now this. She'd been fine once she was securely locked inside the house the previous evening, but her sleep had been fitful, troubled by dreams she couldn't remember upon waking.

She'd call Tuck as soon as she got home, find out what he'd learned from Ricky. His voice would calm her down. And he'd be interested to hear about her lunch with Billy, aka Will too. No, furious was more like it, perhaps it was better not to mention it? Billy looked to be in his early thirties. Was he in Amherst thirteen years earlier when Blythe Leeming had died?

CHAPTER 44

September 16, Saturday

Whispers. Whispers. The past was slowly fading into whispers with Brother only hours from freedom. The duffel bag lay on the kitchen floor, packed and repacked a dozen times. Overalls, painter's cap—he got them for free at the lumber company—plastic sheeting, a small ax, the scalpel would never cut through the bones and he'd been unable to procure a surgical saw, rope and of course, gloves—three pairs. He wanted to be well-prepared and why not splurge? He wouldn't need any of it after tonight.

He patted his pocket, the pocket containing a first class ticket to London. Better to leave it at home, he thought, reluctantly extracting it from his jacket. Wouldn't want to lose it in all the excitement of the outing. He'd packed the money in two large carry-on bags, but that was it. He was taking nothing with him into his new life to remind him of the past. Once he got on the plane, he intended to close the door forever. He'd organized everything before walking slowly through the house to say goodbye to every room, every object he must leave behind. His farewell stroll reminded him of his father, talking him to sleep. Together they'd say goodnight to every object in his room, just like the children's story. If only his father hadn't gone away, things might have turned out so differently.

"Julia, I'm coming," he whispered, running his fingers along the zippered canvas of the duffel. "Soon, you'll be free of those crippled knees. Wouldn't want you to have children and wind up a cripple, saddling them for life! Don't worry, your children will never have to listen to the screaming or feel the cane. I'm coming Julia, I'm coming."

The phone rang.

CHAPTER 45

September 16, Saturday

It was quarter of seven as Tuck bumped his truck down the Marvells' long, gravel drive. Nearly a half a mile into the woods, he finally reached a clearing, two fields, bordered by stone walls. Beyond the fields, the drive dipped to the right and the roof of the small clapboard cottage was visible beyond a stand of sycamores. He brought the car around the next bend, parking in front of a four-stall barn.

As he hopped out of the truck, a voice called out "Hello!" and his host waved as he made his way along a garden path at the side of the house, a basket full of vegetables on his arm. Reaching Tuck, Marvell extended his hand. "Thanks for coming, Mr. Potter. We're a bit out of the way here."

"What a place," Tuck said, returning the other's handshake.

"Yes, isn't it? It's been in my wife's family for three generations. She's always teasing me, claiming I married her for Windbrook, that's what we call this place. We're very lucky."

"I'll say, right on the river, too. You have a boat?"

"Just a small whaler for mucking about in the marshes. The grandkids use it mostly. Betsy and I keep a Beetle cat over in the harbor. You sail?"

"Whenever I can."

"You're welcome to use it anytime, just ask Mickey over at Spindle Rock and he'll set you up, get you the sails and all. You live in the harbor, don't you?"

"Yup, I live in the same house as our office, where you came last week."

"That's right, you're the house sitting people, aren't you? Betsy, my wife, wants me to get your card. She's not home now, it's her bridge night, but she's real interested in your services and would appreciate a call. I'm supposed to be on the verge of retirement, you see, and she's got plans for traveling all over creation. We'll need you if she ever gets her way."

Tuck took a business card from his wallet, handing it to him. "Just give us a call, number's in the corner. The other number's my partner, Julia Whitman's home number." Despite J and T's waiting list, Tuck knew he would take the Marvells immediately should they call.

"Well, now, let's get down to it," Linc said, leading him towards the back porch. "And please, call me Linc. Everybody does. What can I get you, beer, iced tea, wine, soda?"

Tuck started to refuse, but then said, "Beer'd be great, thanks, Linc." He sat in one of the porch rockers to wait.

Linc returned several minutes later with two Heinekens and a brown paper sack full of vegetables. "For you," he said, setting the sack at Tuck's feet. "Betsy and I can't keep up with it all. We're always looking for victims to pawn off a load of this stuff on."

"Thanks. My lucky day."

"You were good to come all this way so I won't keep you all night babbling. There's two things I thought you should know. The first concerns that list of yours, the second is bank business, so I'd ask for your discretion. If they weren't related I wouldn't tell you the second, but.....well anyway, I know you and Miss Whitman lost a dear friend, just as Betsy and I did. We still miss Ellie so dreadfully," his eyes misted over, his voice trailing off to a hoarse whisper.

"Forgive me. Anyway, I know you two grieve as we do and so I felt you had a right to know. If there's any connection, I'd never forgive myself if I didn't tell someone and I don't wish to involve the police if it's simply a wild goose chase." Breaking off, he wiped his eyes with a soiled bandana.

"I understand. You can count on me to keep anything you say confidential, Linc. It's hell, isn't it? My partner's been a wreck since Rosie died. You okay?"

"Yes," the older man had collected himself by this time and went on. "First off, I recognized a name on your puzzle list—Editha Raines. She was a valued client until her death three years ago. Although your list gave no addresses I'm quite certain she is the Editha I knew. It was a demographic list, I believe?"
"Yes. The company agreed to furnish a list from Massachusetts and Rhode Island, but only names."

"I see," Linc replied, absently. "Anyway, I'm quite sure it is my Editha as she was an avid jigsaw puzzler. Is that the correct term?" Tuck shrugged and he continued. "Raines was the name of her second husband which brings me to the other piece of the puzzle so to speak. She had a son by her first husband who is still my client. Since her death I have managed a sizable trust for him, a trust which until yesterday contained a great deal of money as well as a large portfolio of stocks and other investments.

"Last week he ordered us to sell almost everything, much of it at a loss. Many of the bonds and treasury notes had not come due, but he didn't care. Nothing would deter the boy, and so we acquiesced to his wishes and liquidated the account.

"When I began thinking about his behavior in connection with your list, I began to wonder if somehow Ellie could have met him through the bank. He came in once a month to meet with me, you see. He's an odd man, but I can't believe him capable of murder. Still, he had a grim childhood, poor boy, and who's to say what people are capable of, don't you agree?"

Tuck nodded.

"And then I keep going back to something Ellie said just before we were interrupted. She started to say something like, 'you know him' or something to that effect."

"Has he left town, do you know? Sounds like a person ready to pull up stakes and disappear."

"I don't have the faintest idea, he wouldn't tell me anything."

"What'd you say the name was?"

Linc Marvell said the name and Tuck's blood ran colder than the half-finished beer in his hand.

"I have to use your phone, right now," he said, jumping up, his rocker nearly toppling off the porch.

"Oh my, God, you don't think?"

"I don't know what I'm thinking, but I'd rather be safe than sorry." He followed Linc to the kitchen, furiously dialing Juls number. No answer. "Shit," he mumbled, dialing the office. The J. & T. line was busy and he breathed a sigh of relief.

Hanging up, he turned to his host, the older man's face pale and worried. "Thanks, Linc, I gotta go."

"Of course. Shall I keep trying your friend, give her a message, or something?"

"No, I've got my cell phone. She's at the office, I'll keep trying and if I hurry I'll probably catch her anyway." He sprinted to the car and waved before speeding away.

After watching him go, the older man returned to the porch, finding the bag of vegetables lost and forlorn on the step where Tuck, in his haste had forgotten them.

"God keep her safe," Linc said aloud, the wind carrying his whispered prayer out over the open river. "Please God, keep Ellie safe."

CHAPTER 46

September 16, Saturday

It was after seven when Juls arrived home, Joan Nadeau's harangues still ringing in her ears. It had been a grave disappointment to find Joanie at home when she arrived to attend to the mums. She'd been hoping to prune in peace, instead she had had to listen to a three hour diatribe on the trials of gardening "among cretins". No one could do even the simplest gardening chore without her standing over them it seemed.

After her ordeal at the Nadeau's, she'd stopped by the office and left Tuck a note. "Going home, do not disturb."

A hot bath and to bed early, she thought, dropping her things in the small galley kitchen. She'd forgotten to put on the machine so there were no messages. As she slipped out of her jacket the phone rang.

"Shit," she said aloud, tempted not to answer. Finally, after five rings, she caved in.

"Hey Julie, how's tricks? It's Danny, Danny Moniz." He was obviously drunk, slurring his words.

"Danny, I really can't talk now."

"I thought I'd come over and we'd take in a movie, have some dinner, drinks, whatever? 'Member, I said I'd be calling?"

"Sorry, but not tonight. Thanks anyway, I've gotta go."

"Oh no you don't bitch. I'm comin' over there and—"

She slammed down the phone not wanting to hear another syllable. It was the second time today, what was going on? First, Billy Correira, now this.

No longer tired, her quiet, little house, a welcome haven only minutes earlier, now seemed alive, a pulsating menace hounding her every step. She dialed the office number. Tuck was always trying to get her to sleep over, maybe tonight she'd take him up on his offer, wouldn't he be surprised? After four rings the machine came on and she left a message, "Tuck, I need you, please call."

Who could she call? Ordinarily, she'd have phoned Rosie, now there was no one. Her family lived out of town and Bobby didn't answer either. Who was left? One of the Flames? No, she didn't feel up to that tonight. Wilson, that was it, she would call Wilson. The phone rang six times and she was just about to hang up when he answered sounding sleepy.

"Wilson, it's Juls. I'm sorry did I wake you?"

"'Course not, I was out in the shop working, so it took me a while. How are you?"

"I've ...." Her voice trailed off as she wondered if she knew him well enough to confide in him about imagined fears and unseen terrors. Rationality won out in the end. "I've had some strange phone calls and I don't want to be alone right now. Is it possible.... I mean, are you busy tonight?"

"No, I'm just finishing up work on a desk, but I can leave it though and—"

"No," she said, feeling foolish. "I'll be okay, really."

"I know, why don't you come here? I could order take-out and you can keep me company while I work."

"Are you sure?"

"I'd love it."

"Okay then, but I insist on bringing dinner. What do you feel like?"

"Anything's fine, except liver, I've never liked liver. Your choice, surprise me."

Thanking him profusely, she hung up, dug out the Cathay Dragon menu and ordered. Hastily changing into clean clothes, jeans and a cotton sweater, she couldn't seem to get out of the house fast enough. Before departing, she tried Tuck one more time, leaving a second message on the machine. "Sorry if I scared you partner. I'm okay, everything's fine and I'm heading over to Wilson's for dinner. See you tomorrow."

CHAPTER 47

September 16, Saturday

The last vestiges of a brilliant September sunset greeted Tuck as he careened the truck down the drive, screeching to a halt outside the office door. Her car was gone. He raced inside to check the desk, no note. Ignoring the answering machine's blinking light—the clients would have to wait—he ran through to his kitchen. Sometimes she left messages on the table. Nothing.

He grabbed the phone, dialing her number, pacing as it rang again and again. "Shit, Juls, where are you?" After eight rings he slammed down the phone. Before he could dial again, a car pulled up beside the truck. "Thank God," he whispered, throwing open the door to find not his partner, but Ricky Steele standing on the doorstep.

"Shit," he muttered holding the door open for her.

"Hey, I'm glad to see you too."

"Sorry," he said, flashing her a sheepish grin.

She had just enough time to reflect on what a hunk Jack Potter's younger brother had grown up to be when he asked, "What's up?"

"I could ask you the same thing. You look like you've seen a ghost."

"I'm just a little worried, that's all. I can't find Juls and I need to warn her about something."

"Wouldn't have anything to do with the strangler, would it?"

"Yes, it's probably nothing, but damn, I wish I knew where she was!"

"She's more than just a partner to you, isn't she?"

"Pretty obvious, isn't it?" He paced back and forth, his eyes betraying his mounting fear. "I 'spose she might've gone somewhere just to grab a bite. I'll... never mind. What's up with you? Did you hear from your friend?"

"Yup. He did some digging and found out a little more about Blythe Leeming's murder."

"And?"

"Definitely happened on a Sunday in January. She was strangled with a smooth rope or something, the rope was never found. No puzzle pieces but it sounds like our man. The word "blithe" was written on a scrap of legal paper. Block letters, no prints."

"Anything else?"

"One other thing we might wanna check out. Police records didn't show this, but Smith College campus security had an interesting item. Blythe was taking classes there as well as at U. Mass. My friend bowls with the head of security and the guy apparently has records that go way back.

"Seems they questioned a friend of Blythe's, but never spoke to the cops 'cause the guy seemed so broken up about his friend. They figured there was no way he'd have done it. He had an alibi for the time of the murder too, or so they thought. Anyway, the interesting thing is, he's from around here. Might still live here. He'd be in his early thirties. Name's—"

"McCaffrey," they said in unison.

"Wilson McCaffrey," Tuck continued.

"You know him?"

"Know him? Juls has been dating the fucking wacko! His mother's name is on the list from *Puzzle It Out!* We didn't catch it 'cause she'd remarried and had a different last name. Mr. McCaffrey just withdrew a huge load of cash from the bank. He's gettin' ready to run I figure, but what if he has designs on Juls before he goes? Jesus Christ, where is she?"

He grabbed his keys from the kitchen table. "I'm driving over to her place now to check on her."

"I'm coming."

He made the fifteen minute drive to Juls' in eight, the truck's wheels barely touching the ground as they spun into her driveway. "Shit," he said, as they stared at the darkened house, the porch light its sole illumination.

He leapt from the car, fumbling with his keys as he ran up the walk. Checking every room, they met back in the kitchen.

"Now what?"

"I'll check her mom's." He dialed first one number, then another. No success. After exhausting all possibilities, he scanned the bulletin board near the phone till he spotted a small scrap of paper upon which was written, "Wilson" and a phone number in Juls' large, fluid hand. He dialed the number, letting it ring ten times before banging down the receiver.

"No luck?" Ricky stood at his side, her hand resting lightly on his shoulder. "Nope. I'll try the office. Maybe she's called in. He dialed, then punched in the play back code for the answering machine. The two messages played back and Ricky watched as his face turned ashen as he listened to the first call—"Tuck, I need you, please call!" Then, "I'm okay, heading for Wilson's. See you tomorrow."

"She's there," he said, slamming down the phone, heading for the door. "The bastard's got her there right now! She trotted right into his lair, like a lamb to the slaughter! If I'd only checked the machine earlier, we wouldn't have wasted all this fuckin' time!" Juls was always chiding him for not checking their messages.

"Wait Tuck," Ricky called. "Let me call Jack Mederois."

"Hurry, we can't lose a second!"

"Sorry, Detective Mederois is off duty," Sarah, the dispatcher said. "Want me to connect you with—"

"This is Ricky Steele, Sarah. I don't have time to explain, but you need to send a squad car to 18 Riverview in Somerset immediately. Please don't ask questions, just do it. A woman's life depends on them not losing a second! Get the Somerset police if you can, anyone that can haul ass over there right now! And, please, keep trying to reach Jack, it's really important! If you tell him the address, he'll know what it means."

She hung up and tried McCaffrey's number again. Still no answer. Racing out the door she just caught the truck before he drove away. "Hurry up! Jesus Christ Ricky, we don't have time to screw around!"

CHAPTER 48

September 16, Saturday

Three bags of Chinese food jostled against her as Juls crossed the bridge into Somerset. The moist, fragrant heat emanating from the sacks filled the car, steaming the windshield, tempting her to sneak a bite of spring roll. She resisted, turning onto Riverview at last. Hopefully, Wilson had remembered the wine, she mused, but if not, she had noticed a package store just down the street the day they'd had lunch together. She could stroll down and pick up some wine while he continued to work. There was something very comforting about the evening ahead, like the routine of an old married couple. Turning into the driveway, she felt safe and secure, the terrifying vulnerability of a short time ago fading away, almost laughable like a bad horror flick. Her only worry was that she was imposing, inviting herself over when she'd known Wilson for such a short time. What would he think of her and all her crazy fears?

Wilson was talented, his reproduction furniture exquisite, but what did she really know about him? A few times he'd spoken of his father, but no one else. He was an only child, that much she knew, but little else. His family and especially his mother seemed to be a closed subject and the one time she'd tried to draw him out about them, she'd glimpsed uncharacteristic anger in the pale hazel eyes.

Supposing they would eat in the shop while he continued to work, she was surprised to see every window of the house ablaze with light. As she stood on the stoop waiting for him to answer, she glanced through the dining room window spying the table set for two.

CHAPTER 49

September 16, Saturday

"Look Tuck," Ricky said as they drove. "Even if he's the one—and we don't know that for sure, you know—Juls is probably safe. She hasn't a handicap or disability, and he always goes for—"

"Her knees! God, why didn't I think of it before?" he cried, his voice betraying his fears. "She doesn't limp much anymore, so in that way at least, I thought she'd be safe, but the bastard's seen the photograph! Jesus, what an idiot I am! He zeroed in on her from the first day we met him, maybe even sooner. Maybe he knew even before he killed Rosie that he'd eventually go after Juls!"

"What are you talking about?"

"There was a photograph in Rosie's apartment, taken years ago. Juls and I arm in arm, Rosie took it right after her second knee surgery. Juls is on crutches, both legs in walking casts! Can't get much more crippled than that!"

"Maybe the police are already there, if Sarah was on her toes," Ricky said, quietly, praying they wouldn't be too late.

CHAPTER 50

September 16, Saturday

Jack Mederois was taking the wife out, for the first time in months. He'd just finished showering and was splashing on the English Leather when the phone rang. It was Tim Cottrell whom he'd sent up to Amherst to poke around. "You were right, Jack. McCaffrey was there. Just got off the phone with Smith College security. They brought him in for questioning, but never charged him."

"Morons," Mederois grumbled. "Thanks Tim. I'll take Mickey and we'll head over for a chat with Mr. McCaffrey. Won't be easy if he's anything like his bitch of a mother."

Jack Mederois had been well-acquainted with Editha Raines, in fact had recognized her name immediately on the subscription list from *Puzzle It Out.* In his early years on the force, he'd spent many a night poking around the old bat's backyard searching for the imaginary prowlers she was always calling in about. He'd never met the kid, but once or twice he'd glimpsed a small, frightened face at the windows.

He'd questioned Wilson McCaffrey briefly the morning after he'd received the list, but the man had no idea what he was talking about and claimed to have given all his mother's old puzzles away after her death. "To the youth home on Rock Street. They had a rummage sale and were looking for games and puzzles" he'd said and Mederois had left it at that. Like a fucking idiot, he hadn't even bothered to check out the man's story! Still, the thing nagged at him and he'd been unable to dismiss completely his suspicions about Editha's son. Recently, when Juls Whitman had casually eluded to her date with Wilson, his antenna had gone up, prompting Tim Cottrell's sudden trip out to western Massachusetts.

So much for our night on the town, he thought, leaving a note for the wife due home any minute. He'd pay for this for a month or two, easy. Better go quickly, he thought, strapping on his shoulder holster, she was gonna be steamed! As he headed out, Mederois made a mental note to call Juls Whitman, first thing in the morning. Even if he turned up zip on McCaffrey, he figured he owed her a warning.

CHAPTER 51

As he stood in the shadows peering out the window, Brother could see her coming up the walk, laden with bags. She looked happy. Blissfully unaware of what awaited her inside.

They'd eat first—he'd put the sedative in her wine mid-way through dinner—then....he'd set the dining room table with Mother's best Spode. After she was asleep, he'd sweep the dishes to the floor—who cared if they broke—and operate right there on the table. No need to worry about the mess; he'd never set foot in the house after tonight. As soon as it was done, he'd walk out and drive straight to the airport.

His ticket and the two carry-on bags were tucked by the back door. He didn't dare leave the money unprotected even for an instant. What if someone stole his truck out of the driveway? Brother had thought of everything.

The last of them was actually coming to him! It was perfect. There was no need now for him to skulk around outside of her house, plotting his point of egress. What had started with plucky, little Blythe so many years ago would end with Julia on Mother's best damask tablecloth!

It was fitting after all his hard work that the last should come so willingly to him. Like the spider waiting for the fly, he drew back, allowing her to plunge deep into the web, before he struck.

The doorbell rang and he could barely contain himself, so desperately did he want to run for the gloves. Patience, Brother, patience.   He forced himself to walk slowly to the door.

CHAPTER 52

Mederois' radio crackled and sputtered as he pulled out of his drive. The twenty minute ride to Somerset was bad enough, now he'd probably pick up four or five more calls en route.

"Jack, you there? Read me, over." It was Sarah, gorgeous, super-efficient Sarah, the best dispatcher they'd had in years.

"Hey Sare, how goes it?"

"Jack, Ricky Steele just called." He groaned. "She sounded pretty upset. Some kinda problem at eighteen Riverview in Somerset. She wanted me to send a squad car and—"

"Did you, for Christsake?"

"Well, no, I'm checkin' in with you then I—"

"Get on the fuckin' horn and notify anyone that's close by, Jesus Christ! Call Somerset too, have 'em get their asses over there without delay, you hear me? I'm headin' there now, but it'll take me fifteen minutes at least. God, I hope we aren't too late!"

With sickening clarity, Mederois realized that McCaffrey was their man and Juls Whitman his next victim.

CHAPTER 53

"Hi," she said, stepping into his front hall, suddenly shy and uncertain.

"Hi yourself. Come in."

"I thought you were hard at work."

"I've reached the point where I can leave it till tomorrow so I quit. I'm yours for the evening madam." Bowing slightly, he smiled as she handed him the bags. "Chinese, great."

"Wilson, I'm sorry. Now my stupid fears have interfered with your work."

"Nonsense, it's Saturday night. I'd much rather be with you, and Mr. Tyler can wait. Believe me, I'll wait long enough for his check. Come back to the den, I've laid a fire."

Following him, she glanced in at the dining room table candles already burning in silver candelabra.

He poured them each a glass of beaujolais and they settled on the sofa, facing the fire. "Thanks, Wilson."

"For what? You brought the dinner."

"For catering to my ridiculous fears."

"Don't be silly after all you've been through this summer, you have a right to be scared. I'm glad you came. Now, no more—I can't believe I haven't had you here for a proper dinner after all this time. I'm a decent cook, not great, but decent and, speaking of food, I haven't eaten since very early this morning. Those bags smelled delicious."

"Let's have at them then," she said, jumping up, almost spilling the wine. A tension she couldn't quite define hovered over them, what was it? On the surface, Wilson couldn't have been more charming, but underneath the smiling facade, she sensed an unreadable change, a furtive, secretive quality that she had never before associated with him.

Where was the contentment of only minutes ago? Suddenly she wanted to eat and be gone, but why? Tuck must be home by now, she reasoned....yes, that's what she'd do. Head straight to Tuck's as soon as they finished dinner. Only with Tuck, did she ever feel truly safe and protected.

They spoke little during dinner, save his occasional exclamations about the food and how delicious it was. In her haste to be gone, Juls had wolfed down her food and suddenly she found herself uncomfortably full. Putting down her fork, she took a gulp of wine. The room was dreadfully hot and stuffy. An ugly room, she decided, the red brocade walls and dark, heavy mahogany furnishings put her in mind of an Edgar Allan Poe story. As the minutes ticked by, Juls felt as if she were suffocating.

"Oooh," she sighed, yawning. "I've eaten too much and I'm so tired."

"I shouldn't wonder, Julia. You work hard for a living. You don't take time to relax, have fun." The soothing voice of a stranger came to from a great distance. Wilson at one end of the tunnel, she at the other.

What had he said? Was there something familiar that she was missing?

"May I use your bathroom?"

"Of course, end of the hall, to the right. More wine?"

"No," she said from the mouth of the tunnel. "I think I've had enough. That shrimp was really spicy!"

"I've just the thing," he said, rising, heading for the kitchen as she wended her way down the hall to the bathroom through the haze.

Rinsing her face under water, she looked around the small lavette, a hideous floral affair with the violet bouquets splayed across the vinyl wallpaper, blue lilies painted in the bowl sink and matching porcelain faucets and bunches of lilacs embroidered on tea towels that were sorely in need of washing.

She stepped out of the bathroom, starting back to the dining room when she lost her way and her attention was diverted to a small alcove off the living room. An antique card table stood against the wall, its top decorated with a hunting scene, red jacketed men on horseback, beagles and foxhounds yipping at their heels. On the wall behind the table hung a number of photographs in identical black frames. Through the fog she recognized Wilson in several of the photos.

Her eyes moved to the other pictures slowly, trying to make sense of them. Finally, she came to a black and white photo of a woman in a wheelchair, hunched over the very same table that stood before her. What was she doing? Juls tried desperately to see squinting in the thickening fog that swirled all around her now. There were disconnected pieces, small bits of—In a brief moment of clarity, she realized what she was staring at— jigsaw puzzle pieces! The crippled woman was working a jigsaw puzzle!

As she tried desperately to focus on the photograph the descending darkness inched closer, threatening to envelope her. She slapped at her face, trying to clear her head as she peered at the adjacent snapshot. It was the same woman at a much younger age, standing under a bower of trees. She wore a long, flowing dress and was obviously pregnant; one hand caressed her swollen belly, the other waved at the camera. Christine's puzzle, she thought, steadying herself against the door frame as his footsteps sounded from behind.

Turning, she swayed crazily, nearly toppling into the wall of photographs. Wilson stood framed in the hallway. He was smiling, his hands covered with gray film.

What was it he'd said? "You work hard for a living". As Juls fell forward, the blackness overtaking her at last, she realized with horror that she was "Saturday's child".

CHAPTER 54

They parked a half a block from the house.

"Slow, Tuck—go slow!" Ricky pleaded, as they raced towards the house. "He might freak out and hurt her if we scare him."

Tuck sprinted on ahead, slowing down as he reached the yard. The front windows' curtains were drawn, but all the lights were on. They peeked into window after window, cracks in the drapes affording them tiny glimpses of the rooms within.

Ricky spotted her first, her body already laid out on the dining room table. She had been bound, hands behind her back, a silk scarf gagging her and she appeared to be sleeping. Drugged, not dead, Ricky thought, motioning to Tuck. "I don't see him," she mouthed the words.

"I'm going in."

"Wait, he's coming. For an instant they watched in horror as McCaffrey entered the room swathed in surgical gown and mask. In his gloved hand he held a tray with tools laid out on a white cloth. Tuck made a move towards the window, but she held him back.

"Tuck, don't. Go around and try and get in. If he starts anything, I'll distract him."

As she watched in horror, the deranged man moved about the room setting up his surgery. On a card table covered with a damask cloth, he laid scalpels and a small saw. Her body trembling uncontrollably, Ricky whispered, "Hurry Tuck, hurry."

Suddenly there was movement on the table—Juls was waking up, the drug he'd given her apparently wearing off. McCaffrey noticed it, but he seemed unconcerned. As she opened her eyes, he went to her, wiping her brow, soothing her.

His patient began to struggle and he clamped a hand on her neck, shouted something, a warning perhaps, but Juls refused to settle down, wriggling more and more, her legs flailing out at her tormentor.

Holding her down with one hand, he reached into his pocket with the other drawing out the white cord. As he slipped the rope round her neck, Ricky pulled her hand back into her sleeve. As he tightened the noose, her covered fist shattered the window.

"Give it up, McCaffrey!" She screamed, cursing herself for leaving her .38 at home.

Ignoring her, he continued tightening the rope. Juls was unconscious and close to death when Tuck finally burst into the room throwing himself on the green gowned figure. As they struggled, Ricky ran round to the side door where he had broken in. By the time she reached the dining room, the police had broken down the front door and Wilson McCaffrey lay dead, shot by Jack Mederois as he lunged at Tuck with a scalpel.

Loosening the rope, Tuck cradled Juls in his arms whispering to her as she slowly regained consciousness. She tried to respond, but her voice was hoarse and unintelligible from the bruising on her neck. "Juls, Juls, Juls," he said over and over, continuing to hold her, whispering her name until the ambulance arrived to take them to Charleton Memorial.

Left alone after the ambulance's departure, Ricky knelt on the dining room floor, one hundred and twenty eight pieces of a jigsaw puzzle scattered around her. As she sifted through them, she came upon the piece she sought. On the back of it, in precise block letters was the word 'hard'. "Saturday's child works hard for a living," she mumbled as Mederois crouched down beside her, hand on her shoulder.

"Let's get outta here," he said, helping her to her feet.

CHAPTER 55

September 18, Monday

Bright sunlight shone through the slats of the blinds. Juls shielded her eyes against the sharp blades of light until Tuck rose, closing the blinds completely.

"Don't," she said, "the sun feels wonderful. Pull up the blinds, will you Tuck. I'll sit up." She reached down, pushing the button on her hospital bed.

"You're out today, right?"

"That's what they tell me. I didn't need to be here at all if you ask me."

"They didn't. Your windpipe was badly bruised. Everything's okay now though right?"

"Uh, huh. 'Cept for this lovely purple necklace I'll be sporting for a week or so."

"It hurt?"

"Only when I breathe," she replied. Glimpsing his pained expression, she added, "Just kidding. A little sore, but it's manageable."

"Well, we're covered at the office so don't even think about coming in for a couple of weeks. Longer if you need it."

"Couple of weeks! Tuck, I'll be fine in a couple of days, probably could come in tomorrow if there's—"

"No way. Your mom says she's takin' you home for a few days and I've already told her to keep you till the middle of next week."

"Oh you have, have you? Since when are you my babysitter?"

"Since never, but I'm serious Juls. No work till next week or—"

"Or what, you'll fire me? Oh, don't worry," she added, seeing the concern in his expression. "I'll take it easy."

"Fine," he came to sit beside her. "You okay? About things?"

"Mostly I feel stupid. How could I have been so dumb? I mean, not to have known, or even sensed something?"

"None of the others did. And let's face it, he came across as an okay guy and all."

"What are you talking about, you never liked him."

"Well, that's 'cause I was jealous, not 'cause he was—"

"Sad, isn't it? I mean, he had a horrible life, didn't he?"

"Sounds like his mother was a real witch. Some kinda complication at Wilson's birth left her paralyzed from the waist down. She blamed him for her condition, bitching at him day and night. Then to make matters worse, she marries a leech for a second husband and he didn't care about her or the son. Treated little Wilson like shit."

"Where'd you hear all this?"

"From Linc Marvell and neighbors and friends that the police interviewed. Jack knew her too. She was always callin' the cops for Peeping Toms, imaginary burglars, kids runnin' through her yard, whatever. The woman was a loony tune."

"And the puzzles?"

"His old lady was a jigsaw freak and made the poor kid sit all day doin' puzzles with her, screamin' and yellin' at him all the while. Probably the only kid in the city beggin' to get back to school in the fall to get away from her. He was never allowed to play sports or do anything after school. No friends, no nothing."

"So sad," Juls said, thinking about her companion of the last few weeks. She thought back to the day sailing and picnicking on Spar Island and couldn't seem to reconcile the image of gentle, soft-spoken Wilson with the monster who had killed Rosie.

"I guess the old bitch used to torment him with that rhyme about "Monday's child, blah, blah. Always claiming the rhyme was referring to girls, not boys and how much better off she'd be if he'd been a girl."

"Let's not talk about it anymore Tuck, okay?"

"Whatever you say, partner," he said, slipping his arm around her shoulders. "Want to rest now?"

"In a minute. Mr. Marvell is a nice man, isn't he?"

"Very, why, has he been in to see you?"

"No, but those flowers are from him," she said, pointing to a huge vase of daisies, one of the eight flower arrangements crowded into the room. The largest arrangement was from the Flames, an enormous vase of red and white carnations, a red, plastic bat sticking up from the center of the arrangement.

"He called and we talked for a long time. Mostly he talked about Ellen Smith and I told him about Rosie. It felt good in a way, to talk to someone who understands. It helped me to say goodbye. I was even able to laugh about some of the memories, that's a good sign, isn't it? I'm starting to feel Rosie's support again, like she's back with me. I always felt so protected around her, you know? Not physically, but emotionally. Does that make any sense?"

Nodding, eyes misty, his throat in knots, Tuck wanted to say that he'd protect her, but the words were not necessary.

"Of course you know, partner," she said, fingers caressing his cheek. "It's the same way I feel when I'm with you."

ABOUT THE AUTHOR

M. Lee Prescott is the author of numerous works of fiction for adults, young adults and children, among them **Prepped to Kill, Gadfly (Books One and Two in the Ricky Steele series), Jigsaw, A Friend of Silence, and Song of the Spirit.** Her newest contemporary romance series, *Morgan's Run,* debuts in 2014. Three of her nonfiction titles have been published by Heinemann and she has published numerous articles in the field of literacy education. Lee is a professor of education at a small New England liberal arts college where she teaches reading and writing pedagogy. Her current research focuses on mindfulness and connections to reading and writing. She regularly teaches abroad, most recently in Singapore.

Lee has lived in southern California (loved those Laguna nights), Chapel Hill, North Carolina, and various spots in Massachusetts and Rhode Island. Currently, she resides on the river, where she canoes and swims daily. She is the mother of two grown sons, Ransom and Winward, and spends lots of time with them, their beautiful wives, Alexandra and Stephanie, and her three extraordinary grandchildren, Abigail, Ava and Benjamin. She lost her buddy, Rosie (15-year-old golden retriever) last summer and is still looking for her successor. If anyone knows a dog with the sweet temperament of a golden, but half the size, do let her know.

When not teaching or writing (both of which she loves), Lee's passions revolve around family, yoga (Kripalu is a second home), swimming, bouncing, and walking.

Lee loves to hear from readers. Visit her website at *mleeprescott.com* and Facebook page (mleeprescott). Her email is *mleeprescott@gmail.com*.

A Note from the Author

Thank you so much for taking the time to read **Jigsaw**. I love writing about life in a seaside village so, once again, I set this story in a New England town very much like one where I spent a number of years. Although I now live on a river, I return to the ocean often. Was fun to drop in a few local details, as I do in all my novels, even if actual persons and places are figments of my imagination!

Jigsaw is the first mystery featuring Juls Whitman and Tuck Potter, two of my most endearing characters. The tension swirling around the love these friends share for each other was something I particularly wanted to explore in this mystery series. A second adventure for Juls and Tuck is in the works, probably within the next year or two. Many authors have a favorite character, and, I must confess, Ricky Steele (of the Ricky Steele series) is mine, so I decided to have her make an appearance in **Jigsaw**, as a friend of Tuck's. Look for more collaborations between Ricky, Juls and Tuck in future!

If you liked **Jigsaw** and would be willing to write an Amazon review, I would very much appreciate it! In fact, I will be happy to send my first 25 reviewers a free e-copy of another of my titles! If you submit a review, just email me at *mleeprescott@ gmail.com* and I will see that you receive your free copy of whichever title you would like!

If you would like to sign up for future book releases and occasional notices about my books, please email me at *mleeprescott@gmail.com* and I will add you to the list. I promise I will not share your address, nor will I flood you with emails. Do visit my website at *www.mleeprescott.com* to read more about my books and to hear what's next. I am really excited by my upcoming **Morgan's Run** series, set in the incredible United States southwest, another special place I visit often. First **Morgan's Run** title is scheduled for release in 2014!

Finally, this book has been revised, proofed and edited many, many times, but I, and my intrepid assistants, are human so if you spot a typo, please email me at *mleeprescott@gmail.com* and I will fix it. If you'd like to know more about my other books, please scroll ahead to the next section that is followed by a sample chapters of **Lost in Spindle City,** book 3 in the Ricky Steele Mysteries!

Warm wishes,
Lee

Contemporary romances and mysteries by M. Lee Prescott include:

Mysteries
The Ricky Steele series
Book 1: Prepped to Kill
Book 2: Gadfly
Book 3: Lost in Spindle City (coming soon!)

Also featuring Ricky Steele:
Jigsaw

Single titles
Romantic suspense
A Friend of Silence

Contemporary Romance
Well-Versed in Love (coming soon!)
Glass Walls (coming soon!)

Young Adult Romance
Song of the Spirit (coming soon!)

CHAPTER 1

Some days have less than auspicious starts. This was one of them. My third floor office seemed light years away as I dragged up the stairs. My head was fuzzy, legs, wet noodles, and my stomach churned. Other than that, I felt terrific.

Last night was one of the truly dumb ones where I forget that I'm 58, not 28. Had just wrapped up a crappy case, and despite my best efforts to breathe deeply and let go, my shoulders and neck were locked tight as a tick. Instead of taking a bath and hitting the sack, yours truly had to play tough P.I., belting back beers with the guys at the Rainbow.

A little hole in the wall bar frequented by the locals, the Rainbow is a block from my house. Once catching a glimpse of its subterranean façade, no passerby would dare drop in. A small cardboard sign taped to the inside of a grimy front window—Food and Spirits – is the only indication that it's a place of business. The sign, brown and curling at the edges, was penned in red. The ink now faded, it coordinated nicely with the grayish pink, peek-a-boo, half curtains, frayed and dusty after many smoky years.

Once I got started on the beers and a few shots of Tequila, it was all over. My neighbor, Vinnie and I pay cribbage or dice. There used to be an ancient pool table, but Jack, the owner had it removed the previous year, fearing its imminent collapse might injure one of his valued patrons.

The walk home a dim memory, I had slept in my clothes, never a good sign. I woke at 6 A.M. The phrase "death warmed over" sprang to mind. After three aspirin, a shower, juice and muffins, I felt better, but that's not saying much. I'm supposed to have oat bran and lots of fiber to combat high cholesterol and triglycerides, but after ingesting platters of grease and empty carbs the previous evening, that was pretty much a losing battle.

A run? Out of the question. My daily yoga? Probably not wise to invert my body at present. Better to wait until dark to see stars. Maybe a short walk, then I'd treat myself to a coffee cab. The rest of the world calls them milkshakes, but around Spindle City, we call 'em cabs or cabinets—yum!

I hate coffee. Am a tea drinker, mostly Earl Grey and Yerba Mate, but I love coffee cabs and occasionally coffee ice cream, both of which serve as my primary treatment for the occasional hangover I experience as a middle-aged nincompoop. I keep a coffee maker in my office for clients and I've been known to swill a cup to be friendly, but coffee has never been part of my daily routine.

My name is Ricky Steele, given name Dorothy. I've been married, but no kids, have one sister and a father who I see occasionally. I was married for about five seconds and have no children, the latter my one regret. I hold many odd jobs from newspaper columnist for our local paper to waitress and craftsperson, but most recently, I've been working as a private investigator, a profession, which I recently fell into thanks to my own foolishness. Surprise, surprise—I found I liked it enough to put in the requisite hundreds of hours working with two local P.I.s in order to get my license. I'm a private person and this life suits my personality, if not my overall health.

While I've stumbled into several murder cases, most of my work is fairly routine. A good friend, Bud Dixon, runs his own insurance business and throws me a fair amount of work. Insurance fraud is a full-time occupation for lots of folks so Bud's work helps make ends meet. I also pick up a fair amount of work trailing errant spouses, since infidelity is epidemic. About half of this work is accomplished in the real world, the other half online, since the Internet is a cheater's best friend.

Over the past six months, I've become the P.I. of choice for a certain Newport set. Having hubby followed and photographed as he goes about his tedious daily routines seems to be the "in thing" these days for bored housewives and those who have a vested interest in keeping close tabs on the checkbook.

My last case, which I tried mightily to stay out of, nearly got me killed. There are certain cases one does not take in this city, if one wishes to remain among the living. I was out of physical danger now, or at least for the next decade, but I was still emotionally shaken, hence last night's idiocy. I'm not a big drinker – the occasional beer and glass of wine about the extant of it – but sometimes the amnesia of alcohol can be therapeutic. A day spent indulging myself with junk food and sugar and I'd be ready to face the world again.

As I reached the top of the stairs, my stomach turned again. Increased heart rate, beer and tequila definitely do not mix!

My office is in a restored mill building in the heart of the city's Flint District. It's a beautiful structure, the façade still strong and proud, despite acres of advertising splayed across its granite walls. In the city's heyday, its cavernous rooms once roared with the machinery of textile production, hundreds of workers toiling 24 hours a day. For years, the abandoned mill had sat, gutted and empty, left to ponder its fate as the once thriving city slipped into poverty, neglect and high unemployment. Now, although silent, the halls and passageways had been "repurposed" and housed a variety of enterprises.

The ground floor hummed with a ragtag collection of outlet stores and bargain kiosks hawking everything from pocketbooks to silk flowers. The second floor is in imminent danger of succumbing to the same fate. Right now, it's vacant, providing a buffer between Outlet Central and the offices on the third floor. Bud, my insurance friend, began his business here and dragged me along, but as his client list grew, he moved to fancier digs downtown, leaving me alone with several other tenants on the partially renovated third floor. Not exactly a classy location, but it suits me. I have my own rear entrance, insulated from the comings and goings of the outlet crowd.

At the moment, there are four of us on the floor. I'm in 308, a real estate appraiser I rarely see in 312, a salesman for "Boats Afloat" or some nautical magazine in 316 and a writer, in 320, who comes most days at 10:00 AM and departs shortly before 3:00 PM. He told me last week that 320 is his sanctuary, an escape from the bedlam at home. The remainder of the floor is vacant. An acre of empty is a lot of empty. They tell us there are 60-80 potential office spaces, but it takes a certain type to locate here. Cheap and bizarre. It's relatively quiet and fairly secure, at least during the day. They've had to hire extra security to keep the bargain hunters' thievery in check. Apparently for some, no price is cheap enough.

I slid open the heavy, metal fire door and headed down the hall. The walls had been painted dull, asylum gray, but they'd left the beautiful woodwork alone, dark, mahogany moldings smooth and solid as I ran my hand along the chair rail collecting dust. Unfortunately, the renovators had made no attempt to match the old with the new so my cubicle and the others had been slapped together, minus mahogany trim.

As a middle aged spinster set in her ways, I have a little routine I like to follow which involves a cup of tea, a little bill paying, or ignoring depending upon the status of my bank account, a little office tidying, record keeping, and whatever puttering I find to last until the last sips of tea. I do not like to be interrupted before eleven AM. I have found this ritual to be important to my sense of well-being and willingness to face the day. I was not to enjoy my routine today.

All arms and legs, I found her curled up against my door. Her spindly legs were covered in snagged black netting that had been patched in several spots with nail polish. Impossibly long feet were encased in bright red pumps, from all appearances, several sizes too large.

Street people often camp out in the building when they can slip by the airtight security system. In other words, they're regulars. I've kind of adopted one little lady, Irene, who I suspect is around my age, but looks about 100. She's been sleeping in my hall for at least six months. If I forget to lock the office door, I often find her stretched on my couch catching u on her beauty sleep. Irene snores, loudly. She's short and pudgy, not scrawny like this little gal, her bony limbs sticking out all over the place. I decided that I rules and boundaries were in order, as I definitely did not have room on my couch for two.

She was sleeping soundly so I was contemplating how I might sidle around her when Terry, the appraiser banged open the fire door and startled her awake. I turned to give him an icy glare, but he'd already banged into his office, not a glance in our direction. Turning back, I found our visitor rubbing her eyes, looking disoriented and none too happy. That made two of us.

She gathered herself up and ineffectually endeavored to smooth her hair as she inched up the wall like a spider. Her light brown hair, the consistency of my childhood dolls after I'd styled their tresses, stuck up in odd clumps, coarse, wiry and clearly in need of a wash. She wore a red skirt and matching ribbed top, the entire ensemble 100% unnatural fibers. Over her skimpy get-up, she wore an oversized man's grey sport coat in a herringbone pattern, brown suede patches on the sleeves. I suspected she'd grabbed it from the outlet dumpster on her way in, to ward off the April chill.

Several strands of brightly colored beads hung from her skinny, ostrich neck, and she sported matching, dangly earrings. Her left earring was missing its bottom red bead, giving her an off kilter look, and I found myself listing to the side as I gazed down at her. As I stared into dark, round eyes rimmed with thick black eyeliner, I gulped, realizing that I was looking at a child, twelve at most, maybe much younger. Bud's fifth grader looked older than this sad little bird.

"Miss Steele?" She spoke tentatively, voice husky.

I nodded, thinking, at least she can read. My office door has my name emblazoned in stick on black and gold letters, very classy.

"I'm sorry to be crashed here."

I shrugged. "No problem. Happens all the time. Must've had a rough one last night. But, hey, don't you have to be at school or something?"

"Not today. Sometimes we go, but not today. I needed to see you and I snuck in before the guard locked up so I could catch you first thing." She began fussing with her hair again, pulling at her skirt, smoothing out the jacket. Clearly nervous gestures, a way to occupy her tiny, shaking hands until I responded.

I smiled. "Well, you caught me. Come on in." I didn't have a good feeling about this, but what could I do? Besides, my solemn routine had been broken now, so what the hell?